THE JANUS LEGACY

BY LISA VON BIELA

Jeremy looked up and down the hall, and was relieved to confirm he was alone. He'd come again on another pilgrimage of guilt.

He opened the door and stepped inside the Subject's home. He made himself really think about that for a moment, forced himself to open up and allow the guilt to freely wash over him. The Subject had never known another environment in his relatively brief existence. He tried to imagine what that must be like, and could not. Here was a human being whose entire life and environment had been that of a captive lab animal.

He gazed at the Subject, who sat on the edge of his erstwhile bed and gazed blankly back at him. What else did he have to do? He couldn't read, so books were of no use to him. He had no concept of sports or movies, so a television wouldn't be anything more than a strange and useless curiosity to him.

The more he thought about it, the more puzzled he became. What sort of mental or interior life did the Subject have? Did he have anything like that at all? Given his circumstances, it might be more of a mercy if he did lack those things.

Despite Jeremy's professed resolution to do so back when he first learned of the secret project, he'd never had the Subject tested for his cognitive capabilities. Somehow he never did get around to it, partly due to the logistics of finding someone qualified, given the needed secrecy, and partly because he simply didn't want to face whatever the results might show. They didn't even have an informal clue as to his mental capacity, because no one had ever tried to provide any sort of education or socialization beyond the minimum interaction to feed and care for him.

Surely now no one ever would.

Janus: the ancient Roman god of doorways, of beginnings. Often depicted with two faces, each gazing in the opposite direction.

Janus-faced: having two contrasting aspects.

Janus legacy: a dangerous gift.

PROLOGUE

A burst of fresh, cool air rushed over him. He breathed it in, enjoying how it tasted, how it felt. He couldn't remember feeling such a thing before. He couldn't remember anything at all.

His eyelids fluttered open. Bright lights flared and stabbed at him. He shrank back from the unfamiliar, painful sensation, but something hard and unyielding seemed to confine him.

Of their own volition, his knees drew toward his chest, toward the universal posture of comfort and security, but something unseen limited his range of movement. He opened his mouth and gasped for air as panic seized him.

He heard voices, but couldn't understand them. Something reached into whatever container imprisoned him and fumbled with something. A haze settled onto him, dulling his senses. Then he heard a sound, a sound so distant now, like two solid items gently striking each other. The fresh air vanished, as did the harsh light.

CHAPTER 1

"Mr. Girard is expecting you. Please come this way." The receptionist spoke in the hushed tones of one accustomed to dealing with the well-heeled.

Jeremy Magnusson wanted nothing more than to turn right around and get the hell out of there.

The Botoxed wonder stepped away from her sleek ebony desk and led the way to a conference room down the hall. Jeremy marveled at how she could walk so steadily on such high heels. Not one highlighted blonde hair dared stray; her meticulously applied makeup surely involved serious daily prep time. Perhaps she was some sort of automaton designed to appeal to the clientele.

Overpriced artwork and furnishings permeated the place. The rich and obnoxious would feel right at home. Jeremy decided that Ogilvy, Girard, and Snelling looked just like the sort of swank, high-buck law firm his father would have chosen.

"He'll be in shortly. There's water and coffee on the table behind you." Receptionist Barbie turned and shut the door without a sound.

Jeremy glanced around the room and speculated about the operating costs for a firm like this—and its fees. The thick, highly polished cherry wood conference table could comfortably seat twenty. No skimping on the chairs, either. All ergonomic, black leather types. A long cherry wood credenza on the window side of the room featured an array of mugs and glasses, as well as carafes of water and coffee and all the trimmings.

And the view. The firm occupied the 54th floor of the IDS Tower in downtown Minneapolis, and Jeremy had to admit the view was spectacular. It probably went on for miles on a sunny day. Today, however, ominous dark gray clouds hung low, casting the city into a twilight gloom in the early afternoon. Jeremy supposed that was appropriate enough under the circumstances. He selected a chair facing the door, sat down, and doodled restlessly on the notepad he had brought.

Moments later, the door opened, and Kenneth Girard strode in. He presented the very image of the stereotypical law partner: gray hair, a slight paunch, custom-tailored dark suit and a navy-blue silk tie. He extended a hand and smiled, showing perfectly even, capped teeth.

"Pleased to meet you, Mr. Magnusson. I'm sorry for your loss."

Jeremy stood briefly and shook hands. "Thank you."

Girard seated himself directly across from Jeremy, set a thick legal file on the table before him, and got right down to business. "Mr. Magnusson, I'm not sure how much you know of your father's business—"

"Not much. We haven't spoken in some years now."

"Oh, I see. Well, some of this may come as a surprise to you, then. Your father revised his estate plan considerably after your mother died." Girard shook his head and released a regretful-sounding exhalation. "Fortunately, given the unexpected nature of his passing."

Jeremy briefly considered the actuarial odds of dying in a plane crash for someone who spent all his spare time zipping here or there in his private jet, as did his father, the ubiquitous—and now late—Doctor Ivan Magnusson.

Done with his brief display of empathy, Girard carried on. "You have no siblings, and no other beneficiaries are named in your father's will. Everything goes to you: all the liquid assets and investments, the mansion in Minnetonka, the cars and personal effects, and of course, SomaGene. Everything, that is, under one condition."

"And what is that?"

"That you assume his role at SomaGene—full responsibility for the business. Day-to-day operations, planning, R&D, as well as clinical procedures. I understand that you, like your father, are a surgeon as well as an accomplished research scientist. SomaGene is doing quite well, but Ivan wasn't content to rest on his successes. He had progressed in taking his enterprise to the next level, and that is why he imposed the condition as he did. If you are willing to carry on his wishes for SomaGene, then you are entitled to his entire estate—and it is considerable. If you do not wish to do so, then I am authorized to search for a suitable candidate in your place, and to liquidate all non-SomaGene assets. The proceeds would be reinvested in SomaGene."

Jeremy sat speechless as he tried to process what he had just heard—and the implications. SomaGene had been one reason for his estrangement from his father. Jeremy believed the technology his father developed was too risky and pushed ethical boundaries. That said, it had been successful, and there had been no serious adverse events, at least so far. But, what was the "next level" that he'd been working on? Did it merely push the boundaries of ethics, or barge right through them?

"I really don't know what to think. How soon do you need an answer?"

"Ivan specified 48 hours if there had been no one designated as an interim backup for him. Given his unexpected demise, there was no such person, so SomaGene is without a leader at the moment."

"I prefer to make informed decisions. Tell me more about this 'next level,' as you call it. What would I be trying to implement?"

Girard shook his head. "I'm sorry. Ivan specifically chose not to provide me that information. He said it was very sensitive and he did not want it to fall into anyone's hands, other than the person who would implement it. He wanted total commitment up front. He did, however, provide a mechanism for that information to be made available shortly after you—or an outside recruit—began running SomaGene."

Typical Ivan. "That makes it pretty damned tough to decide."

"I imagine it does. I can arrange a tour of SomaGene tomorrow to at least let you see the operations, meet some of the key staff members. I can also show you the house. It's not far from the SomaGene campus. I hope that would be helpful in your decision."

"All right, let's do that. I booked a hotel for the night, so I wouldn't have to head back down to Rochester."

"Good. I'll have our receptionist coordinate things and get you the logistics."

Jeremy yanked his overnight bag into his hotel room and pushed the door shut with a satisfying click. He shook the rain off his coat and cursed himself for forgetting to bring an umbrella. He knew perfectly well that violent thunderstorms could pop up this time of year in Minnesota. This whole business about his father had him distracted, and he'd failed to properly prepare for the trip. He hated distractions only slightly less than being poorly prepared.

He wheeled the bag into the bedroom and hefted it onto the luggage rack. He retrieved his toiletry case and took it into the bathroom. Time for his daily dose of mercaptopurine. Jeremy filled a glass with water and swallowed the pill. He hoped this med would work better than the last one to get his Crohn's under control. It had gotten bad enough for a while that he was missing work routinely, and his doctor warned him if it kept up at that pace, he would need stronger meds, and possibly even surgery to remove a section of his small intestine that was already badly damaged.

The stress of the pain and inconvenience of his disease had created a vicious feedback loop, worsening his symptoms—and now this. With his mother dead and no siblings, it had fallen to him to deal with his father's sudden death. Ivan had been flying off in his private jet to speak at some conference in Denver. The weather turned ugly and the plane went down. Both Ivan and the pilot were killed instantly. The investigation so far showed nothing more than an accident, but there were still some loose ends to deal with.

And now the bizarre condition attached to Ivan's will. They hadn't even spoken for several years, since Ivan got SomaGene off the ground. Jeremy had not expected anything like this to happen. He had half a mind to just say no and go home, but figured he might as well take the tour and see what Ivan had wrought.

Jeremy glanced at himself in the bathroom mirror. The lines on his face and dark circles under his eyes made him look older than his thirty-two years. *Damned Crohn's. Why hadn't Ivan spent his time trying to find a cure for* that? It had killed Jeremy's mother, and unfortunately, she'd passed it down to him. He'd been fine until he hit twenty, when the disease first began to manifest. Before that, he'd been in top physical condition. He'd excelled in both sports and his studies in school. But once Crohn's made its appearance, his whole life became centered on keeping it at bay.

He glanced at his watch. Barely 4 o'clock. Too early for dinner. Dead tired from his drive up from Rochester and the meeting with Girard, Jeremy decided to take a nap for a while, then just order room service in later. The idea of going out for dinner, especially in this downpour, was just too exhausting to consider.

Especially with such a major decision weighing on him.

CHAPTER 2

R ick Granada was going places. You could tell just by looking at him and listening to him. He stood with his head high and his broad shoulders straight, as if he could defy gravity itself. He spoke with confidence, his words and thoughts flowing effortlessly.

You could tell all of this just by being around him, even if you didn't know he was the most respected practitioner of regenerative medicine in the nation.

Amanda McGovern shared a quiet booth with Rick in their favorite restaurant, Ellington's Seafood and Chop House. They went there often enough—and Rick spent freely enough—that the host always seated them in the best booth in the house so they could enjoy the view of Silver Lake as they dined.

Amanda gazed out the window at the reflections of the sun setting on the lake and admitted to herself that perhaps she was a little biased about Rick. They'd started dating shortly after she'd broken up with her prior boyfriend, and she missed few opportunities to compare the two. The old boyfriend lost every time.

She'd wanted to be with someone ambitious, someone who could match her thirst for achievement. Rick had rocketed to the top of his field in record time. He'd published more articles on regenerative medicine than anyone else, and his research was widely viewed as the standard by which all else was judged. Indeed, he felt somewhat stifled in his current position because the funding did not allow him to push the envelope even further.

For her part, Amanda was also a physician, though not a surgeon.

She was a research scientist specializing in genetic therapy for age-related genome degradation. She'd chosen her specialty carefully for its opportunities for advancement. With the aging of the general population, her research stood to bear important fruit in the coming years.

She sipped her Chardonnay and looked at Rick. His face had retained the tan he'd gotten on the trip they took to Bermuda a couple of months ago. That and his dark wavy hair made him stand out even more from the usual Minnesota blond, Nordic types.

He raised his glass of Cabernet and smiled. "I got word today they've selected me to give the keynote speech at this year's regenerative med conference in Orlando."

"That's wonderful! When is it? Can I come?"

"Of course. We can make a week of it. It's not until early next year. Good time to get out of the cold and snow and hit Florida, eh?"

Amanda clicked her glass with his. "Sounds wonderful. I'm looking forward to it already." The last six months with Rick had been the best she'd ever had. She'd made the right decision to leave her old boyfriend for him.

CHAPTER 3

Jeremy drove along the curvy Minnetonka back road in search of the SomaGene campus. Girard had had an assistant phone him that morning with the address and time to come receive the grand tour.

The day was cloudy with remnants of the prior day's storm, though the light was decent. Nonetheless, addresses were hard to spot along this road. Finally, up ahead he noticed a tiny sign next to a long blacktop driveway. *SG.* Amazing that flamboyant Ivan didn't have something with flashing, glaring neon to proclaim his creation. What was he trying to hide?

He turned onto the driveway. It led back through a stand of pine trees so thick he couldn't see any buildings from the road. The front portion of the property consisted merely of manicured grass and the outer part of driveway. The casual passer-by would have no idea what went on there.

Jeremy proceeded along the driveway as he had been instructed. Past the trees, he came upon a sprawling two-story building sheathed in panes of dark glass. It seemed to absorb all the light, and reflect none. He drove around and behind it to the parking lot, which was filled with expensive-looking late model cars.

He pulled his Nissan Pathfinder into a visitor's spot, shut off the engine, and contemplated the SomaGene building for a moment. It might as well have been dropped by aliens into this clearing behind the barricade of pine trees. That light-deadening glass gave it an ominous appearance. The building also featured a covered area by the entrance that was wide enough for two cars to park abreast of each other, safe from the elements. Jeremy wondered why it needed such a thing. He shook his head, got out of the car, and approached the entrance.

Jeremy stepped inside through the double glass doors, then stopped, stunned. The interior seemed designed in another time entirely. The floor was made of a cloudy white material that looked a bit like marble, but had a bluish glow.

Nothing in the atrium touched the floor.

The front desk consisted of what appeared to be a slab of Lucite—suspended firmly in mid-air. The receptionist sat in a chair that had no legs, but instead hovered behind the floating reception desk. There was no other furniture in the atrium. White elevator doors stood behind the receptionist's area. The place had a hush about it, as if white noise were being pumped in.

Trying not to look thrown by the bizarre surroundings, Jeremy walked up to the receptionist and introduced himself. She wore a skin-tight, long-sleeved white jumpsuit and had her chestnut-brown hair pulled back tight against her head. She looked the very picture of cold sterility.

"Welcome, Mr. Magnusson. We've been expecting you." She greeted him *sotto voce*. "Our two most senior staff, Glen Hawkins and Tim Whitman, will be out to meet you shortly. They will give you a tour of the facilities and will be happy to answer any questions you may have." Her smile, though beautiful, looked manufactured and distant.

"Thank you."

The elevator doors opened, and two men approached him. They both wore white lab coats and disposable shoe covers. The one to the right, a slim man of about forty with short dark hair, extended his hand. "Welcome. I'm Glen Hawkins. Pleased to meet you."

The one to the left, a shorter, heavier man of roughly the same age, with short graying hair, extended his hand. "And I'm Tim Whitman."

"Pleased to meet you both."

"I understand from Mr. Girard that you aren't very familiar with SomaGene's operations, is that right?" asked Glen.

"That's right." Jeremy wondered how much these two knew

about Ivan's special plans for the company, and whether he'd be able to glean anything from them during the tour.

"All right. Let's start upstairs." Glen turned and led them into the elevator.

The elevator swiftly and silently delivered them to the second floor. Then the doors opened onto a view that exceeded anything Jeremy had ever imagined of SomaGene's operations.

Before him lay three long Lucite slabs suspended in mid-air just like the reception desk. The slabs ran nearly the length of the room, leaving enough space around and between them to provide full access to all the surfaces. On each rested a number of glass containers filled with a pinkish fluid that bathed an individual organ: a heart, a kidney, a liver, or a trachea. Every container was connected to an individual filter pump that circulated and bubbled the fluid like the water in a fish tank. A strangely unsettling bluish light illuminated the room, though no discrete fixtures were visible.

Jeremy knew that at one time Ivan had aspired to create individual organs from donors' own tissues. He had no idea he'd actually succeeded in generating what looked to be complete organs. He stepped closer to peer at a kidney on the near end of one of the Lucite slabs.

Glen broke the silence. "We're able to autologously cultivate certain organs from clients' own cells. Issues with rejection and immunosuppressants are a thing of the past, at least for transplants of these organs. The solution they're bathing in contains oxygen, cells, and highly concentrated nutrients as well as growth hormones, so we're able to generate a complete organ in a matter of months. Our clients don't have to depend on long donor waiting lists, and of course, the organs are really their own."

"The room—in fact, the entire facility—is designed for minimum contamination," added Tim. "Keeping the floor clear of table legs and fixtures allows us to keep it scrupulously clean. This, combined with a very aggressive air filtration system and antibacterial lighting, virtually eliminates the potential for contamination. Very important for our clients. There is no danger of rejection, so we don't have to suppress their immune systems, but of course, if they're waiting for a transplant, their systems are already compromised. We like to minimize the use of antibiotics to avoid encouraging superbugs—and this design allows us to do that."

"So these are...*cultivated* for specific clients?" Jeremy glanced at all the glass containers. There had to be thirty or so organs in various stages of development.

"Yes. Production has been going quite well. We may have to expand our capacity soon," said Glen.

"Well, then what happens?"

"Then we implant them. Let's show him the surgery," said Tim.

They got into the elevator and returned to the first floor. This time they exited through the back of the elevator and walked a short distance down the hall to a surgical suite.

Lucite shelves ringed the room. On them were various surgical supplies and instruments. Lights and monitors hung from the ceiling. Again, nothing rested on the floor, which consisted of the glowing marble-like material used in the rest of the facility.

"We have the same anticontamination features in the surgical suites as you saw in the atrium and the organ cultivation room. We have nearly no postsurgical infections reported, and again, that is with the use of minimal antibiotics." Glen smiled, clearly proud of the facilities.

"Where are the patients? Do you have a hospital facility housed here as well?"

"Actually, no," said Tim. "When an organ is ready for transplant, we notify the client and arrange for the actual surgery. However, once stabilized post-surgery, clients are transported to a facility more convenient to them so they can convalesce as needed near their families. They come from all over for these procedures, of course."

"That's also more expedient for us. We don't have to staff for convalescent care and we don't need to take up the space to do so. We can focus on the cultivation and actual surgery," added Glen.

"Who does all this?"

Glen chuckled. "Oh, we don't do it all. We have staff who tend to the organ cultivation, tracking progress and making sure the solutions are replenished as needed. There are others who gather the tissue samples from the clients to initiate the organs. And we're not the only ones who perform the actual transplants. There are several other surgeons who do that as well."

"Well, this is more than I realized SomaGene had been doing. Is there anything else?"

Glen and Tim exchanged a look. Glen answered, "No, this is SomaGene's main business. It's grown considerably since Ivan established the company and developed the protocols we use today."

If there was something more going on, he wasn't going to get it out of these two, Jeremy figured. He glanced at his watch. "I'm sorry to cut this short. I'm supposed to meet Mr. Girard out at the house shortly. Thank you for showing me around."

Jeremy got into his Pathfinder and slumped behind the wheel for a moment. He'd wanted to pry further and see if he could get anything out of those two concerning any other lines of business Ivan had been working on, but he desperately needed to just get out of there. Seeing all those bought-and-paid-for organs sitting there in various stages of development in that floating Lucite maze was more than he expected to have to deal with. And now he had to head over to the house to meet Girard and look at what would be his domicile, should he accept this posthumous offer.

He started the car and headed for his next appointment.

Jeremy managed to find the address and arrive about ten minutes before Girard was scheduled to meet him. He stopped the car and regarded the house. It certainly had Ivan's mark on it. Circular driveway, grandiose portico—as if royalty were expected to drive up and not be soiled by the weather. The house, a two-story Tudor, actually had *wings*. The only thing missing was perhaps a fountain in the front. He couldn't imagine living in such a thing.

A few minutes later, Girard drove up in his sleek black Mercedes E550. Looked like it had never experienced weather. Not a speck of dust or a rain spot on its gleaming paint.

Jeremy got out of his car and went over to meet Girard.

"Good afternoon. I trust your tour of SomaGene went well?" Girard stepped out of his car and moved toward the front door of the house. True to form, he wore an expensive dark gray suit as if he were ready to argue before the Supreme Court.

"Yes, it did. It is…quite the facility."

"Well, good." Girard reached into his suit pocket for the house keys. "I hope you'll find the house equally impressive." He slid the key into the lock and opened the front door.

As they stepped inside, Girard reached over to a panel on the wall beside the door and pressed several buttons. "The entire house is electronically controlled. All the lights, heating and air systems, security—even the appliances. There are even sensors and alarms in the event you're not at home and something happens, like a pipe springs a leak. It will try to stop the leak, for example, by shutting off water to that part of the house, and can even notify you via text message." He glanced around with a satisfied look on his face. "It has about every feature you could imagine."

"I'd say so." Jeremy's little rental house in Rochester was a primitive cave by comparison. He had to turn on his lights the old-fashioned way—with wall switches.

"I understand this may be a little uncomfortable for you, given your father's recent passing. I'll just stay here and let you look through the place yourself, if you'd prefer. Your father's belongings are still here, of course."

"Thank you. I would prefer that, actually." Jeremy started with the lower floor. He stepped down into the living room. It was clearly designed for much more active entertaining than he partook in. A shiny black grand piano stood center stage. Several comfortable black leather couches and chairs were arranged to maximize conversations among numerous guests. A large black marble fireplace dominated the far end of the room.

Jeremy passed through the formal dining room. It, too, appeared geared toward large formal gatherings, with the long dark hardwood table set for a dozen, and the matching credenza and china cabinet lining one side of the room. He continued into the kitchen. It looked like a model in a home improvement convention, with black granite countertops, industrial-sized steel appliances, polished cherry wood cabinets, and fancy track lighting strategically placed throughout. The breakfast nook occupied its own glass-paned alcove.

He stepped to the back door to check out the yard. It had the look of expensive maintenance—the lawn was perfectly trimmed, not a dandelion or bald spot to be seen. The trees and shrubs were expertly sculpted. The wood deck glowed in a way that indicated it had been recently and professionally sealed. The teak patio set was artfully arranged beneath an extended awning to protect it from direct sunlight.

Jeremy sighed and stepped back inside. He went upstairs to check out the bedrooms. There were five of them. A quick glance revealed they were consistent with the rest of the house: nothing but the finest furnishings and most expensive paint and detailing. He saved the master bedroom for last. Ivan's. Feeling like a trespasser, he hesitated before going inside.

He pushed open the door to reveal a massive room lit by creatively placed track lights. A black lacquer four-poster bed dominated the scene. A matching armoire and chest of drawers stood at the far side of the room. A small library nook with a bay window and sitting area extended the room on his right. Jeremy stepped inside and opened the door to his left. It led to a walk-in closet the size of a small apartment. He turned and went over to check out the bathroom. A jetted tub large enough for two, a separate glass shower stall, and a granite double-sink arrangement. No surprise given the opulence of the rest of the place.

Jeremy shut the bedroom door and started back downstairs to meet Girard. He'd seen enough for one day.

"What did you think? Quite something, isn't it?" Girard smiled at him, almost sounding like a realtor showing a prime property.

"It's a bit much, frankly." Jeremy moved toward the front door.

"Don't you want to see the garage and cars?"

"No, not really. When is the deadline for my answer?"

"Tomorrow. You can just call me at the office any time

before close of business. You know, I'm not your attorney, but if you ask me you'd be set for life if you accepted. It would be a shame for all your father's work—everything he's accumulated—not to stay in the family."

CHAPTER 4

Glen Hawkins sat in a burgundy leather booth toward the back of the dimly lit lounge at the Minnetonka Bistro, the local hot spot du jour. He briefly glanced at his watch as he swirled the ice in his gin and tonic. He'd asked Tim to meet him there shortly after work. Glen wanted Tim's take on Magnusson's kid—and what it might mean to their work if he took over SomaGene.

He downed the last of his drink, then signaled the waiter for another. He settled back into the booth, letting the warm glow relax him after his busy day.

"Hey, sorry I'm late. I must have left at just the wrong time. Got stuck in that backup on 101. They need to make that a signal, not a stop sign. Ridiculous." His graying hair slightly disheveled, Tim settled into the seat in the opposite side of the booth.

"S'all right. I've just been sitting here, thinking."

Tim signaled the waiter to bring him what Glen was having. "About Junior? So, what do you think? Think he'll take over the reins?"

Glen considered the question for a moment before answering. "I don't know. I did some checking. He's been down in Rochester at some Mayo knockoff clinic for several years now. Hasn't really distinguished himself. Not sure what drives him, if anything. Sounds like he's competent, at least, but just doesn't stand out for some reason."

"Girard was pretty close-lipped, but I presume there's something in it for Junior to take over at this point. I mean, if he had been remotely interested in Ivan's work, surely he would already have been working alongside him." Tim nodded at the waiter as he arrived with their drinks.

"Good point. Must have been some bad blood, or he would have been here, being groomed and all. So, the question is, is there going to be a...*problem*... if he comes in?"

"He seemed pretty taken aback by the cultivation process—"

Glen leaned forward and nearly hissed at Tim. "Yeah, that's not a good sign, and you know that's the *least* of it. What about the other project? That was even more important to Ivan, but he didn't live long enough to complete it."

Tim leaned back in the booth and stared down into his glass. "Yeah, you're right. If the cultivation room bothered Junior, imagine what he'd think of Ivan's latest project." He took a sip. "That could be a problem. A real problem."

"Well, we certainly don't say anything now. Let him make his decision without that bit of information. I don't know if Girard even knows. If Jeremy decides to take over operations, we deal with it then, I suppose. Do whatever's necessary to make sure he doesn't kill it."

Tim took another sip. "Yeah. Probably the best way to go. And hope like hell he buys into it when the time comes."

Glen looked Tim in the eye and stabbed his index finger at the table as he spoke. "It has way too much potential for someone to step in at this stage and stop it. I don't care who he is." He drained his drink again and signaled the waiter. "Want another?"

Tim waved his hand over his glass. "Oh, no. I'm good. I promised Katie I'd get home for dinner at a decent hour tonight. She's been complaining I'm never home in time to give little Johnnie his bath before dinner."

Glen shook his head and grinned. "Makes me glad I'm not married. I like coming and going as I please—and with whom I please—way too much to tie myself down like that."

Tim smiled. "Oh, with the right person, you'd be surprised. I used to think like that, now I can't imagine anything else."

"Yeah, something's warped your mind. Maybe it's all those diaper fumes. I don't know how you stand that stuff."

Tim finished his drink and stood. "Sounds like there's no convincing you, then. I'm off. There's probably a full diaper with my name on it waiting for me."

"All right, then. Knock yourself out. See you tomorrow, Tim."

After the waiter brought him a fresh drink, Glen leaned back in the booth and surveyed his surroundings. He liked places like this, and was glad there were several to choose from in the Minnetonka area. All the hot young things came to strut their stuff and see if they could attract a man with a little money he wouldn't mind spending on them. Fine with him. All he wanted was a pretty face and a hot body—preferably on a short term, no strings basis.

He spotted a good candidate at the bar. She'd just taken a seat with her back to him, and was glancing around as if she, too, were looking for a little company for the night. She had long dark hair that reached the middle of her back, and a tight black dress that scooped low, damned near to her tailbone.

Glen liked what he saw. He scooped up his drink and sauntered over to introduce himself.

CHAPTER 5

His gut felt like it had its own life, and tonight it was in a vicious mood. Jeremy clutched his abdomen and gritted his teeth as another painful spasm rippled through and reminded him to take his meds.

He shuffled into his hotel bathroom and quickly downed his day's dosage. The stress of dealing with his father's death and the necessary arrangements—plus being forced into this all-or-nothing decision concerning SomaGene—amplified the daily turmoil in his gut. Like it or not, Crohn's ruled his life. On his best days, it was an uneasy truce. On his worst days… it took over.

Jeremy headed back to the little desk in the main part of his room. He briefly glanced at the room service menu, then tossed it aside. He was somewhat hungry, but knew from experience that just about anything he'd order right now would create painful repercussions.

Girard wanted his decision by tomorrow. He wished he had more time, but he knew that wouldn't really make it easier. It would only drag out the process. Just as well he was on a short leash, but he felt so overwhelmed since his initial meeting with Girard.

The SomaGene tour alone boggled his mind. He'd had no idea Ivan had gotten that far in developing autologous organs for transplant—let alone in implementing the stunning anticontamination technology within the facility. He'd not seen anything the likes of that in the second-rate research clinic where he worked. His clinic existed deep in the shadow of the infamous Mayo, and was still in the autoclave days with respect to decontamination. Might as well compare stone tablets to an iPad.

Jeremy had felt uncomfortable with the very concept of generating organs for highly profitable transplants when Ivan first came up with the idea. Now he was profoundly disturbed to see that Ivan had managed to put it into production—and amazingly with few, if any, adverse events. Still, did he want to carry on that sort of work? He shook his head, unsure. He had his misgivings about the ethics and safety, though he had to admit it was a lifesaving technology.

And then there was that house tour. What a ghastly display of overindulgence. He'd need somewhere to live if he came up here, but *that*! Maybe he could sell it and buy something more in line with his tastes. *If* he came here.

The other question was whether he was really willing to leave Rochester. Sure, Mayo wasn't going to hire him anytime soon. He could barely keep up his performance at his second-tier clinic. *Damned Crohn's.* It restricted the pace he could keep, the workload he dared tackle. His excessive sick days held him back. But what could he do? The more he took on, the more stress, the more Crohn's took its toll. There was just no way to win.

And Amanda—still a fresh wound. They'd been together for several years, had even talked off and on about getting married. But, once again, Crohn's stepped in to ruin his life. She finally got tired of dealing with the regimen and how the disease held him back in his career. He could hardly blame her, but that didn't make him miss her any less.

Jeremy stared at his cell phone on the desk in front of him. He hadn't spoken with Amanda for maybe six months—since the day she'd told him she just couldn't deal with the constant worry of whether their very relationship was harmful to his health. She always seemed to attribute the severity of his symptoms to something she must have done.

He shook his head. Amanda was so wrong. If anything, their relationship helped smooth things out for him emotionally. The real culprit was Ivan and the bad blood between them. He also couldn't deny that it stung for him to labor at a second-rate research facility when he really wanted to work at the vaunted Mayo Clinic.

Jeremy reached out and rested his hand on the cell phone, hesitant to call Amanda after all this time and after how things had ended between them. Yet he had to talk to someone about his quandary, and there was no one else he would rather talk to than Amanda, no one's opinion he valued more.

He picked up the phone and hit the speed-dial.

"Hello?"

"Um, hi Amanda. It's me, Jeremy."

A long pause. "Hi. I…um…didn't expect to hear from you." Another pause. "I heard about your father in the news. I'm sorry."

"Yeah, thanks. I'm up in Minneapolis right now dealing with some things." Jeremy gave Amanda a summary of the situation and the decision he faced. "Amanda, I know we haven't spoken in some time, and it's not fair for me to ask this, but I don't know who else I trust right now. What do you think?"

"I can't decide this for you. You must know that."

"I know it's not your decision. I just really need to talk to someone who has an independent view of it—someone who also understands the backstory. That's you. There's hardly any time left to decide, and there is a lot at stake. You of all people would know why I'd be conflicted about accepting all this from my father."

"Jeremy, you know you've always been the idealist and I've always been the pragmatist. You should know what I would say if it were my decision. Take it, run with it—kill it if that's what you really want. At least you'd be the one deciding, not some third party. You'd have all the options in your control. What do you have right now? A research position in a crappy institution. Sorry to be so blunt, but if you want options, you take this and go from there. Simple as that."

Jeremy bowed his head and nodded. Amanda always could cut right through the haze. She was right. If he took the reins, he also had the power to kill SomaGene if he decided that was the right thing. Taking the offer really did put him in the best position possible all around.

"You're right. I hadn't thought of it that way. Hey, I'm really sorry to have bothered you, but… thank you."

Feeling incredibly awkward, Jeremy abruptly hung up and made a mental note to call Girard tomorrow with his decision.

CHAPTER 6

Jeremy set the groceries down on the glossy granite countertops in his cavernous new kitchen. Somehow, a couple of bags of groceries for one person appeared lonely and pathetic in all that space.

The move from his Rochester rental to his father's house had been a pain in the ass, but it was, thankfully, over. He'd integrated his modest belongings into the ostentatious house as best he could manage, and had gracefully severed all of his Rochester ties. Now he'd even fetched his first round of groceries from the nearby Lund's market. Time to settle in and try to have a halfway restful evening before he faced his first day at SomaGene tomorrow.

Despite being on the brink of taking the reins, Jeremy remained torn about his own intentions and what message he wanted to convey to the staff about those intentions. One side of him relished taking over and controlling SomaGene's destiny—even if it meant deliberately murdering his father's creation—and another side of him just didn't want the burden of assuming that control in the first place.

He shook his head. *The hell with tomorrow.* Tonight was his final respite before whatever lay before him at SomaGene, so he pushed the topic from his mind and finished putting away the groceries. He searched several cupboards before finding a plate and a wineglass. He had to hunt through several drawers before finding a bottle opener. He opened a bottle of Chardonnay, laid out his store-bought sushi on the plate, then took everything out to the deck.

Jeremy set his dinner down on the patio table and settled into one of the high-backed, padded chairs. He took a deep breath and enjoyed the scent of fresh growth and blooming lilacs. Nothing was more beautiful than an early summer evening in Minnesota. All was green after the interminably long winter, but the mosquitoes and brutal humidity had not yet brought their misery.

He sampled a piece of the sushi—quite good for store-bought. He savored it with a sip of his wine, and listened to the call of a cardinal in one of the nearby trees. He gazed out at his meticulously landscaped yard, and made a mental note to arrange for less frequent service. The evergreens and maples, as well as the various smaller shrubs, looked way too controlled and symmetrical. Trees should be trees, not sculptures. He bit into another piece of sushi.

Inevitably his mind returned to his plans for the next day and his ever-present animosity toward Ivan and everything he stood for. Jeremy liked to plan and control things himself, and not be at the mercy of others. Ivan had forced this situation upon him with the all-or-nothing condition imposed in his bequest—and he resented that, despite his luxurious surroundings and generous inheritance. He didn't yet know where to begin to manage a company whose business it was to cultivate and implant organs for pay. He had a lot to dig into to even decide how to manage— and whether to kill—this thing his father had created.

But that was something he'd have to face tomorrow.

Jeremy again tried to set it all aside for now, and instead focus on enjoying the rest of the beautiful early summer evening.

CHAPTER 7

Jeremy briefly scanned the roadside portion of the SomaGene campus before turning into the driveway. The lawn was that deep green characteristic of early Minnesota summers. The evergreens had lighter green tips as they took advantage of the warmth to regenerate. And all this was now his.

He drove to the lot in back and parked in his reserved spot. He'd have to change the name on the sign; it still reflected Ivan's reign. But he didn't want to change everything. He had decided to keep his Nissan, at least for now. Ivan had left behind his ridiculously huge Escalade, and Jeremy just could not picture himself in such a vehicle. Ever.

Jeremy stepped out of the car, folded his arms, and stood there to take it all in for a moment. He gazed at the exterior of the SomaGene building and marveled at the outer skin. He'd learned that the reason the glass seemed to absorb the light striking it was because it did—and it converted that energy to electricity to supplement the power needed for the facility. The floating Lucite desks and surfaces were suspended by a system of powerful magnets, and that took considerable energy.

He squared his shoulders and took a deep breath to ready himself for whatever lay ahead, then locked the car and approached the building. He stepped inside, again amazed at the atrium and how clean and uncluttered it looked. He'd never seen anything quite like it. He smiled to himself—Ivan had managed to create something grander than even Mayo. He'd give him that. Anxious to get settled in, Jeremy briefly greeted the receptionist and went straight to his office.

As he entered the room for the first time, Jeremy realized

he'd be chasing ghosts for a while yet. After all, this had been Ivan's office, and it showed. He glanced at the walls, festooned with awards, pictures, and various certificates. He'd have to swap those out for his, though that would leave the walls quite a lot emptier.

The desk looked like Ivan had just left it temporarily, which of course he thought he had. In addition to a computer with a flat panel monitor, it held various stacks of papers and periodicals that would take some time to sort through. Some may have been works in progress that would simply die with Ivan; others might be important for Jeremy to digest and take on himself. A brief pain rippled through his abdomen as he considered all the work ahead of him to just pick up where things had left off, let alone set a course for SomaGene and pilot it.

He seated himself behind the desk and prepared to dig in. Where to begin? He glanced at the framed, formal portrait of his mother Anna and Ivan that occupied the left corner of the desk. Jeremy was surprised to see it there, and not just because his mother had been dead for several years now. No, there was a little history before that, when Ivan had flagrantly carried on with whatever young, attractive lab assistant was available at the time. Given his stature in the research world, it was easy for him to find ambitious female assistants who hung on his every word. And he took full advantage of that for years, while Mom did her best to turn a blind eye to it.

She had been beautiful in her day, though in later years the ravages of Crohn's took a toll on her appearance. Mom had been a student back when Ivan was teaching at the University of Minnesota. To avoid scandal, they'd concealed their relationship for several years, then married right after she graduated. While Ivan went on to fame in his career, she gave birth to Jeremy, and never returned to post-grad work because her Crohn's began to hold her back. She'd always felt inferior and weak, and so chose to put up with Ivan's philandering rather than leave him and try to make it on her own.

His mother opened her eyes and blinked a few times. She appeared to be trying to focus them. The scleras were bloodshot and slightly yellow.

Her color was terrible. She moved her mouth a little, then moaned softly, wordlessly.

"I'm here, Mom." Jeremy took her hand as she lay, thin and frail, in the hospital bed.

She closed her eyes again. A tear slipped from the corner of her right eye and trickled down the side of her face. "Ivan," she whispered.

She lay amidst numerous tubes and wires and monitors in Intensive Care. Her doctor had stopped by a little while ago, and he had no encouraging words to share. Anna had not been careful about staying on the meds to control her Crohn's and it had viciously attacked a segment of her small intestine. A fistula had formed, and had finally worked its way to the surface of her abdomen. It had set up a raging infection in its path, and the doctor wasn't certain his mother would withstand it. Not this time.

Jeremy could see right through the doctor's attempt at a soothing bedside manner. He, too, was a doctor, and he knew how to read between the lines. She likely wouldn't see another day.

And where was his father?

He'd tried to reach him, but he didn't pick up his cell and he'd been forced to leave a terse voicemail for him. Supposedly he'd been speaking at yet another conference out in New York, but Jeremy could swear it was supposed to have ended a day or so ago. Yet he hadn't returned home.

Unfortunately, such a thing was not unusual with Ivan these days. He enjoyed the convention groupies he could garner with his good looks and fame, and he'd become much less fastidious about hiding it.

Bad timing this time with Mom so desperately ill.

Helpless to do much else, Jeremy stared at the monitors and held his mother's hand as she began to slip into a coma.

Jeremy tucked the picture in a drawer for the time being. He'd never forgiven Ivan for being unreachable when Mom was slipping away. He'd finally showed up at the hospital just minutes before she died. Ivan's treatment of her was another reason Jeremy had deliberately distanced himself from him. He didn't want to be reminded of it again now.

He glanced at his watch. Almost time for the kickoff meeting with his senior people, Glen and Tim. Jeremy was grateful to have them. They had been with SomaGene since the beginning, and apparently ran the place while Ivan had been out waxing grand at all the various functions and conferences he attended. They would surely help ease his transition into running the company. Coming from his prior grunt researcher position, this was going to be quite the adjustment for him as it was.

A knock sounded at the door. "Come in."

Glen and Tim stepped in and took their seats in front of his desk. Glen spoke first. "Welcome to SomaGene. How's your first day going?"

Jeremy smiled and shook his head. "There is a lot to absorb, that's for sure."

"That's understandable. Let us know how we can help," said Tim.

"I guess the first thing I want to figure out is where things stand with the...um, *cultivation*, as you call it."

Glen waved his hand. "That's easy. You can pull a computer report from the tracking system that gives all the information you need in real time: client, client's underlying condition, what organ, what stage of development it's in, scheduled date for transplant, and more. The development stage data is broken down even further. For example, does the tissue still need to be gathered from the client to start the process, or what development stage is that tissue in, up to when the organ is fully functional and ready for implantation." He leaned back in his chair.

"That *is* impressive."

"We can show you how to run the report whenever you want." Tim smiled. "It took a while to hone it just so, and it really makes operational tracking pretty effortless. Couple that with the strong demand for the services SomaGene provides, and things nearly run themselves. So, are you planning to perform implantations?"

"Yes, I plan to. I'd like to assist you in a couple first."

"Good. We could use the added surgical capacity. As Tim mentioned, business has been very, very good."

"All right. Well, thank you. This was helpful. I think I'd like to work my way through some of these papers and see if there is anything hiding in there that I need to address." Jeremy rose and shook hands with Glen and Tim.

After they left, Jeremy took another look at the stacks on his desk and sighed. He admitted to himself he was using the paperwork as a bit of a stall. He still felt uneasy about the ethics of building organs for money for wealthy clients, especially when the uninsured and less well-to-do languished on waiting lists—sometimes for years, sometimes until death—for tissue-matched organs from donors.

CHAPTER 8

He could hear the screeches of assorted lab animals through the walls. He did not know what those noises were, but he knew they were good noises. When he heard them, food soon followed. He had been restless today, climbing up and down the metal rungs placed inside his enclosure so he could get exercise in the confined space. Now he was hungry.

He rose from the padded shelf that served as both bed and seating area and approached the front of his enclosure, where the food came in. Anxious, he paced back and forth, stopping periodically to cling to the cold metal bars and press his face between them, as if that would give him a better view.

But there was nothing to view in the space between the front of his enclosure and the wall through which the White Coats would come. It is the White Coats that brought his food. The White Coats were good.

He paced some more, ignorant of the concept of time, yet very conscious of the tie between the screeching noises and the coming of his food.

The wall opened up, and a White Coat came in.

Tim opened the door and stepped into the Subject's room, which was located down a locked corridor, carefully isolated from the main part of SomaGene's facility per Ivan's instructions. He carried with him a tray which held a large plastic tumbler of water, as well as a cube-shaped portion of specially designed food. The shape and solid consistency made it possible to eat without utensils, and he and Glen varied the nutrition and hormone content to suit the stages of the Subject's development. If medications were needed, they could also be included in the cube for easy administration. The Subject had accepted the food and had thrived on it.

He stepped to the opening built into the front of the Subject's enclosure, unlatched it, and slid the tray inside onto the waiting shelf. "Here you go." He gazed at the Subject as he picked up the cube and began eating. He wondered what he understood of his surroundings, of his situation. While, thanks to the special nutrition and hormones packed into the designer food, the Subject appeared to be a young adult, he likely had the mental capacity of a two-year-old. With his relative isolation, it was hard to know what language he had or had not picked up.

Tim sighed and shook his head. Ivan's project had gone according to plan so far, but he often thought they never should have attempted such a thing in the first place. And even if the project itself didn't push the bounds of ethics, was it right to keep the Subject so isolated, without any opportunity for education?

The Subject focused completely on eating, and paid Tim no attention at all once he had been given his tray. Tim just stood and watched while he revisited his misgivings about the project, as he had done countless times before.

"Hey, how're things in here?" Glen entered the room and glanced at the Subject with a satisfied look. "Appetite looks good today. Seems to like the food, though I can't imagine it tastes all that good with the enhancements we put in it."

"I suppose he wouldn't know the difference since he's never been exposed to seasonings."

Glen cast a sharp glance at Tim. "We don't season the food for any *other* lab asset. Let's not lose sight of his origin and why he's here."

"Yeah. Sometimes that's hard, because of, you know, how he looks."

"Well, don't let that distract you from the goal of the project. Which reminds me, what do you think about Jeremy? Still seems a little reserved about taking over SomaGene, don't you think?"

Tim paused before answering. "Well, maybe. I don't know how to read him, really. He did just lose his father, and they were estranged, so there's probably some baggage there if nothing else."

"I hope that's all it is. If he still has reservations about SomaGene's mainline business, I can't imagine his reaction to our special project. I don't think it's quite yet time to tell him, do you?"

"No, not yet. Let him get settled first. It is only his first day."

"You know, I think we should be extremely careful. We need to be sure about him before saying anything." Glen gazed at the Subject. "After all this work, we cannot take the chance that he would kill the project. I'd rather keep it under wraps indefinitely than have that happen."

"You can't be serious. Like it or not, Ivan is dead and Jeremy owns SomaGene now. It's one thing to let him settle in before telling him, but we can't keep something like this from him indefinitely. He has a right to know what's going on, and unfortunately, he has the right to stop it if he sees fit."

Glen glared at Tim. "He's an idiot. He doesn't have half the vision Ivan did, and he never will. He didn't get SomaGene because he deserves it and is the right person to run it. He got it because of a freak accident. Damned right I'll keep this project secret as long as I have to if there is any chance of him killing it."

Tim opened his mouth to object.

Glen stabbed an angry finger in Tim's direction. "Don't you dare go around me on this. I promise you will regret it." He stalked out of the room, slamming the door behind him.

Tim flinched and noticed the Subject looked up briefly, then continued eating as if nothing happened. *Innocent as a baby. No idea his life depends on how we handle Jeremy.* Tim wondered if he should side with Glen, but for a completely different reason. If the project were killed, what would become of the Subject? Was his very existence worse than if he were to be...disposed of?

CHAPTER 9

Kenneth Girard gazed out his office window at the early fall sky. Pink and orange hues lit up the clouds as the sun crept toward the horizon. It had been a busy day, and he was just now able to get to the stack of tickle files his legal assistant had dropped off that morning.

Reluctantly, he tore himself away from the sunset view and focused on the task at hand. He pulled the stack to the center of his desk and took the first file off the top. *Magnusson.* He flipped it open to remind himself of the case's status and why he'd set a tickler for it.

He skimmed through the various memos and documents. All the work appeared to have been completed. Ownership of the business, SomaGene, had been officially transferred to the son several weeks back. All the property had been formally transferred as well—the house, the liquid assets and other items. The son had assumed responsibility for the business, and so had satisfied the sole requirement to receive the assets of the entire estate.

Kenneth shook his head. Given the value of that estate, it was a wonder the son had to think about that condition at all. For that matter, why did it even need to be a condition? He was no scientist or doctor, but surely the chance to own and run a company like SomaGene would be reward in itself. Why did the pot have to be sweetened with the conditional inheritance? He smiled. Well, if there were nothing else he'd learned in his years practicing estate law, it was that people could be funny about things.

So what remained to be done? He flipped farther through the file. *The letters.* Ivan had prepared sealed letters to be sent simultaneously to the son and the two key SomaGene people, Tim Whitman and Glen Hawkins. Kenneth had no idea what was in the letters, but Ivan had been very clear and very insistent that they go out about a month after everything had settled, if Jeremy chose to take over SomaGene. If Jeremy had not taken over, they were to have been destroyed.

Kenneth idly turned the envelopes over, wondering what they contained that was so crucial. Well, they were sealed and he had clear instructions. Whatever they contained was none of his business. He prepared them to go out in the next day's mail, and selected the next file from the stack.

CHAPTER 10

Jeremy settled in at his desk late in the afternoon. He liked having a formal work routine, and that meant attacking the mundane, but necessary, paperwork at the end of the day when his energy tended to flag anyway. He reached for the stack of mail his assistant had left in his In box.

He quickly sorted through the obvious solicitations and junk, then abruptly stopped. A letter addressed to him in his father's writing caught his eye. Feeling like a character in a Twilight Zone episode, Jeremy held it in a trembling hand and examined it more closely. Then he realized the return address was that of Ivan's lawyer.

He opened the envelope, unfolded the pages of the letter within, and spread them out on his desk. It was all written in his father's hand, but it was dated about a year ago. He hesitated for a moment, then began to read.

Jeremy,

If you're reading this, then I am deceased and you own and are running SomaGene. I provided this letter—and one each for Glen Hawkins and Tim Whitman—to Kenneth Girard to forward upon my death. He does not know the contents of any of these letters.

There are some things I need to tell you. Some of this concerns your mother. I think you've always blamed me for her early death. It's the best I can surmise since you haven't spoken to me since. I admit the rumors were true. I did see other women, and Anna was certainly aware of it. But she died of complications from Crohn's. I know there was some talk that she had perhaps deliberately chosen to stop her meds in some sort of suicidal effort. I don't believe that was true. The disease was simply too much for her, and for the therapies that were available at the time.

But as you must surely know, stress can aggravate the disease. So on that level, I've come to believe my behavior did at least contribute to her death. I now look back and regret what I did, and for what it's worth, I sincerely apologize. I can't change what happened now. I really wish I could—for your sake and hers.

I can't change what I've done, but I hope to change Crohn's power to destroy lives. As I write this, I've begun work in that vein, and I hope it comes to fruition in time to help you fight—or perhaps even conquer—your own disease. My letters to Glen and Tim instruct them to inform you of the details of this work and its current status. I don't wish to provide that information in letter form; you will surely have questions and they can answer them for you in person.

I know we haven't seen eye to eye in quite some time, and you have expressed reservations about my work, but I hope you will keep an open mind, and take SomaGene to new heights of success—both financially and in terms of continued advances in what it can offer patients to alleviate their suffering.

Good luck to you.

Love,
Ivan

Jeremy set the letter down and rubbed his face with his hands. Damned straight he blamed Ivan for his mother's early death. "Seeing other women" was such an understatement it would have been laughable under other circumstances. It wasn't just a matter of quantity; Ivan didn't seem to mind flaunting it as well. His picture was always in the paper or on the Internet with some new beauty or another. If he had at least been discreet, it would have been one thing. But the public humiliation of it—despite the fact of Mom's ill health. That was unforgiveable. *And now he's sorry. He says.*

Casting aside the posthumous apology for the garbage that it was, Jeremy wondered about Ivan's second point. What Crohn's project had he been working on? Neither Glen nor Tim had mentioned anything along those lines in any of the status meetings they'd had since Jeremy had taken the reins. Why not?

Tim set down the letter from Ivan, stood up and began to pace around his office. He and Glen had established a rather uneasy truce concerning the project. They'd both agreed to keep it from Jeremy indefinitely, albeit each for different reasons. Now Ivan had managed to force the issue from beyond the grave by instructing Jeremy to contact them for details.

He wondered if Ivan had considered the possibility that informing Jeremy would backfire and result in the destruction of the project and all he had worked for. And if so, what would become of the Subject?

His office door burst open and Glen strode in, brandishing an envelope. "Did you get one of these, too?"

Tim nodded. "Yeah, I was thinking it's not yet the right time to tell Jeremy. He still doesn't even seem fully on board with the mainline business. I wish Ivan hadn't arranged for simultaneous letters."

"Yeah, bad move considering their history. But now we're stuck with it. We'd better think this through—and fast. We've got to do whatever it takes to convince him to let the project continue. It's too damned important to let the fool scuttle it."

"I know. Well—" Tim's phone rang. He cast a panicked glance toward Glen, then picked it up. "Hello, Tim speaking."

"Jeremy here. Get Glen and come to my office immediately. I think you know better than I what we need to discuss." He hung up abruptly.

Tim paled and set down the receiver. "He wants to see us. Now."

Glen frowned. "Better be ready for a fast tap dance."

CHAPTER 11

Jeremy fidgeted at his desk as he waited for Glen and Tim. He was so keyed up, he could almost visualize his nerves as a network of tight, thin wires throughout his body—pulsing with electricity and close to snapping.

He didn't know what to expect, but he did know his trust in those two was severely damaged. He'd been at SomaGene for several months now, and they'd let on nothing whatsoever about this. What else were they keeping from him? And they were supposed to be his right-hand men in running SomaGene. *Great.*

A knock sounded. "Come in."

Tim and Glen entered and took their seats in front of his desk. They looked uneasy, glancing around and avoiding eye contact. *Good.* Ivan's overdue and wildly inadequate attempt at an apology had already put Jeremy in a foul mood; the secret project angered him even further. He had no intention of letting these two off easy—even if they had been following Ivan's instructions.

He waved his letter in the air. "I presume you also received your letters from Ivan. Let's cut to the chase. What is this Crohn's project he's talking about—and why has it been kept from me?" Jeremy slapped the letter onto his desk, leaned forward and glared at them both.

Tim and Glen exchanged a desperate look. Tim started to open his mouth, but Glen cut him off.

"It was Ivan's pet project. No one else at SomaGene knows anything about it. We're the only ones who've ever worked on it. He wanted to develop a non-drug treatment for Crohn's that would be 100% effective, or nearly so."

"So? That describes *all* of SomaGene's line. Why has this been kept secret—even from me?"

Glen shifted in his chair. "That's how Ivan wanted it. He was very clear with us about that. This project is…more ambitious than any prior work. I suppose he didn't want to risk word of it getting out and perhaps into the hands of competitors."

Jeremy slammed his hand down on his desk. "That does not explain why *I* would not be informed. I am ultimately responsible for this company and all it does. Ivan is dead. You should have informed me right at the outset."

Glen and Tim muttered vague apologies.

"All right, so explain the project to me. All of it."

Glen took another quick glance at Tim, who paled and motioned to him to go ahead. He took a deep breath and began. "Well, Ivan was somewhat obsessed with Crohn's, given what it did to your mother. He also told us that you've inherited it, so he really wanted to find a solution. The drug-based treatments, though improved in recent years, are no cure and have terrible side effects, as I'm sure you know all too well. He wanted to change that."

"So why not just develop another transplant protocol like all the rest?" Jeremy swept his arm in the general direction of the cultivation room.

Tim cleared his throat and spoke up. "There are some significant differences. One problem with using our normal cultivation and transplantation protocol is that the recipient's Crohn's will, over time, again attack the transplanted intestine. And of course, the very genes that are implicated in Crohn's would also be present in any organ generated by a client's own tissue, and that would exacerbate the problem."

"Not only that, intestines are not yet amenable to cultivation in the *in vitro* environment—not like more solid organs. Because they're tubular in shape and not rigid like a trachea, there is yet no known way to provide them a developmental framework to give them the appropriate form," said Glen.

"Well, so maybe it's not possible to develop a solution for Crohn's using cultivation and transplant as the therapeutic approach. SomaGene should stick with what works. It's certainly successful enough. Sounds like a waste of time and money chasing something Ivan's ego was driving," said Jeremy.

Glen looked down at his hands for a moment, then spoke in a low tone. "We have an approach that addresses all those issues, and so far looks quite promising."

"And what is that?"

"The protocol addresses the genetic issue by using source tissues from a Crohn's-free relative close enough to be compatible. We haven't found a way to stop the eventual Crohn's attack on the transplanted intestines, though, so we have to allow for potential repeat transplants." Glen pressed his lips together for a moment before continuing. "We've addressed the cultivation problem by using a different host modality."

"What, transgenic sheep?"

"Um, no. Native host. We've cloned the entire organism." Glen cast another quick glance at Tim, who sat silent and deathly pale.

Jeremy paused, the realization of what Glen was trying to sugarcoat slowly hitting him. His mouth suddenly became dry. "You've cloned a human being?" He couldn't believe he had uttered such a sentence.

Glen continued, appearing to choose his words carefully, as if navigating through a verbal minefield. "Uh, yes. Ivan provided the source tissue. He, uh, intended this—if it worked—to be a sort of gift to you. He believed his tissue would match yours, hopefully closely enough, but without the genetic predisposition to Crohn's that Anna's tissues would have carried."

"How long?" Jeremy could barely choke out the words.

Tim found his voice and answered. "Nearly a couple of years now. We developed a special diet that included hormones to speed the growth process."

"Where is...this...?" Jeremy's mind reeled trying to fathom what he should even call such an entity.

Glen cleared his throat. "The Subject is kept separate from the other lab assets. Ivan designed the enclosure himself and it's in a location not accessible to other SomaGene employees. We can show you, if you like."

Lab assets?

"Take me there now." Jeremy rose on unsteady legs. He wanted no part of this, wished he still knew nothing of it, yet felt ultimately responsible. He wanted to throttle Ivan for putting him in this position.

Glen led the way as the three walked down the hall in uncomfortable silence. He entered a number on a keypad that controlled the door that walled off the project from the rest of SomaGene. They walked a short distance farther through a featureless white hallway to another door. Glen paused before proceeding. "Jeremy, I realize this must be difficult for you. Are you ready?"

"I suppose."

Glen opened the door and motioned for the others to enter.

Nearly queasy, Jeremy forced himself to take it all in. The room was painted off-white, and was devoid of furnishings. Most of the space was taken up by a barred enclosure that extended from floor to ceiling. Inside the enclosure stood a man dressed in a one-piece sort of hospital gown.

A man who looked like a younger Ivan.

Slowly, walking on legs he couldn't feel, Jeremy stepped forward. The man—the *Subject*—stood at the front of his enclosure and silently stared back at him. He wore a trusting, innocent look.

Jeremy didn't know what to say, or whether to speak at all.

Tim broke the spell. "He's pretty much nonverbal. He has achieved adult size due to the nutrition and hormones we've provided, but he's only a couple of years old. We don't know what he understands."

Jeremy turned to Tim and spoke slowly as he tried hard to control his rage at the inhuman, the impossible. "You've kept a human being in this…*cell*…for a couple of years? Like a lab animal?"

Shaking his head, Glen waved his hand to stop the line of discussion and briskly interrupted. "We grew him from Ivan's tissue sample, specifically for the purpose of cultivating large and small intestines for eventual transplant. It's not like he was… born. You need to keep that in mind."

Speechless, Jeremy turned back to the Subject. He looked into his eyes, trying to discern what lay behind them.

The Subject smiled at him.

CHAPTER 12

Tim quietly closed the front door behind him. He leaned back against it for a moment and shut his eyes. He wanted to leave the day's developments at SomaGene behind him, outside that door, but he hadn't succeeded. Every bit of it continued to replay in his mind even now at home, hours later.

He tried to savor the few moments of peace and quiet before Katie and Johnnie realized he was home and competed for his time and attention. He was completely exhausted from the tense interplay among himself, Glen and Jeremy today. Each of them was at odds with the other for different reasons, and he could see no way to resolve the conflicting motives. Not now, likely not ever.

And the Subject. Tim was still haunted by the image in his mind's eye of how he had smiled at Jeremy. He hadn't seen him smile like that before; it was almost as if he knew there was some sort of connection between them.

"There you are! What are you doing, sneaking into your own house?" Katie stood in the kitchen doorway, holding Johnnie on her hip. A curl of her strawberry blonde hair strayed into her eye. She first tried to blow it out of the way, then had to deftly juggle the baby so she could irritably swipe it aside and tuck it behind her ear with one hand. "Well?"

"It's been a tough day. I'm just tired, is all."

"*You're* tired? Try keeping up with this little guy all day. He gets everywhere, and faster than you'd think. I have to run after him constantly."

Tim would have gladly traded a day watching Johnnie for the dilemma he now faced at work. Katie thought his job was all glamour, effortlessly transplanting lifesaving organs into rich, grateful clients. She didn't miss too many opportunities to remind him that she had given up her career as a business development consultant, albeit temporarily, to take care of Johnnie until he was school-aged. The combination of boredom and exhaustion did not work well for her.

"It was just especially intense today."

"Why? What happened? Did a surgery go badly?"

"Um, yeah. We had one that was a little touch and go." He didn't want to lie to her, but he didn't dare open the door to discussing the real problem. It was way too volatile to even mention outside of SomaGene.

"Well, it's OK now?"

"Yeah, it is."

"Well, then why don't you take Johnnie for his bath while I fix dinner?" She came up to him and before he could say anything more, she'd plopped Johnnie into his arms, given him a quick kiss, and made a beeline to the kitchen to work on dinner. Smelled like the kid came complete with a loaded diaper, too.

Relieved that Katie hadn't chosen to pry further into the day's events, Tim carried Johnnie into the bathroom where all his baby-washing paraphernalia was kept. He started the bath water and changed the little guy's diaper while he waited for the tub to fill.

He gently lowered Johnnie into the little plastic safety seat set within the tub. The baby started splashing the water and cackling with delight. Tim smiled. The kid sure did love his bath. He soaped up a soft sponge and started to bathe the wriggling child. Pretty soon he became so focused on bathing little Johnnie and making sure he didn't slip that his mind was able to unwind a little from the day's crisis.

CHAPTER 13

"Thanks." Glen tossed several bills on the bar to pay for his gin and tonic. He picked it up, tasted it, then began to survey the room.

He enjoyed unwinding at the Minnetonka Bistro after a busy day, at least for now while it was still the trendy place to be. In a few months, it would probably be yesterday's news, replaced by some new hot spot in town.

The bar area featured a small dance floor, but it was still too early for it to see much use. All the singles stood around the room with their drinks in hand, nodding in time with the dance music being pumped in through the sound system. They all tried to look nonchalant, but every one of them was doing the same as Glen—checking out the other singles of their preferred sex.

Glen smiled. He loved the game, loved to see what he could come up with for the evening. Some men liked to fish; he liked to chase women and enjoy the evening's catch. Minnetonka seemed to be loaded with beautiful babes who took exceptional care of themselves. They had tanned and toned bodies from the spa nearby, and they dressed in the latest and slinkiest clothes.

A tall blonde in a shimmering turquoise minidress soon caught his eye. She stood back in the corner, a bit apart from the others. She lifted her drink slightly and seemed to beckon him. He sauntered over, not wanting to look too impressed or overly anxious.

"Hi." She looked up at him from under bangs that fell just below her eyebrows, and smiled. She wore glossy lipstick that was an unabashed shade of blood red.

"Hi. Don't think I've seen you here before, have I?"

"No. I just moved here recently. Great place, huh?"

"Yeah, it is. Gets even more crowded on the weekends, if you can believe it."

They exchanged small talk for a while, then made their way to a booth that had opened up. She slid in, and he slid in beside her, rather than across from her. "So, what do you do?"

"Oh, I'm between jobs at the moment. Just moved here from Chicago. I worked for an insurance company."

Glen nodded. "Ah. I work for SomaGene. I'm one of the surgeons there." He sat back and let SomaGene do its work for him. His position there never failed to impress his dates.

Her eyes widened. "Wow, really? I've heard about them. That must be really exciting work."

"Oh, it is. We get to do amazing things every day. People come to us in terrible condition, and they walk out with new lives."

She looked down at her drink. "I wish I could do something that important." She shook her head. "My work at the insurance firm—well, it was really just clerical." She looked up at him again. "I bet you make really good money there, huh?"

It was working. "I do. You know, it's getting really loud in here. Would you like to see my place? It's only a block or two from here. I could make us a little dinner, if you like." He placed his hand on the table so the edge of it just touched hers. He noticed she left her hand right there.

"Sure I would."

He opened the door to his apartment. "Well, here it is. Let me open the curtains over there—the windows overlook Lake Minnetonka." He stepped over and pulled the cords with a little flourish. He'd done this many times, and knew the view would have the desired effect.

She followed him to the floor-to-ceiling window and stood open-mouthed. "Wow, what a great view!"

Lights from boats on the lake twinkled in the twilight. Some were docked, some were taking an evening cruise.

"Would you like some wine?" He started toward the kitchen, satisfied he was off to a good start with this one.

"Yes, thank you." She glanced around the apartment. "You have a great place here. It's near everything, and I like your décor. And that view—just amazing."

He handed her a glass of wine. "Yeah, I love it here." As they stood side by side gazing out the window, he slid his arm around her waist. She put her arm around his waist and nestled closer.

After a few minutes, he lightly ran his hand up her back, to the nape of her neck beneath her long blonde hair, then leaned over and kissed her cheek. He liked how warm and soft she felt. "Why don't we sit down?" he whispered into her ear as he led her to the trim, Euro-style black leather couch.

He took their wineglasses and set them down on the low glass and chrome table in front of the couch. Then he took both her hands in his and sat down. He maintained eye contact while trying to gauge her thoughts and what she might be into. She seemed to hesitate for a moment, then sat down beside him.

He reached out and touched her neck. He could feel her tremble ever so slightly. He found himself mesmerized by her blood-red lipstick, the gloss of it, the shape of her mouth. It looked soft, yet firm—and inviting. He leaned in and kissed her on the lips. She responded by taking him in her arms and kissing him hard, slipping her tongue inside his mouth.

Pleased to have chosen well for the evening, he reached behind her and slowly unzipped the back of her dress. He reveled in the sound of her quickening breathing. He could feel his own pulse pounding and his body throbbing with anticipation.

She broke free of his kiss and sat back. She breathed rapidly, her mouth slightly open. She gazed directly into his eyes as she pulled her dress down to her waist in one fluid movement and lay back on the couch, waiting for him.

He inwardly congratulated himself for getting that vasectomy a few years back. At times like this, he never had to concern himself if the woman was careful about birth control.

Right now, his pants were painfully constraining him. He hastily removed his clothes and carelessly cast them aside as she watched his every move. Her watching him so intently aroused him even further. Once stripped down, he displayed himself to her, enjoying the way she looked at him.

"Is this what you want, baby?"

"Yeah, that's what I want. Come help me out of this dress first."

She lifted her hips as he pulled the dress and her panties the rest of the way off and flung them aside. Naked and panting, she reached for him and pulled him toward her.

Glen gasped as he felt how warm she was inside. She began to wildly thrust her hips up toward him and he matched her rhythm. He forgot all about who she was, what she was doing, whether she was yet satisfied, and thrust faster and faster until he went over the brink of his own release.

CHAPTER 14

Jeremy arrived home late, slammed the front door shut and stomped his way toward the kitchen. He took off his jacket and flung it toward a chair, not noticing he missed it by a foot.

He'd stormed back to his office right after seeing the Subject, leaving Glen and Tim behind without another word. He just couldn't be in that room with them another minute. He'd locked himself in his office and spent the last several hours alternately pacing and sitting and wrestling with his own thoughts. He finally left the SomaGene facility a little while ago. His hands still trembled, and he didn't really remember the drive home.

He didn't even know how to begin to deal with the situation. The fact that the project had been kept secret from him paled in comparison to the larger ethical issue that had just fallen into his lap: what to do about his father's clone?

Did it make him any less human because he originated from a piece of Ivan's tissue—because he was *cultivated* in a lab? Yet, his very development had been highly manipulated. He had achieved adult proportions in less than two years, thanks to whatever cocktail of nutrients and hormones he'd been fed. That made him more of an engineered living thing, like some of the lab animals at SomaGene.

What would the public think if his existence ever came to light? Some of the animal rights types were always up in arms about keeping primates in the lab and how cruel and unfair it was to experiment on them—as if they were sentient human beings. Those people would have a field day if they learned of this.

Jeremy leaned against the kitchen counter, hunching his shoulders and bowing his head. He sighed deeply and reached into the cabinet for a glass. Then he stepped over to the shelf where he kept various hard liquors, mostly in case of company. He reached for the vodka, splashed a generous amount into his glass, and took a big swallow. He was not used to hard liquor, let alone straight, and the vodka forged a blazing hot path down his throat and into his stomach. He set down his glass and coughed until tears ran down his face.

A spasm of pain ripped through his abdomen. He clutched his stomach and groaned, cursing himself for neglecting his meds. His Crohn's had been relatively quiet lately, and he tried to take the smallest dose possible to keep the side effects at bay. Given this new situation, he figured he'd better go back to full doses to ward off any further stress-provoked attacks.

As soon as the attack waned, he made his way upstairs to his bathroom. He had moved his things into one of the other bedrooms, choosing to close off his father's grandiose suite rather than occupy it himself.

Jeremy took his meds at the sink, then regarded himself in the bathroom mirror for a moment. Ivan had manipulated him into taking over SomaGene—and had deliberately withheld information on this project until it was too late. Jeremy realized he'd unwittingly been made a party to this debacle. His name was now indelibly associated with SomaGene, and so he was now responsible for all that went on.

Ivan had created the perfect trap. Jeremy dared not reveal the project publicly, and yet he didn't know what to do about it. He couldn't simply end the project and dispose of the Subject as he could a lab asset he no longer required. But what was he supposed to do with him? Did he owe him some sort of meaningful existence?

Yet there was even more to the trap. Ivan claimed to have done it for *him*, to possibly help him conquer his Crohn's and live a normal life. Jeremy glanced at the line of prescription vials adorning his bathroom counter. None of them provided a cure. None of them even offered complete symptomatic relief. All of them came with serious side effects.

Jeremy mused for a moment on what it would be like to be free of Crohn's, free of its debilitating effects and his dependence on the meds. It was more than a matter of personal comfort and convenience. It had stymied his career.

And it could kill. He knew that firsthand.

Jeremy clutched his head in his hands, as if he could still and organize the warring thoughts swirling in his mind. He needed to talk to someone he could trust, someone who could help make sense of it all. He reached for the cell on his belt.

"Hello?"

"Amanda, it's me, Jeremy. I've run across something I…just don't know how to deal with. I really need to talk to you."

A pause. "Why me? Is it something to do with SomaGene? Don't you have an entire staff there?"

"It is, and I really can't discuss this with my staff. They're part of the…problem."

"Well, I don't know what *I* can do."

"Just hear me out. This is going to sound hard to believe, but I saw it myself, and now I have to figure out what to do. I need you to keep this to yourself, OK?"

"Well, all right."

Jeremy proceeded to explain the situation to Amanda. A long silence ensued.

"I don't know what to say. I didn't know this was possible yet on a technical level. Goes without saying you're on thin ethical ice."

"Amanda, I have to ask a big favor of you. I really don't know what to do, and there is no one else I can talk to who I trust to keep quiet—and to be a sounding board I can rely on. Would you consider coming up here for the weekend? Just…to talk about this."

"Jeremy, I…"

"I'm not trying to push you into anything. It's not that. I have a guest bedroom you could use. I just really need to work through this, and a phone call isn't going to do it."

"I can't just drop everything, and I thought we went over this all before."

"I'm only asking for the weekend, just to try to sort this out. Nothing else. Please, Amanda."

"Well, all right. Just for the weekend."

Jeremy pressed the End button after giving her the address. *Thank God she agreed. Maybe with her help I can see a way through this.*

CHAPTER 15

Amanda set the phone down and let out a frustrated growl. She'd thought her relationship with Jeremy was over and done months ago and had mostly put him out of her mind. She'd loved him at one time, but couldn't deal with his Crohn's and all that went with it—the physical toll, the drag on his career, and the baggage from his mother's death. She just couldn't picture herself assuming the caretaker role if he sank into decline. Maybe it was chickenshit on her part, sure. But Rick helped her envision a different life for herself, and so she had decided to end her relationship with Jeremy.

Now this.

She had no reason to think Jeremy was making this all up, but the story was nonetheless damned difficult to swallow. She shook her head. She didn't know what she could possibly do about it, what brilliant insight she might be able to contribute. After all, it was his decision. She wasn't a part of his life any more, but maybe just talking it through would help him figure things out.

Though she had to admit, she was more than a little curious about the technical details. How had they managed to do it? Could you tell it was a clone by looking? What did it do all day?

Amanda picked up her phone and dialed Rick. "Hey, about Saturday night. I need to be out of town this weekend, and won't be able to make it after all."

"But I made the dinner reservations weeks ago. Becker's Beach Club is really hard to get into on a Saturday."

"I know. I'm sorry. I was really looking forward to trying them out, too."

"Can't you move it to next weekend?"

Amanda weighed her response, and decided she didn't want to rock the boat with Rick for no good reason. "An old girlfriend is having some…health issues. She needs a little moral support."

"Well, all right. If you really can't get out of it. I'll reschedule and let you know."

"Thanks, bye."

She rose from the couch and went into her bedroom to pack. Just a weekend's worth of things. Nothing more.

Amanda stopped at a nearby gas station to fill her tank and get something to drink before setting off on the couple-hour drive from Rochester to Minnetonka.

She got back into the car, set the soda in the cup holder, then opened her Forester's sunroof to let in that crisp fall air. She took a deep breath and savored it. At least the scenery along the drive would be pretty this time of year, with the fall colors close to peak. She left the radio off so she could think while she drove, and pulled out of the gas station.

As she eased onto northbound US-52, Amanda started to have second thoughts about agreeing to go up to Jeremy's. She had no intention of getting back with him, and hoped her visit wouldn't encourage him to think along those lines.

But what about the ethical dilemma he had described to her? Could she be exposing herself to any professional repercussions just trying to help him figure out what to do? As far as she knew, this situation was totally uncharted territory in the field of regenerative medicine. And it was certainly way out of her league. All her subjects were incontrovertibly lab animals, and her use of them was, she believed, not controversial. Oh, sometimes she got some flak for her use of primates, but at least that was nothing new.

But a *human* clone?

She decided to set aside her worries for now and settled back in her seat. She inhaled the fresh fall air and began to enjoy the easy drive and the scarlet-tinged leaves in the roadside trees. Soon enough she would arrive at I-494 and have to battle Minneapolis metro traffic.

CHAPTER 16

Jeremy finished putting away the groceries he'd gotten in preparation for Amanda's visit. He hoped she'd agree to just stay in for the weekend so they could talk through this thing freely without fear of being overheard in a restaurant.

The doorbell rang. Jeremy hurried to the front door and opened it.

Amanda stood there, dressed in jeans and a sweatshirt, a gym bag in one hand and her purse over her shoulder. Her short dark hair rippled slightly in the breeze. "Hi. I, uh, just parked in front of the garage, if that's OK."

"Yeah, come in." Jeremy stepped back to let her in and reached for her bag. He suddenly felt awkward in her presence, even though he had invited her. It had been months since she had broken things off, and here he was asking her to help him make an incredibly personal and difficult decision.

"No, it's all right. It's pretty light." Amanda moved away from him and glanced around. "So this is the house, eh?"

Her body language was not lost on Jeremy. "Yeah. I pretty much hate it, especially now, after what I've found out about Ivan's doings. It was convenient to have a place to move into right away, though. I'll probably just sell it, take the money and buy something else."

"It is a bit…ostentatious, I suppose." Amanda took a brief tour of the lower level, poking her head into the rooms as she went. She made her way back to the bottom of the stairs. "Which room will be mine? I'll set my stuff in there so it's out of the way."

Jeremy led her upstairs. "There are several to choose from, actually. The one at the end was Ivan's. I've left it as it was. Can't stand it. The next one over is mine, and these others—"

"I'll take this one." Amanda selected the one farthest from Jeremy's and stepped inside to drop off her bag and take a quick look around.

"I got some wine and cheese. If you like, we can have that in the living room, relax a bit, and talk."

"Sounds all right. I'll be down in a minute."

Jeremy went to the kitchen to retrieve the prepared plate of cheese and crackers and little snacks that he'd purchased at Lund's. It was a bit of a cheat, but he figured things would be awkward enough without trying to demonstrate any particular culinary expertise. He opened a bottle of Chardonnay, grabbed a couple of glasses, and went into the living room to set everything out for them.

Amanda walked in moments later. Judging from her choice of clothing and lack of makeup, Jeremy guessed she was trying not to look attractive, given the circumstances. It wasn't working. She looked every bit as beautiful as he recalled, perhaps even more so. She sat down on the couch, separating herself from him by an entire cushion's width. He tried to set aside their personal discomfort with each other, as he had something far more pressing than their prior relationship to discuss. He poured them both some wine.

"So, where to begin?" He lifted his glass and sighed.

"Jeremy, I did some quick research after you called, and unless someone else has also managed to do this under wraps, it looks like Ivan did what had been considered impossible." She took a sip of her wine. "And of course in doing so, he did put you pretty much in the position you surmise—totally unsupported by any sort of ethical precedent."

"I just can't wrap my head around it—that clone." He set his glass down, and twisted his hands in his lap as he spoke. "What *is* he? *Who* is he? And what are my obligations to him?"

"I can't figure that out, either. Given that he already exists, I don't see how you can risk raising the issue with an outside ethicist and getting a formal opinion." Amanda frowned and stared down for a few moments, then looked at Jeremy. "You know, I think it's all or nothing. You either keep him in the lab indefinitely and keep this whole thing quiet—or you get him out of that lab and somehow prepare him to live independently. But then the whole project goes public and you'll have to deal with God knows what sort of fallout. And who knows how he would be received in the outside world anyway."

Jeremy shifted in his seat as the implications sunk in. "I bet it'd bring the company down."

"True enough. And if you let him out, then I suppose you would have to treat him as a vulnerable adult. How would that work? Who would be the guardian—you? You say he physically appears to be a grown adult, but has only existed for a couple of years. His mental development can't possibly be normal. What sort of life would he have anyway?"

Jeremy stood and began to pace the room like a trapped animal. His hands balled into fists at his sides. "I can't believe this! *What* am I supposed to do? If I keep quiet, I'm sentencing a human being to life as a lab animal. If I take him out of the lab, I have no idea what it would mean for him to exist in the outside world, no idea if he would ever be capable of self-sufficiency. I don't know what he thinks, *if* he thinks, nothing." Jeremy stopped pacing. "And of course, it would destroy SomaGene to admit we even did such a thing."

"Maybe you don't know enough to even try to make this decision now."

"What do you mean?"

"Well, you just said you don't know if he thinks. You don't really know if he is sentient. I don't think you know enough about him and how he is or is not functioning to be able to guess at what he really is."

Jeremy returned to the couch and sat down heavily. "You're right," he said softly.

Amanda gathered momentum. "So maybe you start by testing his cognitive function, see what you're really dealing with. Give yourself a little time to do that before you make a decision."

"That sounds—" Jeremy moaned and clutched his stomach as a searing pain shot through him.

"What is it?" Amanda jumped up.

"Fucking Crohn's. It's getting active again. Gimme a

minute." Jeremy curled into a fetal position on the couch, trying to ride out the wave of pain.

"I thought you'd told me the meds had been keeping it in check." Amanda crouched down next to him.

"It had been pretty quiet the last few months, but the stress from this damned situation seems to have kicked it into high gear again." Jeremy groaned.

"Can I do anything?"

"No, just give me a minute. It's starting to taper some." Jeremy let out a long breath. "OK, it's a bit better now." He slowly sat up.

"When did you last get evaluated?"

"I went in for a full workup at Mayo right before I moved up here. Barium, sigmoidoscope, the whole thing. They found a section—a few inches—that is pretty compromised. They said as long as the meds keep things at bay, to stay on them. But they said it was likely that section would eventually constrict or develop a fistula, and that would mean surgery." Jeremy gasped as another, briefer, wave of pain struck him. "Problem is, I've been trying to keep the meds to the minimum possible dose because the side effects have been getting worse over time. And surgery isn't even a permanent solution—the problem would return at some point, just in a different section."

Amanda stood, walked over to a window and gazed out before she spoke. "You know, Jeremy, you have another decision you need to make."

The worst of the pain over, Jeremy sat up straighter. "What are you getting at?"

Amanda turned toward him. "I'm not saying I'm comfortable with this, mind you, but remember why he exists in the first place. Ivan made him for you. To try to cure you. If it worked, maybe SomaGene could try to come up with a less ethically challenged way to achieve the same result. What a breakthrough that would be—think of it."

"Well, I didn't ask him to do this!"

"Jeremy, that doesn't matter anymore. It's done. The only question concerns what *you* are going to do now. You need to separate your resentment of Ivan from what's presented here.

Your disease has progressed, and the meds aren't working as well as they used to. You could be pushing away a cure."

Jeremy bowed his head, exhausted. "Maybe you're right. I just can't think about this anymore now. I'm really sorry—I just want to go to bed right now. I got groceries. You can make whatever you want for yourself—the kitchen has about anything you could imagine. Sorry."

Without another word, Jeremy made his way up the stairs to his room. He flopped down onto his bed without changing clothes, and tried to sleep. Tangled thoughts raced through his mind and refused to let him rest. Thoughts of his moral duty, his own dire medical dilemma…and of Amanda and how much he really still wanted her.

CHAPTER 17

"I think you need to see him." Jeremy and Amanda, each nursing a hot cup of coffee, sat at the little table in the glass-enclosed breakfast nook the next morning.

She gazed through the glass at the tree-lined back yard as she warmed her hands on the mug. "I don't know. I was thinking of heading back home a little later today." She'd reflected on the situation last night after Jeremy had abruptly gone to bed. The last thing she wanted was to get any deeper into Jeremy's ethical snake pit—let alone reopen anything concerning their relationship. She thought she'd given all the advice she was capable of in their discussion last night, and saw no need to prolong her visit just to go over the same ground.

"You made a good point about evaluating his cognitive function before making a decision, but I think if you saw him, too, it might bring something else to mind that could help."

Amanda waved her hand as if to ward off Jeremy's words. "Look, I understand the gravity of this, believe me, and that's all the more reason I don't want to get further involved, see?" She took a sip of her coffee and set the cup down hard.

"All right, Amanda. I understand. Just this one last thing. Come see him for a few minutes. The campus is a really short drive from here, and it should be empty on the weekend. Just this, please?"

Amanda weighed it in her mind. She was curious to see the clone—as a scientist, of course—but that had to be it. She would not let Jeremy draw her in further. "All right. Then I'm heading home."

Jeremy opened the main door and ushered Amanda inside the SomaGene facility. She stopped, astonished, when she saw the inside of the atrium. "I've never seen anything like this. All the surfaces *float*?"

"Yes, the outside skin of the building draws in solar power to assist. Special electromagnets are used to suspend various surfaces throughout the facility, like here in reception, in the surgical suites, and in the cultivation room. Also, the air is very aggressively filtered. The idea is to keep the surroundings so clean that we can use the absolute minimum of antibiotics and anti-rejection meds in our procedures. Results in much better surgical outcomes, and helps avoid creating more resistant organisms."

"This is truly impressive. I thought Mayo was advanced. They have nothing on this."

"I can show you the cultivation room if you're interested. I'd like to take you to see him first, though. Then you can decide if you want to stay longer—or not—to tour the rest of the place."

Renewing her resolve to stay as uninvolved as possible, Amanda replied, "Yes, of course, thank you."

They walked in silence as Jeremy led her to the door to the Subject's enclosure. "All right, this is it." He paused to look her in the eye. "You ready?"

"Yes." Amanda did her best to look nonchalant, but she felt a burst of adrenaline as she realized she was about to view something that had never been done—that she knew of.

Jeremy opened the door and silently motioned her to follow him in. He paused in front of the Subject's enclosure.

Amanda stepped inside, riveted by the sight of the Subject. He stood at the front of his barred enclosure, staring at them both with a look of what appeared to be innocent wonder. Clad in something resembling a hospital gown, he certainly did appear to be a young adult version of Ivan. Amanda moved closer. "Does he speak?"

"Glen and Tim say he's not verbal. They've fed and cared for him all this time, but they don't know what he might understand."

"Hello." Amanda looked into the Subject's eyes and wondered what, if anything, he was thinking. He continued to gaze back at her with a seemingly trusting look. Or was she seeing what she expected to see?

It would be so incredible to run tests on him. Had the brain developed at an accelerated rate along with the body due to the nutrient and hormone regimen? Did it only lack education and training to make the Subject a fully functional adult? Or was more required to develop cognitive function—was experience needed along with the physical cell development? Was the brain even of adult size within the cranium? Her scientist's mind nearly ran wild before she brought it up short. To involve herself in any meaningful way would likely expose her to an ethics probe and end her career.

Amanda drew back. "All right. I've seen him. I'd like to go now."

The Not White Coats shut the door, leaving him alone in his sparse and silent enclosure. He gazed at the door for several minutes afterwards, then reached out from between the bars with one hand. He had wanted to do that while they were there, but had been afraid.

The White Coats were always nice. They brought him food. He did not know what to think of the Not White Coats. They did not bring him food. They did not stay very long. They made few sounds before leaving. Were they nice, too, or not?

One of the White Coats would often sit with him, making sounds for him. The other White Coat often brought food, but never stayed very long. Sometimes they both came, and they made sounds to each other. He wondered what those sounds meant, wondered if he could make them, too.

CHAPTER 18

Jeremy heard footsteps on the stairs as he was putting some dishes into the dishwasher. He stepped out of the kitchen to the foyer in time to see Amanda coming down the stairs. She had her gym bag and purse slung over her right shoulder, and looked ready to leave.

Jeremy slumped a little with disappointment. He'd hoped she'd at least stay the whole weekend. They hadn't come up with anything approaching a neat and tidy solution to his dilemma, though he wasn't sure they ever could no matter how much time and effort they put into it. Even so, just having her around to talk to comforted him and made him feel less alone in facing it.

He admitted to himself he wanted to rekindle their relationship, even in the midst of all this turmoil and the resurgence of his Crohn's. She'd broken things off, not him, and he missed her terribly to this day. He'd had no interest in dating other women because he could still think of no one else he'd rather be with.

"Do you really need to leave so soon?" He hoped he didn't sound like he was pleading with her to stay.

"Yeah. I have a busy week coming up, and want to have some time to relax at home before the end of the weekend." Amanda did not make eye contact.

Jeremy could tell she had no intention of entertaining any further discussion, so he suppressed what he really wanted to say. "Well, it was good to see you again. Thanks for coming up. I really appreciate it." He reluctantly opened the door for her.

"You're welcome. Take care, Jeremy." Amanda gave him a quick glance, then turned and headed for her car.

Jeremy lingered at the door and watched her as she drove

off without waving or looking back. He slowly shut the door, then leaned against it, suddenly feeling empty, hopeless, and terribly alone. The house already seemed cold and cavernous without her there.

He trudged back to the kitchen to finish loading the dishwasher. He mindlessly placed dishes in the racks and silverware in the little plastic corrals as he thought about the week ahead of him. After their last encounter, he dreaded having to face Glen and Tim again on Monday. He considered their working relationship irreparably damaged because of their secrecy, yet he knew he needed them on so many levels. How he was going to get past his anger with them to keep the relationship functional going forward, he had no idea right now.

As far as the Subject went, he'd decided to let the situation ride for the time being, uncomfortable as that would be. Amanda was right. He didn't know enough about the Subject's cognitive function to make an informed decision about what to do about him. He'd have to figure out a way to measure that, and then decide.

CHAPTER 19

"Thanks for rescheduling. I hope it wasn't too much of a hassle." Amanda glanced toward the packed, neon-lit bar at Becker's Beach Club. All the denizens were dressed to impress—and most of them were likely there only for some drinks. Entry to the dining area was far more elusive.

"I think we got a little lucky, only having to wait a couple of extra weeks to get in." Rick smiled. "I've heard nothing but great things about the food."

"Right this way." A razor-thin young man with a clean-shaven face and precisely trimmed short dark hair led them to their booth. He wore an old-school uniform of black matte pants and vest, and a crisp white long-sleeved shirt.

Amanda felt like she'd stepped back in time, between the young waiter's demeanor and the piped-in notes of Ol' Blue Eyes Sinatra. She'd looked forward to trying out this restaurant for months, and had felt terrible for causing Rick to have to reschedule after snagging coveted reservations.

She'd heard the owners wanted to create an experience that combined cutting-edge cuisine with an old-fashioned sort of class—the first of its kind in Rochester. As she evaluated her surroundings, she thought they'd certainly succeeded with the atmosphere. All the reviews said they'd succeeded with the food, too.

The waiter seated them in a deeply padded black leather booth lit only by tiny track lights suspended above. He asked what they wished to drink in a tone that was cool and professional, yet inviting. Falling into an old-school mood, Amanda ordered a dirty martini—extra olives.

Rick ordered the same and began to scan the enormous, leather-bound menu. "Finally, some great dining that isn't in Minneapolis or St. Paul."

Amanda opened her menu and flipped through the pages. "No kidding. I'm going to have a hard time choosing. Look, they have sablefish. They put it on a bed of grilled asparagus. I'll have that." She took a sip of her martini. "Ooh, haven't had one of these in a while. They make a mean one."

Rick took a sip of his drink. "That is good—best ever. Glad we finally made it here." He smiled and reached across the table to take her hand. "So how's your girlfriend doing?"

"My what?"

"Your girlfriend—the one you stood me up for a couple of weeks back."

Amanda took another sip and tried to hide her misstep. She hadn't expected Rick to bother asking weeks after the fact. "Oh, she's much better now."

Rick scowled slightly. "Well, that's good. Must have been something pretty serious for you to skip town at a moment's notice like that."

"Yeah, it was. It was kinda sudden and she needed someone to talk to pretty badly. Can we, uh, change the subject? It was pretty intense at the time, and I'd rather not think about it right now." Amanda smiled at Rick. "I'd much rather enjoy our belated evening out."

"Sounds good to me. Maybe we should plan a weekend away together soon. Would you like that?"

"I would. Let's pick a place soon. So, what are you having?" Amanda was relieved Rick got off the subject of her little weekend away. She hoped he'd leave it at that and she wouldn't have to come up with more supporting details for the lie. And she hoped she'd heard the last about it from Jeremy. She didn't need to be involved in his crazy complications, and she didn't want to risk derailing her relationship with Rick.

CHAPTER 20

Jeremy returned to his office after assisting Glen and Tim in a successful liver transplant. They had developed a truly impressive protocol for the cultivation and transplant processes prior to his taking over the company. The business nearly ran itself with the high demand and fees they were able to charge their well-to-do clientele. And the actual procedures had been honed to elegant simplicity.

He gazed out his window at the grassy clearing and border of evergreens that comprised his view. The first serious snow of the season had dropped several inches on the grass and had coated the pine needles like trees in a Christmas postcard. He still intended to sell the house, but on days like this the extremely short commute was a nice perk. He wouldn't have to fight snarled traffic for an hour or more, unlike most commuters in the area.

Good thing, too. He was tired and just not up for a tough drive home. As smoothly as the surgery had gone, it seemed to take more and more out of him these days to stand for several hours like that. His Crohn's had been slowly ramping up since the fall, despite his returning to the full prescribed doses of his meds. He wasn't sure any more if it was Crohn's or the meds—or his poor sleeping patterns—that contributed most to his constant fatigue.

His sleep had been troubled for the past several months as he continued to wrestle with the question of what to do about the Subject. No good answer presented itself, no matter how he approached the problem or how hard he tried to resolve it.

For the time being, he was taking the path of least resistance and keeping the project under wraps. He still hadn't even figured out the best way to conduct the cognitive testing that might help him decide. He was no expert in such things, and did not dare enlist outside assistance. So he kept spinning in circles—and his inability to decide tormented him daily.

Jeremy considered just going home for the day and trying to rest. Suddenly, a pain seized his stomach that was so intense it took his breath away. He hunched over and tried to breathe deeply until it subsided.

There was a knock at his office door.

"Not now," he said through clenched teeth.

"It's me—Glen. I need to talk to you about tomorrow's scheduled procedures."

"Not now!"

Glen entered the room anyway and cast a questioning look at Jeremy. "What's the matter?"

"Crohn's is acting up." Jeremy tried to pace his breathing to get through the pain.

"You've been taking your meds, haven't you?"

"Yessss…but they're not working as well as before, and the side effects are getting worse."

"Jeremy, you know there is a solution. It's waiting for you. Tim and I can perform the procedure."

"I can't…"

Glen moved closer to Jeremy's desk and spoke forcefully. "The whole point of Ivan's work was to make this possible. Your meds are failing. You know as well as I do the longer you wait, the more debilitated you get, the bigger the risk. We should start planning the procedure. We'll need to decide how much to transplant, for one thing."

Jeremy writhed in his chair. He didn't want to have this conversation at all, let alone when he was in such pain. "What do you mean?"

"I've given this some thought. There are two main approaches we could take. One is a minimalist approach. Just replace the segment that is most compromised, and leave the rest of the Subject intact. If—and likely when—you had another intestinal segment that became compromised in the future, we would use the same Subject to replace that segment, and so on as needed. Or we could transplant the entire small and large intestine in one procedure. It would provide more complete relief, but of course, your disease would eventually attack those tissues again. It would buy time until that day, though, and we could regenerate another Subject by then if we just plan accordingly."

Jeremy waved him away. "I just can't talk about this right now, all right?"

"OK. But let's talk about it as soon as you're up to it. I think it's time to act." Glen let himself out and shut the door behind him.

Jeremy put his head down on his desk, clutched his stomach, and concentrated on taking slow, deep breaths to push Glen's words from his mind and to get him through the painful spasms.

Glen spotted Tim walking down the hall. "Hey, wait up a minute." He caught up to him.

Tim stopped. "What is it?"

"I was just in Jeremy's office. He was in a lot of pain, looked terrible. His Crohn's is getting worse and the meds aren't working so well any more. I suggested we start planning the procedure."

"What did he think of that? He still seems pretty conflicted about the project in general. Can't imagine he was too receptive."

"He pretty much shooed me out of there and wouldn't talk about it. I think it will take some convincing, but the longer he waits, the worse his chances. Meanwhile, we need to decide on whether to transplant only the most critical segment, or the entire large and small intestine. There are tradeoffs, of course."

"Well, if we take only a segment, the Subject should be able to withstand that, given some additional nutritional support. But the entire intestine? That would kill him—or would put him on some form of life support that would be pretty ghastly to live with."

"Tim, remember why the Subject is here: to potentially cure Jeremy. That's what Ivan intended. So if we need the entire intestine, then that is what we use. If it kills him, we clone another so we're ready in the event Crohn's eventually compromises the transplanted organs."

Tim paled.

"I'd better not have to fight both of you on this. We need to move soon to get the best odds of success, and we need to take whatever portion is going to provide the best relief. Simple as that." Disgusted with Tim's unprofessional attitude toward the Subject and unwilling to listen to any more protestations about the project, Glen stalked off toward his office.

CHAPTER 21

The procedure Jeremy, Glen, and Tim were performing was going so smoothly, it was as if it were the most mundane of surgeries. Jeremy never dreamed he would think such a thing of something as complex as a heart transplant.

Thanks to the unique clean-room environment, there was no need to pump the patient full of antibiotics. And of course, because the organ was autologously generated from the patient's own source tissues, there was no need for the dangerous and debilitating antirejection drug regimen, either. Side effects and recovery time were stunningly minimal.

SomaGene's transplant success rate was nearly 100% due to careful patient selection and the unique protocols. No other clinic came close. Jeremy smiled a little behind his surgical mask. At least this part of the business was smooth and noncontroversial, except for the have-and-have-not aspect of providing such a service to well-heeled clients while people of normal means waited, dying a little each day, for a donor organ they *might* not reject.

"Jeremy…clamp!"

Glen's urgent demand snapped Jeremy's attention back to the present task. He chided himself. No matter how honed the protocol, inattention was still unacceptable and dangerous.

He passed Glen the clamp.

Tim sat by the patient's head, managing the anesthesia. "Looking good."

"Ready to switch to the artificial heart." Glen turned on the machine that would pump the patient's blood during the brief time between clamping off the defective heart and connecting the new heart. Moments passed as they all watched the monitors.

"Stable," said Tim. "Vitals good."

"New heart, please." Glen removed the diseased heart and dropped it into a stainless steel pan, then reached out, palms up, to receive the organ and gently place it in the patient's chest.

Jeremy turned to the special container that held the precious organ, bathed in nutrients and warmed to body temperature. He carefully lifted it from its protected glass environment and placed it in Glen's outstretched hands.

Glen accepted the organ, turned back to the patient and began to place and connect it within the chest cavity. Despite the nearly commonplace occurrence of such procedures within the walls of SomaGene, all three men were reverently silent as Glen made the placement.

Jeremy felt his stomach clench, then the familiar and increasingly frequent searing pain cut through him again. He felt a little dizzy, and wished he could get off his feet and try to breathe through the pain for a few minutes. But there was no way he could do that. The procedure was at the most critical juncture—the switchover from the artificial heart to the new one. He just had to hang on through the pain for a little while longer. He grimaced, but thought neither Glen nor Tim noticed. He surreptitiously reached for the far end of the surgical table to help steady himself.

"I've got all the vessels connected and ready. How's he doing?" asked Glen.

"Vitals good. Go ahead with the switch," said Tim.

Jeremy flipped the switch to shut off the artificial heart, just as Glen administered a shock to start the new heart.

"It's beating. Watch…"

Tim scowled at the various display screens that surrounded him. "Good…good…"

Another wave of pain seized Jeremy. Darkness crept in on the periphery of his vision for a moment, but he thought he recovered pretty quickly from it.

"Blood pressure dropping!"

"Shit! One of the vessels isn't holding. Clamp!" Glen waited for a brief moment. "Clamp, Jeremy!"

Jeremy had only heard their words in a sort of fog. He shook his head to try to clear the haze, grasped the edge of the table a little harder to try to steady himself and get back into what was happening.

Glen turned to Jeremy and snapped, "He's going to bleed out—hand me a goddamned clamp!"

Jeremy stumbled to the instrument tray, selected a clamp, and slapped it into Glen's gloved hand as decisively as he could—which wasn't very much so.

Glen snatched the instrument and silently bent to the task of stopping the bleeding.

Tim stared at Jeremy, but did not speak.

Glen wiped beads of sweat from his brow with his right gown sleeve and sighed. "All right, got it. What do you see, Tim?"

Tim viewed his monitors for several moments before answering. "Looking better...better. OK, all good now."

Glen bowed his head for a moment. "Good. Good." He glanced briefly at Jeremy. "You look like shit. Get out of here. We'll close." He turned back to the patient's open chest and began to meticulously stitch the various layers of tissue, then skin.

Jeremy, still feeling weak, tottered backward, then quietly made his way out of the surgical ward and into the little atrium where they scrubbed and gowned for the procedures. He stripped off his gloves and flung them into the receptacle. Then he sat heavily in a chair, lowered his head, and breathed deeply to try to ward off the pain for a while.

After several minutes, the worst of the pain subsided and he could see and think clearly again. *My God, I nearly blew it in there. I wasn't paying attention. That patient could have died because of it.* He put his face in his hands.

A little while later, the surgery door burst open and Glen strode toward him. "What the fuck was that? Where were you? That patient could have bled out waiting for a simple, fucking clamp!" He jabbed his index finger in Jeremy's face. "That can never, ever happen again!"

Tim pushed the gurney out the swinging doors of the surgery. "He's ready to go to the recovery suite. Someone want to help roll him?"

"I will." Glen took one end of the gurney and helped guide it out and to Recovery.

Jeremy watched them go, knowing Glen was right—and hating what he'd have to do to keep this from happening again.

CHAPTER 22

Jeremy stumbled slightly and leaned against the hallway wall for support. Darkness stole in at the edge of his vision as he fought off a wave of dizziness. Running his hand along the wall to guide himself, he faltered toward his office, just a couple of doors away. Once there, he gripped the door jamb like a lifeline, pivoted into the room and quickly took the last few steps to his desk, where he flopped into his chair.

He rested his head on his desk until the spell passed. It had only been a few days since he had the attack during the heart transplant. He licked his cracked lips, then reached for the tumbler of water he kept on his desk. He drank cautiously.

He'd just returned from his fourth visit to the bathroom that morning. Each visit had been more agonizing than the last, as Crohn's viciously attacked his intestines. His meds seemed to be doing nothing to fend it off, and he knew after this morning's activity he must be significantly dehydrated. He sipped some more water, then set the tumbler down with a trembling hand.

Jeremy raised his head, leaned back in his chair and tried to sit up fully. He winced as another spasm racked him, and hoped he could stay out of the bathroom at least for a while. He felt empty, torn apart.

And he realized a decision was being forced upon him—a decision he wanted no part of.

He sipped some more water, hesitated for a minute, then picked up the phone and dialed Amanda. He leaned forward again, resting his elbow on the desk and his forehead on his hand.

Mercifully, she picked up on the second ring. "Amanda,

it's me, Jeremy. I…um…sorry to bother you, but…I don't know what else to do."

"What's wrong? You sound awful."

Jeremy explained how much his Crohn's had worsened since they last spoke. "I don't want to do it." He closed his eyes and slowly shook his head.

"What, Jeremy? Are you thinking of going ahead with the procedure?" Amanda paused. "I know how you feel about it, and I have my reservations, too, but if your condition has really degraded that much, well, I don't see any other solution."

"Do I have the right?" He forced himself to say the words aloud. "It could kill him."

Amanda sighed. "I still don't know, and I really can't be the judge anyway. It's your life. I don't know what I would do if I were in your position. I do know that if your meds aren't working any more…your mother, you know."

"Yeah, I know."

"Didn't you mention two possible protocols? One was much more conservative, just taking enough of a section to replace the most damaged portion. That would leave him compromised, but it shouldn't be fatal."

"Yes, that was one of the approaches. Maybe that would be enough to take care of the worst of this without…sacrificing him. Sort of like a healthy person donating a kidney. They compromise themselves somewhat, but still have the other." Jeremy paused, gathering the nerve to ask his next question. "Amanda, I know this is a huge imposition, but if I do this, I'm going to need a little help while I recover. I hate to ask this of you, but I can't very well hire someone, given the circumstances." He held his breath as he waited for her answer.

Amanda paused for a long time before answering. "I would need to rearrange my schedule, but I think I could manage it. I imagine you wouldn't be up to running up and down those stairs for at least a little while afterwards."

"Are you sure?"

"Yeah. Yeah, I can be there. You shouldn't be alone for this."

Jeremy felt the first and only shred of reassurance he'd felt in some time. "Thanks, Amanda. I really appreciate you doing this. I'll get things arranged and let you know the schedule."

After he hung up, Jeremy sat for a moment and let his decision sink in a bit before calling Glen. Having Amanda to help him through it was more than he could have hoped for, but even the more moderate surgical approach still didn't sit right when he dared to look into his conscience.

He called Glen and asked him to bring Tim to his office to confer on an important matter, then he sipped some more water and tried to prepare himself for the reality of actually committing to this decision.

Moments later, Glen and Tim stepped into his office.

"What's up?" asked Glen.

Jeremy explained the morning's events and why he had asked them to come to his office.

"Well, if it's progressed that acutely, why not address it in one procedure—take the entire large and small intestine?" Glen sat forward in his chair, his eyes positively alight with excitement at the prospect.

"That would mean death, or at minimum an extremely unnatural and painful existence for the Subject." Jeremy shook his head. "I'm just not prepared to go that far. I'm barely prepared to even take *this* step."

"Well, aren't *you* having the unnatural and painful existence right now?" Glen folded his arms as Tim sat silent, his lips pressed tightly together.

"That doesn't mean I have the right to inflict it on someone else. No, I don't want to discuss that version of the procedure. I want the most conservative possible, to try to solve my problem and still leave him in the least compromised condition."

Glen waved a dismissive hand and took on a patronizing tone. "All right, if that's how you feel. Given what you describe, I think we'll be having that discussion at some point anyway."

"I'll deal with that if and when it comes up. So, what do we need to do to prepare?"

Tim spoke up. "Jeremy, you look horrible. I think the first thing to do is some pre-op blood work, of course, but we also need to get some fluids into you. You're certainly dehydrated, and it would be too dangerous to proceed until that's cleared up."

Glen nodded. "That sounds sensible. We should also put you on some stronger steroids temporarily just to get your tract calmed down so you can build a little strength back up. I wouldn't want to operate with you in an active flare-up situation unless there was no other choice. Let's get conditions as optimal as possible first."

"How soon for the procedure, then?"

"Let's plan on a week out, and work on building you up in the meantime." Glen glanced at Tim, who nodded in agreement.

Jeremy wished he felt better about his decision. Not only was he undertaking something beyond his ethical comfort zone and inherently risky, but he also was being forced to place his trust—and his life—in the hands of the very two people who had concealed the project from him in the first place.

CHAPTER 23

"Just lie back on the table, Jeremy." Tim turned to the counter at the side of the treatment room and prepared the IV kit.

Jeremy lay down and rolled up his right sleeve. The heavy steroids had calmed the pain and irritation in his bowels, but of course such doses were not something that could be tolerated by the body for very long. Still, he was grateful for the relief for now.

Tim turned around, hooked a bag of saline on the bracket above the head of the gurney, then placed a tourniquet on Jeremy's arm. "You ready?"

Jeremy nodded. He hoped Tim was good with needles, because he hated them. He already felt woozy from being dehydrated and full of steroids in the first place.

He flinched as Tim jammed the needle home into the vein on his upper wrist. He then taped it down, removed the tourniquet, and adjusted the flow of the saline.

"All right. Now just rest there. This should take maybe an hour to infuse. I'll check on you in a while and we can see if this will do it, or if another bag would be advisable. You OK?"

"Yeah."

"OK, just relax. I'll be back in a while. There's a panic button over on your left if you need anything."

"Thanks."

Tim left the room, gently closing the door behind him.

Jeremy settled his head on the paper-covered pillow and closed his dry and tired eyes. The saline felt cool and tickled slightly as it flowed into his vein. He welcomed it. After the repeated gut-tearing bouts of diarrhea he'd had in recent days, he felt as if no amount of water he could try to drink would get to his tissues and refresh him like this.

He tried to relax, tried to focus on positive thoughts. He looked forward to seeing Amanda again, though he certainly would have preferred to see her under far different circumstances. How strange it would be to have her in his house taking care of him, given that they had split up mainly because she didn't want to end up caring for someone incapacitated by a debilitating disease.

And of course, there was the elephant in the room. The Subject. The unwitting donor. Whatever you wanted to call him. It was probably too late to question whether he had a right to this transplant without becoming a complete hypocrite—even more so than he already felt himself to be. The wheels were in motion; he'd made the choice, such as it was. Jeremy supposed the best he could do was to be sure the Subject was kept as comfortable as possible, and given the best available care to recover from the procedure. He tried to make peace with that position and doze a little.

After a while, Tim returned to check on him. "Perfect timing. Bag's just about empty." He pinched the skin on the back of Jeremy's hand to test his hydration. "Well, it's better than you were. How do you feel?"

"I think a little better. I'd like to get up and move around now anyway."

"OK, we can give you some more later if we need to." Tim quickly slipped the needle out and taped a piece of cotton over the site. "There. Let me help you sit up. Don't get up too quickly." Tim cranked the gurney so that it elevated Jeremy's torso at about a 45-degree angle. "Rest like that for a few minutes."

"I really do feel quite a lot better than earlier today."

Tim chuckled. "Well, that wouldn't take much. You really looked like shit when you called us in." He raised the back of the gurney just a bit more, and changed to a less conversational tone. "Jeremy, I know you're not completely comfortable with the idea of the procedure. I understand. I think it's a huge advance that can bring a lot of relief to patients if we were to commercialize it, still…it's disconcerting, on the edge." Tim looked off into the distance.

Jeremy was somewhat surprised at Tim's admission. He had just supposed that Tim and Glen were completely in concert on the project. But, now that he thought more about it, Glen was the more vocal one. Maybe they weren't equally committed after all.

Jeremy rolled his sleeve down. "Hey, thanks, I'm feeling all right now. You don't need to babysit me anymore." He smiled.

"OK, thanks. I do need to get to some work in the cultivation room. We've got some more new starts in there to check on." Tim left the room.

Jeremy was relieved to see him go. He wanted to be alone so he could take care of something he needed to do.

Jeremy glanced up and down the hallway to be sure he would have a little bit of private time, then he opened the door to the Subject's enclosure and stepped inside.

He softly shut the door behind him and stood staring at the Subject, who had been sitting on the padded shelf that served as both seating and bedding. Upon seeing Jeremy enter, the Subject stood and moved to the front of his cell. He grasped the bars and quietly stared back at Jeremy. He seemed to expect something.

Jeremy stepped about halfway to the Subject and looked into his eyes. He wondered what he was thinking, *if* he was thinking. What sort of things went through his head? He looked so vulnerable behind those bars, dressed in that surgical gown. Did he have wants, desires? Could he even conceptualize such things? Surely he had basic drives, like the need to eat and drink. Like the desire to be free from pain. Jeremy winced as he thought of what the Subject would soon undergo. For *his* benefit.

Jeremy stepped even closer. The Subject did not move away. Instead, he returned Jeremy's stare, almost as if he knew him. *Is he searching* my *eyes for a clue to why I'm here?* A chill chased up Jeremy's spine. Soon they would be joined, in a strange sort of way. On an impulse, Jeremy reached out, tentatively, and lightly touched his fingertips to those of the Subject. He instantly wished he hadn't, as he experienced a strange sort of thrumming on his fingertips where they contacted the Subject.

The Subject gently grasped his fingers in his hand. And then he smiled.

Startled by the Subject's move and the strange sensation in his fingers, Jeremy flinched and reflexively snatched his hand out of the Subject's grasp, as if he'd accidentally touched a cobra.

Looking as if he was going to cry, the Subject recoiled and sat back down. He then rolled over to face the wall as he curled into a fetal position.

Jeremy didn't know what to say or do, and so he quietly left the room and closed the door behind him. He didn't want to encounter Glen or Tim, so he quickly headed back to his office so he could be alone to reflect on what had just happened.

Maybe that was it. White Coats are good. No White Coat, not good. Can't trust.

The Subject looked closely at the hand Not White Coat had touched. How strange it had felt. White Coats had never touched his hand like that. White Coats cleaned him. White Coats changed his clothes. White Coats never touched without a purpose.

What was the purpose of No White Coat touching him?

The Subject could not understand; he became uneasy.

He curled up even tighter, then fell asleep for a while.

CHAPTER 24

Amanda hung up the phone. *Why the hell did I let him talk me into that? Now I've let myself get sucked into this thing. Great, just great.* She'd have to do some serious scrambling to juggle her work schedule to accommodate such an absence.

And then there was Rick.

They'd already made plans for their weekend away, and she'd have to cancel it. Surely he'd not be thrilled with that hassle and disappointment. It had been all they'd been talking about since he nailed the reservations. They'd planned to drive to a fancy lakeside cabin in Wisconsin. She shrugged. At least they wouldn't have plane reservations to redo as well.

But what to tell him? Her true reason for cancelling had to be kept secret—even if the patient didn't happen to be her former boyfriend. The mysterious sick girlfriend would have to resurface. The continuity would likely bolster the story's credibility, and she could lean on it being some female issue to avoid getting into details.

She took a deep breath to prepare herself for a nice, elaborate—and hopefully successful—lie, picked up her phone and dialed.

"Hey, Rick, how're you doing?"

"Fine. What's up?"

Amanda closed her eyes and hoped she could pull it off. "Well, um, remember my old girlfriend who had the medical issues a couple of months back?"

"Yeah, what about her?"

"Well, she's having problems again. This time she needs surgery. I need to go back and stay with her for a while."

"When?"

"That's the problem. I'll need to be there over the time we're scheduled to go to Wisconsin." Amanda held her breath. She knew he'd be pissed; it was only a matter of how much.

"Are you serious? I've already made the reservations and put down the deposit."

She replied quickly to try to sidetrack his rising anger. "I know, I'm sorry, but the scheduling just worked out that way."

"Since when are you a nurse, anyway? Are you the only one who can do this? Maybe she should just hire someone to help her."

Amanda hadn't thought ahead to this line of objection. She struggled to come up with a quick, yet credible, response. "Well, it's serious enough she will need some help getting around, but not so bad I can't handle it. Given the sort of problem it is, I just don't think she'd be comfortable with a stranger in the house."

"Well, maybe there's a compromise. Maybe she can get paid help just for the weekend we're in Wisconsin. Couldn't that work?"

Knowing her position had a serious flaw, Amanda tried again. "Well, I really can't talk about what her problem is, but she would be really, really uncomfortable with a stranger in her home with her, even for that short time. She really needs me the whole time. It's hard to explain." She hoped that would do it.

"Well, this is an awfully big favor you're doing her, I'd say. You've never even mentioned this friend to me before, yet she's someone you're willing to drop everything for to assist like this—twice now. I'll have to meet her sometime when she's better. What's her name, anyway?"

"Yeah, maybe someday. Her name is Jen. You know, I need to go. I have a lot to do to rearrange my work in the meantime." Amanda hoped Rick would forget about his newfound desire to meet her friend—and that she wouldn't get tripped up on the name in some later conversation.

"All right. Take care and keep me posted, OK?"

"Yeah, sure thing." Amanda hung up and let out a long breath. She did not need all this intrigue in her life.

Amanda scowled as she clicked off the remote. A major snow

storm was fast approaching right through the route she would have to travel. She wished she had been able to get on the road before now, but she had to go into work most of Saturday to prepare for her absence. Her work generally involved long hours, which made it all the more difficult to arrange to be gone for possibly several weeks on such short notice.

She shrugged. Might as well put that behind her now. She'd wrapped things as best she could with work and with Rick, and it would just have to suffice. She returned to her bedroom, where a large bag lay open on her bed and clothes lay strewn everywhere. She checked her watch. Not even getting a good early start on the day. Her inability to decide on what to pack and just get it done reflected her underlying misgivings about the whole situation.

On so many levels, she wished she hadn't agreed to help. She didn't like lying to Rick and making him cancel their plans on such short notice. She'd had to push off some work deadlines that gave her cause for worry. Even more, she feared getting drawn back into Jeremy's life, especially now that he was involved in such a questionable experiment.

But what choice did he really have? It sounded like his condition was deteriorating rapidly—just as it had with his mother. His decision was a life-or-death matter. And ethical qualms aside, it was still going to be a tricky procedure. He'd need help while he recovered. How could she have said no?

Still, she wondered if she'd experience any professional backlash, should her involvement ever come to light. Granted, she was only caring for him after the procedure and had nothing to do with the underlying experiment, but…did she have any professional duty to report it? She'd never found herself in a situation remotely similar to this, and so had no idea.

And yet, that was part of the attraction. Ivan's boldness and vision in setting the project up and driving it this far—even after his death—tantalized her. She could never admit that to Jeremy, given how he felt about his father. But Ivan had set up what might be the answer for Jeremy's severe Crohn's. It was, frankly, brilliant, and she wanted to witness it, to see it succeed.

She glanced out her window. Storm clouds blocked the midday light, making it look as dark as early evening. She had to get on the road now, else risk delay by getting caught in dangerous conditions. Jeremy's surgery was tomorrow.

Amanda pulled another, smaller bag from her closet, flung it onto the bed beside the larger one, and proceeded to just toss all the clothes into them as fast as she could. Time to quit screwing around. She'd lived in Minnesota long enough to know things on the road could get ugly—and fast.

She set the bags down by the front door, then hurried through her apartment, making sure she'd turned everything off and secured things suitably for being away for a couple of weeks. She could call the landlady to check on things if she ended up being gone longer.

Only about twenty minutes into the drive, Amanda lost her race with the weather. Big, fluffy snowflakes began slapping against the windshield. To anyone who didn't live somewhere like Minnesota, these would resemble the innocent, picture-postcard sort of flakes. The snow globe kind. But Amanda knew better. These were the most dangerous kind. She glanced at the temperature gauge in her dash. Thirty-two. Just as she feared.

Warmer snow meant deeper drifts because the snow itself was not compact, and the snow would be heavy and sticky because of its increased moisture content. This would be the kind that would accumulate on the wipers, eventually rendering them useless. Amanda mentally calculated the added travel time from having to stop periodically to knock the blades free of the accumulation so they would actually function.

But worst of all was the potential for black ice. She knew despite her all-wheel drive, she could still slide unexpectedly if she hit a patch of the damned, invisible stuff. She gripped the steering wheel tighter, as if that would keep the car on course.

She slowed a bit more as the snow thickened and swirled around her. It had begun falling so suddenly and so quickly that the plows had not yet gotten out and made a dent in it. The whiteness accumulated on the road, obscuring the lane lines. She cursed herself for not getting on the road way ahead of the storm.

Amanda came upon a light-colored car partway in the ditch.

With all the snow, she didn't see it until nearly the last minute, and had to swerve to avoid clipping it. She fought down panic and tried not to overcorrect her steering as she felt the rear of the Forester fishtail with the sudden movement. She just got by the ditched car without hitting it, and the Forester regained its footing. Thank God there had been no one in the lane next to her. She took a few deep breaths to try to calm herself.

This was going to be a very long drive.

Amanda pulled off in Zumbrota. It had taken her an hour longer than it should have just to get that far. Her wiper blades were thick with snow and nearly useless. She wanted to knock them clean, get some gas and coffee and stretch a little before getting back on the road.

Anxious for some really good coffee, she turned into the Casey's station. After topping her tank and clearing off her wiper blades, she pulled into a parking spot, went inside and used the restroom. Once she'd finished, she ventured back out to the store, poured herself some coffee and went to the counter to pay.

"Terrible driving weather today." The older clerk brushed aside a strand of gray hair that had crept into her line of vision. "Makes me glad to be in here, at least I'm warm." She smiled.

"Yeah, pretty bad. I'm still trying to get to the Twin Cities in this mess."

"You crazy? They say it's not going to let up until sometime tomorrow. Why don't you just find a room in town here? They're saying people should avoid driving until the plows get on top of this."

Amanda sighed. "Can't help it. A friend is having surgery tomorrow. I've got to push on."

The clerk shook her head. "Well, be careful, then, dear."

"I will." Amanda smiled, left the store and hurried to her car.

She sat inside and savored her coffee for a few minutes before venturing back out. She pulled out her cell phone and noticed there was a voicemail. She hadn't even heard it ring. She'd been focusing all her attention on peering out through the cramped clearings in the windshield that her wipers had managed to eke out.

She listened to the message. It was Jeremy, calling to see where she was. She checked the timestamp—nearly forty-five minutes ago. She quickly called and updated him. Then she started the car and braced herself for the remainder of the drive.

CHAPTER 25

Jeremy glanced at his watch for maybe the tenth time in the last fifteen minutes. Nearly two hours had passed since Amanda called from Zumbrota. She should have arrived about an hour ago, but all bets were off when there was a snow storm like this. He'd checked the weather, and heard they were pulling the plows off the road in some spots because conditions had become too dangerous, even for them.

He wished he could have simply hired a local contract home care nurse. Then Amanda wouldn't be out in this weather trying to get to Minnetonka. Of course, that wouldn't have worked. How would he have explained what procedure he was to undergo, and under what conditions? He was damned lucky Amanda had agreed to come. Now he just hoped she arrived soon—and safely.

Jeremy puttered around the house, too nervous to know what to do with himself. Too nervous about Amanda. Too nervous about the procedure that awaited him in less than twenty-four hours. He'd already taken care of everything else that was in his control. Glen and Tim were well positioned to handle anything that arose at SomaGene while he was convalescing. He'd already stocked up on enough groceries for Armageddon and beyond. He'd even caught up on all the laundry and general straightening around the house—a first.

Unfortunately, he'd completely run out of things to do except worry. On that score, he had plenty left to do. He still couldn't shake off his encounter with the Subject. He'd been rattled by the Subject's response to him and the strange sensation that had coursed through his fingertips—and his reaction had clearly upset the Subject. The whole scene kept replaying in his mind as if it happened moments ago.

The Subject. He doesn't even have a name.

Probably just as well. To have a name would humanize him even more, and Jeremy felt guilty enough. He wondered what would go through the Subject's mind when he was brought into surgery—and after.

A terrifying thought occurred to Jeremy. What if a more extensive portion of intestine needed to be removed than they anticipated? It was certainly possible once he lay open on the table and Glen could see everything firsthand, rather than relying on imaging equipment.

For that matter, how much did he really trust Glen? He was so hell-bent on trying to convince him to accept the total large and small intestine transplant. He'd made his wishes clear, but... what if Glen went ahead with the full procedure anyway?

The doorbell rang.

Distracted from that disturbing line of thought for the moment, Jeremy hurried to the front door to find Amanda standing there, two bags slung over her shoulders. She was bundled up in a thick down coat. Her hair was askew, and she looked exhausted.

"That had to be the worst drive ever." She stepped inside and dropped her bags to the floor. "Lost count of all the ditched cars, and did a fair amount of fishtailing myself." She gave a small smile. "But I'm here."

Jeremy resisted the urge to take her in his arms. Barely. "I'm glad you are. I've been so worried. You must be hungry. I've got just about everything imaginable in the kitchen."

Amanda shed her coat and gloves. "Actually, I am. I didn't eat much today, and it's been hours since I even stopped for gas."

"Here, let me take those. Why don't you just settle in and relax and I'll make us something." Jeremy reached for her coat and gloves. In doing so, he touched her hand, then gently squeezed it. "It's the least I can do before I'm the one who needs to be waited on for a while." He tried to smile. "Thank you for coming. I..." He gazed down at the floor for a moment, then looked back up at her. "I really don't know what I would have done if you hadn't come."

She smiled, almost shyly, and squeezed his hand in return. "I guess I just couldn't leave you to face this alone."

"I'll get started on dinner, then. I have to limit my portion, then I have to take that stuff that clears out the colon so things are…ready."

Amanda cast him a concerned look. "Oh, I suppose. Any other prep?"

"No that's about it. No more solid food after, say, eight, then be sure to drink that awful stuff. They want me to report to surgery about eight tomorrow morning."

"Better make it an early night, then."

"Somehow, I doubt I'll sleep."

CHAPTER 26

Tim worked alone in the surgery early that morning, laying out the necessary instruments and supplies with gloved hands. Enough for two. He glanced behind him. He and Glen had brought in a second gurney, as well as a second set of monitors and anesthetic equipment, to prepare for today's procedure. It promised to be a challenge on so many levels.

They had planned for Tim to administer the anesthetic and monitor both patients. He fervently hoped if any problems arose, it wasn't with both of them simultaneously. Of course they couldn't bring in another doctor to assist, so they were going to have to make it work. Glen would also pull double duty in performing both procedures, but at least he could focus on one patient at a time.

Tim returned his attention to the instruments. He had arranged them on two separate rolling trays, one for Jeremy's procedure, and one for the Subject. That way, Glen would be able to more readily reach for them himself near each patient, in the event Tim was too occupied with monitoring or adjusting the anesthetic.

They had met together for many hours to prepare and work through likely scenarios and how they would handle them. Even so, this procedure had never before been attempted, and a live procedure was always a far cry from any brainstorming or blackboarding they could possibly do. They'd taken all the precautions they could in terms of pre-op testing of both patients, and double-checking the tissue typing. They were as ready as they could be, he hoped.

Glen strode in. "How's it going? Are we nearly ready to get started?"

Tim bristled at Glen's nonchalant tone. He sounded like this was nothing more than a test run on lab rats. "Yes, I've got everything laid out now. I suppose we can begin any time once Jeremy gets here."

Glen glanced around at the instruments and equipment. "This looks good. I think we have things arranged optimally, considering the nature of the procedure." He looked at Tim. "Which reminds me. Have you laid out the instruments we'd need if we did the complete transplant?"

Tim hesitated. "Well, no. We're doing the subsection only, so I selected only those instruments."

"We need a full set. What if we get in there and find the damage is too extensive to just transplant a section? I don't want to be scurrying for instruments if that happens. There won't be time for that."

"Glen, I know you want to do the complete procedure, but Jeremy made it clear—"

Glen glared at Tim. "Yes, Jeremy indicated his wishes. But as you should well know, despite all the pre-op tests in the world, things can happen once you open up a patient, and sometimes the patient's wishes are not in his own best interest."

Tim sighed. "I know. I'll set out the additional instruments, but Glen, we've got to be conservative if we possibly can. We haven't begun to address what would be required for the Subject's care if it turned into a complete transplant."

Glen shrugged. "That's not the critical issue here. The quality of *Jeremy's* outcome is all we need to worry about, all right? I'm going to see if he's arrived yet."

Tim suppressed a caustic remark and tried to refocus himself on the task ahead as he augmented the surgical trays with the additional instruments. He prayed nothing would happen to give Glen an excuse to go ahead with the full procedure.

CHAPTER 27

"D o I turn here?" Amanda glanced anxiously toward the side of the road as she hunched over the steering wheel.

"A little farther. See that small sign and long driveway over there?" Jeremy pointed toward the inconspicuous SomaGene sign.

"Got it, OK." Amanda drove up to the driveway, signaled, then turned.

The snow storm had weakened since the prior day, but it had not stopped. Four-foot-high drifts lined the edges of the road where the plows had done their work. Fortunately, whatever service SomaGene used to plow had also done its job. The long driveway was cleared and the parking lot was in pretty good shape, though it did have an enormous pile of plowed-up snow in the far corner.

Amanda pulled into Jeremy's parking spot and left the car running with the heater and defrosters on. "You ready?" She cast a concerned look at him.

He looked down at his hands, only then realizing they were clenched into tight fists in his lap. He noticed all his other muscles were bunched tightly as well. He closed his eyes, breathed deeply and tried to focus on relaxing. As if he could. "Almost. Let's wait just a couple more minutes."

"Sure."

He opened his eyes again a few moments later. A thin layer of snow already covered the windshield and seemed to cut them off from the outside world, at least for now. Jeremy felt a strange feeling of peace, of safety—and of distance from what he had to face in a matter of minutes. He took a little bit of comfort from that, then turned to look at Amanda.

She stared at him, her eyes wide with concern. On an impulse, he reached out, cradling the back of her neck in his gloved hand. He gently pulled her toward him and kissed her—at first lightly, then more urgently, as if it might be his last kiss ever. She leaned over, wrapped her arms around him and pulled him as close as possible given the console between the seats.

Jeremy wanted to get lost in the moment, in her warmth, but he knew he couldn't, not now. He forced himself to pull away, then looked at her closely. "I still love you, Amanda. Maybe when this is over…"

She sat back, looking flushed. "I…um…need to think a little. This is all a bit sudden."

"Sure. I understand." Jeremy sat back up in his seat, then glanced at his watch. "I suppose it's time." At least he could dare hope he might be able to get back together with Amanda. That thought alone gave him a little more courage to get out of the car and report to surgery.

Amanda turned off the car, and they hurried through the freezing wind to the entrance. Once inside, Jeremy steered Amanda toward his office. There they took off their coats and gloves and hung them on a rack by the door. "This is probably the best place to wait. Make yourself at home. I presume this is going to take a while." Jeremy took both her hands in his and bent down to kiss her.

"Good luck, Jeremy," she whispered. "I'll be here."

He smiled, then turned and began walking down the hall toward the surgical suite.

CHAPTER 28

He clutched his stomach. It made noises and it hurt. This had never happened before.

Empty, so empty.

A White Coat came yesterday. Gave him something to drink. It tasted funny. He didn't like it, and the White Coat forced him to drink it.

A White Coat had never been forceful with him before. He did not understand.

All night, he could not sleep. He had to get up over and over again in the dark and empty himself. It made him tired. Made him feel weak.

Empty.

Now he sat, waiting. He'd already heard the screams from the room next to him. Seemed a long while ago. Usually it was only a short time after those sounds before he got something to eat. He wondered if he had been forgotten.

He hung his head. Had he done something wrong? That No White Coat had come. He'd touched him, then he seemed repulsed. He wondered if that had something to do with this. Maybe No White Coat was a bad thing.

The door opened and both White Coats came in. He stood, anxious for his food.

But they did not have his food with them. He looked at them, asking questions with his eyes.

They didn't usually come see him together. Only sometimes.

They both came toward him. They opened his enclosure and entered. He shrank back, confused. They never opened it without bringing a bucket and water and a thing they wiped the floor with.

They didn't have any of those things with them.

One of them grabbed his arm roughly. He flinched. They had never done that to him. The White Coats had always been nice to him.

He was scared.

They briefly made sounds to each other, then one of them moved very suddenly.

He felt a small, sharp pain in his arm.

One nodded to the other, and they started to take him out of his room. He'd never been out of it before. He didn't know what was going to happen now. Nothing was as it usually was.

Everything started to look fuzzy. He felt very tired. His legs didn't work like they should, and the White Coats were holding him up, moving him along.

He was tired, so tired.

And he was afraid to be out of his room. He tried to move away, to get back toward it, but the White Coats wouldn't let him.

They moved him down a white tunnel. He could hardly feel his legs. They didn't work. His head bobbed around.

They turned a corner with him. The lights were so bright now they hurt. He shut his eyes against them.

Suddenly he was lifted up. He opened his eyes again, and he was lying down. Something was holding him in place. He wanted to get back to his room, but it was so far away now.

Something was on his face. Something over his nose and mouth. He panicked, took in a big gasp. Everything blurred even worse.

He felt like he was floating.

Darkness came at the sides of his view.

"All right, that went pretty well." Glen snugged down the strap that restrained the Subject's legs, then raised the hospital gown. He swabbed the abdomen with antiseptic and arranged the surgical drapes around his intended incision site.

Tim looked up after he finished inserting the IV needle. "He must have been horribly confused by all this. I wonder if he'll be traumatized by the memory."

"Tim, you keep forgetting what he is. *A lab asset.* It would behoove you to keep that in mind. Stay objective. You can't get wound up in what he might or might not even be capable of thinking. Just get him under and ready to go. Jeremy should be here any minute."

Tim clenched his teeth and decided to remain silent. It would be tense enough during this procedure; he decided not to add to it by arguing with Glen right now over his inhumane attitude. He checked the Subject's vitals, then prepared to intubate him.

CHAPTER 29

Jeremy paused outside the surgical suite. He rested a hand on the hallway wall and leaned against it for a moment. Aside from not having eaten, he didn't feel too bad. The potent steroids had done a wonderful job. Oh, if only those doses could be tolerated long-term—he'd be plenty happy to skip this procedure.

But he couldn't stay on such potent meds for long, else he'd trade one destructive process for another. Either way, he'd be on a downward spiral. He tried to remind himself that this was his only chance to avoid ending up dying like his mother.

He glanced up. The door to the suite was only a few feet away. Seemed like a mile. He smirked at the irony. Usually a surgical patient would be initially prepped in a special room, drugged up to the point of not giving a damn, then wheeled down the hall to surgery. He had to walk himself in there directly to ensure no other SomaGene staff member got wind of the procedure they were undertaking. The comparison to a death row inmate walking to the chair on his own steam was not lost on him.

He thought of Amanda for a moment. Was it possible they would get back together? He tried to hold on to that thought as he forced himself to take the last few steps to the door.

He stepped inside to the small atrium that led to the actual surgery. He peered through the porthole in the door and saw both Glen and Tim in there—and the Subject, draped and hooked to all the necessary tubes and wires. He turned, picked up the surgical gown that had been left for him and changed into it. Then he took a deep breath and entered the surgery.

Glen motioned him in. "Hi Jeremy, we've been waiting for you.

Come have a seat." He pointed to the empty gurney. "Right here."

Jeremy wasn't so sure he appreciated the false cheer, like he was being welcomed into the dental chair for a mere cleaning. But he supposed in light of the seriousness of the situation, there was no need to add to the tension of the moment.

"OK." He straightened his shoulders, stepped over to the awaiting gurney and positioned himself on it. He couldn't help but turn his head to steal a glance at the Subject who lay parallel to him on his own gurney. He felt a little ill when he noticed that the Subject was actually bound to the table. He tried not to think of what sort of panic and confusion he must have experienced on his way in here.

He looked away.

Both Tim and Glen were in full surgical garb, and had apparently scrubbed. He could still recognize them behind their masks. Tim approached him, while Glen appeared to be rechecking the various instruments spread out before him.

"How're you doing, Jeremy?"

"OK, I suppose. Nervous."

"Sure. Can't say as I blame you, though we've prepared and tried to think through all the possible scenarios ahead of time. The Subject is already under, so the clock has started. You ready?"

"Yeah, let's do it."

Tim fitted the mask over Jeremy's nose and mouth and urged him to breathe slowly and deeply. It only took a few breaths before Jeremy was out.

He was gazing into a mirror. It was foggy, as if someone had taken a hot shower in the room and not let the steam out. The room itself was not familiar, but for some reason he cared only about the mirror.

He reached out, wiped a clear spot in the center. Something was strange. He looked more closely. No reflection.

He wiped harder.

He looked again. Now he could see it was as if his reflection were approaching the other side of the mirror from a distance. He grew larger and clearer as the moments passed.

Jeremy stood mesmerized, his hand still suspended near the mirror where it had been wiping.

The image came closer. It seemed so strange for the mirror to do that. Why wasn't it just *there*, like always?

The image finally came up to the mirror and assumed the appropriate size.

But something was still very wrong.

Jeremy got his face right up to it and peered closer still.

It looked like him, but not totally. He rubbed his eyes and looked again.

It was the Subject!

Jeremy quickly stumbled back and nearly fell.

The Subject reached a hand right through the mirror. The mirror rippled and parted to let it through as if the hand were coming up through water.

Jeremy screamed.

The Subject then used both his hands to part the mirror and force his entire head through. He stared at Jeremy.

Then he opened his mouth.

Help me.

Jeremy pressed himself against the wall behind him in a complete panic. His legs buckled and he slid to the floor. Then he noticed something that had somehow escaped his attention.

He looked down in his lap.

Forgetting about the Subject coming through the mirror, he screamed again.

In his lap was a complete large and small intestine, just like the glossy color pictures in his med school books. It throbbed and pulsed in peristaltic rhythm.

He tried to shimmy away from it, tighter against the wall. He didn't dare touch it, but it was somehow connected to him, and stayed on him as he tried to squirm away.

In his terror, he had not noticed that the Subject had somehow come all the way through the mirror and now stood before him.

Jeremy could feel his heart pounding all through his body as he watched the Subject slowly bend, then kneel before him. The Subject gazed upon the glistening intestines, seemingly ignoring everything else around him. He bent lower, lower, then reached out and carefully touched them.

Jeremy could feel his touch, could feel it on those intestines sitting out there, impossibly exposed. Were they his? Whose were they? What was the Subject going to do?

At first he'd thought the intestines were just resting on him, now he feared they were somehow part of him. He didn't know what to think.

Then the Subject looked up at him. His demeanor somehow began to change. He was caressing the intestines as he looked back up into Jeremy's face, only inches away.

Jeremy was terrified, his breath coming in brief hitches. He didn't know what to expect. The Subject's caresses felt strangely... good. He looked down again, briefly wondering how the intestines were connected. They couldn't be functional exposed like that, but they pulsed and seemed to respond to the Subject's touch.

The Subject suddenly grasped one of the loops of intestine, as a snarl played across his face.

Mine!

And then he pulled. Hard.

Unimaginable pain tore through Jeremy's abdomen, a thousand times worse than the worst Crohn's attack he had ever experienced.

He was lying on his side on a cold, white floor. Alone. He gingerly touched his abdomen with his hand.

It was empty.

Open.

And empty.

His hand was covered in blood.

He curled into a fetal position, his hands over his midsection.

And shut his eyes.

CHAPTER 30

"Hey, hey, calm down. Let me get the doctors."

Jeremy snapped his eyes open, and was shocked to see Amanda's face filling his vision instead of the Subject's.

"What happened?" he muttered.

"You were agitated, trying to talk in your sleep. They told me to call them when you came to." Amanda reached for the buzzer at the side of Jeremy's bed and pressed it.

He quickly glanced around to try to orient himself. Gradually, he realized where he was and why. He lay his head back down on the pillow, grateful to have made it to the recovery room. He felt groggy, yet was in minimal pain. *Must be some good drugs.*

Threads of his nightmare hung with him, though, weaving an undercurrent of dread beneath his relief at having come through the surgery. He closed his eyes.

"How're you feeling?"

Jeremy opened his eyes again to see Tim standing next to the bed, checking the blinking and beeping monitors. "Not too bad. How did it go?"

"Quite well, actually. You tolerated the procedure better than we expected, all things considered. You now have about six inches of new small intestine—the portion right before the colon. Yours was in bad shape—strictures, the beginnings of several fistulas—I doubt you could have gone much longer without even more serious symptoms than you were having. Good thing we got in there now."

"How is…the Subject?"

Tim adjusted the IV flow for what seemed an extended time, then turned away as he answered. "He's doing as well as can be expected. We removed the needed section, then rejoined his remaining small intestine right to the colon. His ability to absorb nutrition will be somewhat compromised now that he's short a bit of intestine. We think we can adjust his diet to ease that problem. Otherwise, he appears to be recovering."

Glen stepped over to the other side of Jeremy's bed and cast a sharp glance at Tim as he spoke. "Don't spend your energy worrying about that. The important thing is that your procedure went well. Now we want to be sure your resection heals properly. How's your pain level?"

"OK, thanks."

"Well, your buzzer is right over here. Don't hesitate to use it if you need more pain meds or anything. One of us will be present on site at all times over the next 48 hours to make sure everything is proceeding as expected." Glen leaned over, adjusted Jeremy's bed sheet, then smiled. "You're doing very well so far. Now you should just get some rest and let your body heal." He glanced at both Amanda and Tim, who stood on the other side of the bed.

Tim gently put his hand on Amanda's shoulder. "Yes, Jeremy needs his rest right now. We should let him sleep."

Amanda bent down, lightly kissed Jeremy on his cheek. "Rest well. I'll be back."

All three quietly left the room, and someone dimmed the lights. Jeremy lay alone with his thoughts. But his thoughts soon became tangled in the cottony confusion of the pain meds.

He edged closer to sleep. And he hoped that nightmare would not return.

CHAPTER 31

"All done now." Tim pulled the giggling baby out of the water and dried him off. He opened the tub drain, put on Johnnie's diaper and pajamas, then carried him out to his high chair at the dining room table.

He sat down in the chair next to him with a small groan of exhaustion, then offered his finger to the little guy to play with while they waited for their dinner. Johnnie gripped it firmly with the saliva-laden hand he'd just removed from his own mouth.

Katie stepped out of the kitchen with a bowl of salad, took one look at Tim, and declared, "My God, you look like a wreck. What happened today? Tough surgery?"

"Uh-huh," he grunted, hoping she would leave it at that. Katie always showed a keen interest in his work and liked to talk about it over the dinner table, which he usually appreciated. It helped him unwind from the day and reflect on what cutting-edge work they did at SomaGene.

"What this time? Heart, liver? Maybe a trachea? Those seem to be a little trickier, eh?" Katie set down the salad bowl and folded her arms as she waited for his answer.

"Yeah, a trachea." Tim decided to go with it and steer clear of the truth this time. "This one was a lifelong smoker, and the lungs were in tough shape. Made the whole procedure a lot more delicate than usual. Looks like the patient will make a good recovery, though." He was surprised by his ability to spin a fast lie, and hoped that little story would satisfy her tonight.

Katie shook her head. "Wow. It's amazing what you do every day. You must really feel good about how much you improve the quality of your patients' lives—and some of them are in pretty tough shape when they come to you." She glanced over at Johnnie as she spoke. "Sounds a lot more exciting than swapping out dirty diapers all day."

Tim chose to ignore her last remark. The last thing he needed today was to get into it with her about her stay-at-home status and how bored she was. "We do. I don't think any other clinic comes close to our success rate—and many can't even offer some of the procedures we do." He tried desperately to get the image of the Subject out of his mind. He'd chosen his specialty as a way to help people, not tear them down by harvesting their organs for the benefit of others.

"Well, you really should be proud of yourself. You do important work." Katie turned and headed back into the kitchen to get the rest of dinner.

Tim wondered if Katie would think quite so highly of him if she knew the truth of what he had participated in today.

He glanced at Johnnie as they waited for their dinner. The boy stared back at him with wide, innocent blue eyes. The same sort of look the Subject gave him when he came in to feed him each day.

A chill ran up Tim's back as he fully grasped that he had helped steal—yes, steal—part of a human being's intestinal tract for the sake of another. Without consent.

Today they'd been complicit in more than just pushing the biotech envelope to discover new surgical and treatment modalities. They'd played God.

Katie returned from the kitchen bearing their dinner plates.

He waved her off. "Sorry. I'm not hungry. I've got a horrible headache." Ignoring the quizzical look on her face, he got up from the table without another word and headed for the bedroom. He couldn't bear to sit through dinner right now. He just wanted to be alone, in the dark and quiet.

CHAPTER 32

Amanda stared down at the eggs frying in the pan. The edges of the whites were bubbling in the layer of oil, starting to crisp just as Jeremy liked them. He liked crisp edges, but he didn't like the eggs overly hard. She watched closely until just the right moment to slip them from the pan and onto his plate.

She figured eggs would be relatively easy for him to digest, and would offer some good protein to help him heal. She had decided against toast for the time being—too rough. Glen and Tim had initially only allowed him a liquid diet, but now, a week later, they were letting him graduate to soft proteins and starches.

But bland. Amanda had to fight off her natural reflex of adding seasonings. She wondered how Jeremy could stand his food totally unseasoned; she didn't think she could have, at least not without complaining bitterly. But he'd not complained at all, not a word.

He hadn't brought it up overtly, but she was sure he was feeling some level of guilt in doing so well because of a live—and forced—partial organ donation. Tim had assured them both that the Subject was doing reasonably well after the procedure, but neither had actually seen him yet. Tim could be covering something up to try to give Jeremy the peace of mind he needed to heal.

But she could tell Jeremy was not at peace. She knew he wanted to get to SomaGene and see the Subject's condition for himself. Of course he wasn't ready for that right now. He was healing well, but it had been a major procedure and the resectioned intestinal segment needed to be allowed to properly heal before he undertook much of anything.

Amanda placed the breakfast plates on a tray, picked it up, and went to deliver it to Jeremy's bedroom.

As she reached the top of the stairs, she paused briefly and glanced toward Ivan's room—or suite, really. She wondered if Jeremy would ever make peace with his memory. She set the thought aside and headed for Jeremy's room with the tray.

She knocked at his door. "Jeremy—you awake? I have your breakfast."

"Yeah, I'm awake, come in."

She pushed open the door with one foot and stepped inside. She set the tray down to avoid tipping it, then turned on a small lamp on the dresser.

Jeremy had propped himself up to a sitting position with several pillows. His color was quite good, considering how badly he had been doing before the surgery and how extensive the surgery itself had been. She picked the tray up again and set it on the bedside table next to him.

He smiled, but his eyes were serious. "Amanda, thank you."

She waved her hand at him. "Oh, you don't have to—"

"Yes, I do. You didn't have to do this, didn't have to take off from work and make all those arrangements, just to be with me." He looked down for a moment. "I really just want to thank you." He looked back up at her. "You've done a great job helping me out, and...I'm really happy you're here. It's almost like we were never apart."

A guilty twinge passed through Amanda's stomach as she thought of Rick and the cover story she'd fed him. In spite of herself, she could feel the remnants of her resolve crumbling.

She'd broken up with Jeremy after she saw what Crohn's did to his mother. She hated to admit it to herself—let alone him— at the time, but she just couldn't bear knowing any future with him would likely take a similar course. She knew she couldn't handle that, so she broke it off and convinced herself that the reason for their breakup was his apparent lack of ambition. She'd started seeing Rick, someone she felt was the complete opposite of Jeremy in terms of personality and drive, and she'd been happy with that choice.

And now this. She looked closely at Jeremy. He really did look miraculously better. She dared to picture him living a relatively normal life.

She dared to picture them together, living that normal life, with the secret kept between them, and of course, Tim and Glen. She tried to push the Subject from her mind. What was done was done.

She reached out and caressed his face. "You're right. It is almost like we were never apart. Almost." She kissed him gently. "I'm glad I came."

CHAPTER 33

"I've always thought this was the most amazing time of year here. Look at all those fresh green leaves on the trees. There are even some daffodils coming up already." Amanda strolled with Jeremy along the dirt path at Purgatory Park. "It's great to be able to leave the down jackets and heavy boots in the closet, too."

A young couple with a small child in tow passed them going the opposite direction. The child looked up at them, waved one of his pudgy hands, and shouted, "Hi!"

Jeremy glanced at the trees lining the walking path. Any Minnesotan whose mood could not be lifted by the glorious display of spring regeneration after a long, cold monochromatic winter must be in tough shape indeed. He drew in a deep breath. It felt so good to be able to breathe like that without pain, and without frosty air clawing at his lungs.

He felt as rejuvenated as the landscape around him.

"It certainly does feel good, Amanda." He slipped his arm into hers. "I really can't remember a time when I've felt quite this good."

She glanced up at him and smiled. "You've really done well. Looking at you now, it's hard to believe what condition you were in only a few months ago." She furrowed her brow. "I wasn't entirely sure you were going to make it through the procedure."

"I'd forgotten what it was like to feel normal. I didn't even realize how much the disease was dictating my life—what I did, what I ate. Everything." He squeezed her hand. "I feel like I'm finally free of all that."

"I'm really glad it worked out so well." Amanda sighed.

"Too bad it's Sunday already. I need to head back in a few hours. At least it should be an easy drive with the nice weather."

Jeremy hesitated for a moment, then decided the time was right. "Amanda, I want to talk to you about something." He spotted a wooden bench under a maple tree a short distance ahead. It sat on a small rise and overlooked a peaceful meadow. No one else was around. "Let's sit over there."

Amanda shot him a questioning look. "Sure, what is it?"

They sat down on the bench. Jeremy desperately wanted to hold Amanda's hands in his, but instead he clasped his hands together in his lap and cleared his throat. "I know you can't keep driving up here every weekend forever, and I'm recovered now and don't really need help…"

Amanda stared at the ground. "Oh, I suppose you're ready to get back to a normal rhythm and all…"

"Well, no, that's not it. Not exactly." They'd gotten closer and more comfortable with each other over the last several months, but neither of them had spoken of what might—or might not—come next. Their focus had been primarily on his recovery. "I just…well… I'd just… Oh, screw it. Would you move in with me?"

She looked up at him. She seemed to weigh the question for a few moments, then she smiled. "Yes. I want to be back with you, Jeremy. I love you." She threw her arms around him.

Jeremy stole a quick look around. Still no one nearby. "I love you, too. I never stopped loving you." He kissed her long, hard, and recklessly. He'd never been so happy.

He scratched his side, noticing it was no longer smooth there. He encountered a series of hard, rounded ridges there when he scratched now. He looked at the back of his hand. Where it used to be smooth, there were parallel ridges there, too, thinner than the ones on his side.

Something wasn't right, but he couldn't understand it.

He didn't feel much like moving around. Sometimes he felt weak if he stood up too quickly.

There was something else, too. A dark line went across his stomach now. He couldn't remember it being there before. It looked angry and twisted. Sometimes it hurt. Sometimes it itched. It used to hurt a lot more all the time, back when there were white things pressed over it. Not so much now.

The White Coats acted differently, too. They measured and examined and collected things from him much more than before.

Before what, though?

There was something else he didn't understand. He had a recollection of something bad happening with the White Coats, but he couldn't quite recall what it was.

The screeching next door started again. He didn't care like he used to. The food the White Coats brought used to taste better. Now it tasted so bad he didn't really want to eat it.

But the last time he didn't eat it, one of the White Coats had done things to him. He'd tied him down to his bed, then hurt his arm with something sharp. Then he let him lay there for a while with a bottle hanging above him.

This didn't use to happen.

Things were better before.

Before what?

The Subject scratched another itch and lay down, too tired to try to figure it out.

CHAPTER 34

Jeremy set the report down on his desk. He'd read the same paragraph about ten times, and still hadn't comprehended a bit of it. Time to admit it was a losing battle.

He simply couldn't focus. He was way too happy to concentrate.

Crohn's had lost its grip on him, and he felt better than he'd felt in years. And now Amanda had agreed to move in with him. He'd loved her since the day they met back in their undergrad days. Now they would be back together—with him healthy.

Yet a darkness lay beneath that happiness. He knew it had a price, and he wasn't the one who had paid it.

Right after the procedure, such thoughts didn't enter his mind because it took everything he had to focus on his recovery. It had taken some weeks before he was really up and around, let alone ready to return to the SomaGene offices.

Since he'd been back to work, though, he'd indulged in purposeful avoidance. He'd buried himself in catching up on the state of the business and deliberately pushed aside thoughts of what really lay beneath his miraculous recovery. He'd even avoided any mention of the Subject with Tim and Glen. And they seemed happy enough to let it lie.

But it was catching up with him. His good fortune had a dark lining, and he knew he had to face that at some point. Right after the surgery, Glen and Tim had assured him they had only taken a section of intestine and that the Subject had survived his part of the procedure and would go on to live a relatively normal life. Well, as normal as one can live locked up like a lab animal.

Yet he hadn't had the nerve to see for himself.

Jeremy rose from his desk and started down the hall toward the Subject's quarters.

Fortunately, the Subject was housed in a segregated section of the facility, away from the general staff, but today he didn't even want to run into Tim or Glen. He was uncomfortable enough without getting into a situation where he might have to explain his presence to either of them.

Now he stood outside the door, his heart pounding and his mouth dry as paper. It would be so easy to just accept Glen's and Tim's word that all was well, and spare himself the firsthand encounter. But they'd kept things from him before, and maybe they were doing it again. What if the Subject hadn't survived? Did they replace his entire large and small intestine after all? He'd been forced to trust them with his life while under the knife, but his overall trust in them had shattered when he discovered they had initially kept the existence of the Subject from him.

He reached out and slowly opened the door. As he stepped inside, he felt immediate relief to see the Subject lying on his little padded shelf. He'd survived the surgery; they'd told him the truth to that extent anyway.

He stepped closer, and his initial relief dimmed. The Subject stared back at him listlessly, his eyes set in dark circles. His face was thin, far thinner than Jeremy recalled.

The Subject sat up slowly and soundlessly without breaking his stare. His hospital gown hung on him. His legs stuck out from beneath it like pale sticks. Even from this distance, Jeremy could tell he had lost noticeable muscle mass. He approached the bars of the enclosure for a closer look. The Subject leaned back against the wall and drew into himself as if trying to keep as much distance as possible between them.

Thinking back on their last encounter, Jeremy figured maybe he had frightened the Subject with his own reaction to his touch—and to that strange sensation he'd fleetingly experienced. Maybe he shouldn't be surprised to elicit this sort of response now. He decided not to attempt any sort of firsthand physical examination. He'd seen enough to just take it up with either Glen or Tim.

He turned and left without speaking. He felt like he should

say something, but didn't know what he could say that the Subject would even understand. As he shut the door behind him, he tried to soothe his guilt by viewing the Subject's condition in the best possible light. He had survived the months since the procedure, and he apparently was doing so without extensive medical intervention. There had been no sign of a feeding tube or other sorts of painful or inconvenient devices required for survival. That was something, anyway.

Jeremy headed down the hall toward Tim's office to ask a few questions. He felt somewhat more comfortable speaking with Tim. Glen seemed focused solely on the purpose and goals of the experiment and didn't seem to even recognize there were ethical questions.

"Tim, got a minute?" he asked as he poked his head into the office.

"Sure, come in. What's up? I was just checking the upcoming surgical schedule. Pretty good pipeline." Tim motioned toward the computer screen he had been peering at when Jeremy came in.

Jeremy took a seat in front of Tim's desk. His hands intertwined and fidgeted as if of their own accord. "Hey, that's great to hear. I, uh, have a question or two."

"About what?"

"The Subject."

Tim's face became more serious and he sat up straight in his chair. "Sure, what do you want to know?"

"What's his condition?" Jeremy decided not to let on he had already seen the Subject in the event it might color Tim's response. He wanted to see if he was going to play straight with him.

Tim briefly scratched behind his ear before answering. "Well, he's doing as well as can be expected."

Jeremy waited for more, then prompted, "What do you mean?"

"Well, we only took a section of small intestine, but of course, that's where the body absorbs most of its nutrition, so we've had to change his diet to provide more readily absorbable nutrients."

"And how well has that worked?"

"As we calculate it, the altered diet should be enough to compensate for that loss of function. Problem is, he doesn't seem to like it very much, and it's hard to get him to eat enough of it. We don't really know what he does and doesn't understand, so we can't simply explain to him that he needs to eat all that we give him. Thing is, we've also been trying to avoid having to implement any ancillary supplementation."

"You mean like a feeding tube?"

"Yeah. We're trying to keep the changes to his daily life as nonintrusive as possible, yet still make up for the loss of absorption. We're particularly trying to avoid anything that would be inconvenient to live with—or uncomfortable." He sighed. "We also don't know how he would handle anything like that, whether it would disturb him enough that he'd try to remove it himself and create more problems."

Jeremy nodded. "That makes sense. So how would you gauge his current condition?"

Tim looked directly at Jeremy. "Honestly, he could be better. He's lost noticeable muscle mass. He's a bit weakened. Nothing life-threatening—unless he were further compromised with something else, like a bad flu or some other additional health issue. I'd like to see his condition improved over what it is, but given that he's isolated in a controlled environment, I don't think he's in any immediate danger."

Jeremy started to ask another question, then thought better of it. He nearly asked if the Subject was suffering or if his quality of life was diminished by living that way. Why even bother to go down that path—he'd been created in a lab and had never lived as a human being. Seemed like there was no good answer to that question even had the procedure never taken place.

He rose from the chair. "Thanks, Tim. Appreciate your time."

Once back in his office, Jeremy shut the door and set his phone to go straight to voice mail. He sat down heavily in his chair, rubbed his eyes, and rested his face in his hands while he considered what he had seen and heard.

He had to put this to rest, one way or the other. The situation had been weighing on his mind and conscience for the better part of a year now. He began to consider his options, then realized he had none. Maybe in the beginning, when he first found out about the Subject, he had the chance to lay it all on Ivan, cut Glen and Tim loose as scapegoats, and free himself and the rest of SomaGene from the fallout as best he could. But time had passed and he had said nothing.

And worse, he had sealed his and the Subject's fate when he submitted to the procedure. He'd partaken. He'd benefited. There was no way he could disavow the project now.

Jeremy decided he was just going to have to accept Ivan's gift, package up and compartmentalize his guilt, and move on. He'd make sure the Subject got the best and most humane care possible. Any other approach would expose Amanda for her involvement, and would most certainly bring him and SomaGene down.

CHAPTER 35

Amanda paced in her living room. Rick was due to arrive at any moment, and she wasn't ready. She tried to mentally rehearse what she was going to say, but nothing seemed right. She didn't know *what* she was going to say to him.

Surely her post-surgical girlfriend story had worn thin by now. She'd stretched it far beyond its intended use when she continued visiting Jeremy on weekends even after he was able to fend for himself. Rick had become increasingly impatient with her excuses, but he hadn't yet pressed her hard on the matter. Surely that wouldn't last. And now that she'd accepted Jeremy's invitation to move in, she had to break things off without revealing anything concerning Jeremy's miraculous cure.

She now understood her feelings for Rick for what they were. She'd thought she'd fallen in love with him, but she really had fallen in love with who he was. He was smart, successful, and attractive. He exuded confidence in every situation. She liked that. But deep down, he pursued his achievements for purely selfish—not altruistic—reasons. When he developed a new surgical technique, it was all about what it meant for his reputation and persona, not for the human value of how it improved patients' outcomes.

Jeremy wasn't that way. If anything, he tormented himself with concerns for what SomaGene's developments meant for its patients, not for his potential personal glory. And she knew he carried a tremendous burden of guilt for the real cost of his newfound health.

The doorbell startled her from her reverie and she stopped in her tracks. "Be right there." Her heart racing, she tried to gather

her nerve as she went to open the door.

"So what's up?" asked Rick as he stepped in, bearing a bottle of Cabernet.

"I, uh, need to talk to you about something. Something serious." Amanda dodged his attempt at a kiss, sat down on the couch and stared at the floor, not knowing how to begin the conversation.

Rick followed her over, put the wine on the coffee table, and sat beside her. "What is it? Are you mad at me for something?"

"No, it's not that. It's not your fault."

"What, then? You know, you've been avoiding me a lot lately. Something's going on, isn't it?" He eyed her suspiciously.

Amanda wished she'd been able to plan ahead of time what she was going to say, because the tension in the room was becoming unbearable—and fast—and she was having trouble thinking at all coherently. "Rick, I'm planning to move up to the Twin Cities."

Rick drew back, a surprised look on his face. "Why? Did you get a job offer?"

Amanda suddenly needed some space to say what came next. She stood, stepped around the coffee table, and kept her back to him while she stared straight ahead. "No, no job offer." She knew she'd have to say enough to make the break clean. She couldn't have him trying to come up and visit. "Well, when I was spending all that time up there to look after my girlfriend, I ran into someone I used to go with a long time ago. It was pretty serious at the time, and, um, we've decided to get back together."

Rick was silent for a moment. "Anybody I know?"

Amanda decided to steer clear of mentioning Jeremy at all costs. "No, someone from way back. You wouldn't know him." She turned to face Rick again. "I'm sorry. I don't know what else to say."

Rick stood. "I don't think there's anything else *to* say." He cast her a sharp glance. "You don't think I really believed that bullshit about some unnamed girlfriend, did you? I figured I'd let you play out whatever you were playing out, and that you'd be back when you were done. Obviously, our relationship wasn't that important to you."

"Rick—"

He waved her off. "I'll let myself out. Have a good life." He walked out the front door, shutting it firmly and finally behind him.

Amanda collapsed onto the couch. She was exhausted from the encounter, yet relieved. It didn't go that badly, all things considered. So he did suspect she was visiting someone other than an old girlfriend all this time. Well, he was probably seeing someone else while she was gone anyway. It's not as if women didn't flock around him all the time. She felt less guilty thinking that he hadn't been sitting around all alone, and probably wouldn't miss a beat in his love life.

She glanced at the wine he had left behind. Maybe she'd open it and have a little to celebrate her new life with Jeremy.

CHAPTER 36

"You know, I used to hate this place, but you've transformed it. Maybe I'll forget about selling it and just redo Ivan's room some time." Jeremy stood next to Amanda in the archway to the living room. It was a Sunday afternoon, and the late spring sun shone through the windows and cast cheery light onto the gleaming wood floor. The room had been grand to the point of haughty before, but now that Amanda had interspersed it with her own decorations and what-not, it had become downright inviting to sit in there and talk over the day's events before dinner each night.

Amanda had already snagged a plum research position with a local firm. Her reputation for excellent, meticulous work had made the job hunt short and sweet, and she was happily settling into her new environment. Jeremy had offered to hire her at SomaGene, but in the end they decided it was probably safest for her to secure outside employment. Just in case anything ever leaked out about the Subject, she would need all the insulation she could get.

SomaGene's services remained in high demand. Things were going so well, in fact, that Jeremy had recently hired several new surgeons to keep up with the flow. Naturally, any and all knowledge of the Subject was carefully kept among himself, Glen, and Tim.

At Jeremy's urging, Tim had revamped the Subject's diet to be more palatable, yet still provide the added nutritional support he required. The Subject had started accepting his meals better, and had even replaced some of the lost muscle mass in recent weeks.

Amanda broke into Jeremy's reverie. "You'd better *not* sell this place now, not after I've spent this much time humanizing it. Now I know what you meant. As big and well-equipped as this house is, it just wasn't a very inviting place to be." She glanced around and smiled with satisfaction. "Much better now."

Jeremy turned to her and took her in his arms. It felt so right to hold her close, to feel her warmth. He couldn't imagine being without her again. "Maybe it's not so much the stuff you brought with you. Maybe it's just having you here."

She looked up at him. "I'm so glad things turned out this way. I never should have broken up with you."

Jeremy leaned over and kissed her. She slid her warm fingers onto the back of his neck, pulling him even closer as she gently slipped her tongue inside his mouth. Then she suddenly pulled away, her face flushed.

"Upstairs," she whispered, as she took his hand in hers and led him up the staircase and to their bedroom.

He started toward the bed, hungry for her, but she stopped him in the doorway. "Not yet." She reached up, kissed him once on the lips, then lightly along his neck down one side and back up the other. She gently took his earlobe in her teeth. He could feel her warm breath on his skin.

"Now." Driven mad, Jeremy reached down, scooped her up, carried her over to the bed and placed her on the soft down comforter. He knelt over her, pinned her arms, and kissed her neck, her ears, her eyes, and her mouth as if making up for every minute they had been apart. As she began to pant and writhe beneath him, he wanted her more now than he had ever wanted any woman.

He slipped his hands beneath her shoulders and raised her up. She pulled her T-shirt up and off and flung it to the floor. Then she lay back down, and he slowly unbuttoned, then unzipped her jeans. She raised her hips to help him slide them off. She wore no underwear.

Still clothed, Jeremy took his time kissing and licking Amanda all over until she became frantic and he could no longer wait. Then he quickly stripped off his shirt and pants and moved to enter her. But just before he could, she suddenly pushed him aside and ordered him onto his back. He complied with a frustrated groan.

She knelt over him and started to lower herself toward him. Jeremy lay back and closed his eyes, waiting for that moment when he would first feel himself inside her. And that moment came—briefly, oh so briefly. She barely let him inside, then pulled away. And then again. And after a tormenting pause, yet again.

Unable to stand it any longer, Jeremy reached for Amanda's shoulders, flipped her onto her back and pushed himself all the way inside her, as slowly as he possibly could. Her teasing had heightened the sensation for him so intensely that nothing in the world existed except where their bodies met. They moved in a slow rhythm together for a time, their fingers entwined, then Amanda started to move her hips more urgently, and Jeremy stopped holding back.

Afterward, they lay exhausted and entangled on the bed. Jeremy whispered in her ear, "I love you, Amanda."

She squeezed his hand. "I love you, too."

Jeremy closed his eyes and smiled. He couldn't remember ever being so happy.

CHAPTER 37

"Is the patient ready, Tim?" Jeremy glanced at the new kidney that lay in its bath of pinkish nutrient fluid in a gleaming stainless steel tray. It struck him how the unblemished, newly cultivated organs resembled precious gifts in their shiny receptacles. He supposed they were, in their own way.

"Yep, looks good. We should get started."

"All right. Going in." Glen picked up a scalpel and made the initial incision.

The client in this case, Mr. Abbott, was a ninety-year-old man with far more money than time. His kidneys had begun to fail, largely due to his advanced age rather than any specific disease process. He was fortunate to be able to afford in-home dialysis, rather than having to sit with other patients in a room full of machines for multiple hours per day. But of course, no one wants to be tied to daily dialysis if there is an available alternative.

So, money in hand, he'd approached SomaGene for the solution to his problems. And SomaGene had been more than happy to oblige him.

But Jeremy had concerns about taking this particular client. While it had become commonplace for SomaGene to safely and reliably produce suitable new organs for its clientele, Mr. Abbott was undoubtedly the oldest client to approach them so far. Jeremy worried that his overall condition presented a greater than normal risk. Of course, they required pre-op testing and evaluations of all prospective clients, but Mr. Abbott's results had been just barely within the acceptable values. He was so very old and frail in general. In reality, his kidney issues were only part of his problem.

Jeremy tried to set aside his concerns and focus on the procedure taking place. They'd accepted him as a client, so there was no point worrying about it now. Besides, all clients had to sign a release that was supposed to limit SomaGene's liability to providing competent surgery to implant a new organ derived from the client's own tissues. Once that was done, even the post-op care was outside of SomaGene's hands. It was so much simpler and cleaner that way.

Glen finished clamping off the offending kidney, removed it, and tossed it into a waiting steel bowl with a somewhat disdainful flourish. "Ready."

Jeremy lifted the new kidney from its nutrient bath and guided it into place in the patient's waiting cavity.

"That's it. Thanks. Got it from here." Glen bent over and prepared to resect the new kidney onto the blood vessels and awaiting ureter. He began to work, deftly and quietly.

"He's flatlining!" Tim jumped up and reached for the paddles. "Step back!"

"Wait a second." Glen quickly pressed a wad of sterile gauze into the cavity and slapped a strip of surgical tape over it. "All right." He stepped back, hands raised in the air.

Tim applied the paddles and sent the lifesaving jolt through Mr. Abbott. He briefly arched on the operating table. Tim glanced at the monitor readout for a moment. "Again!" He applied the current. And again, Mr. Abbott arched forcefully on the table.

"Jesus, I only had that kidney partly resected." Glen hissed through clenched teeth. "Hope nothing tears."

Tim glanced at the monitor once more, and exhaled. "OK, he's back. Better wrap it up fast as you can. I don't trust him."

"You got it." Glen bent down, carefully removed the surgical tape and gauze and worked on completing the implantation.

Jeremy realized he'd been holding his breath through the entire crisis. He inhaled slowly and deeply to purge himself of the adrenaline burst that now caused his hands to shake. He made a mental note to review the records in this case against their client acceptance protocol to see if any adjustments should be made in the future. They'd dodged a bullet this time, but he didn't want a repeat occurrence. They might not be so lucky next time, and it's not as if they needed the business badly enough to take such risks.

He admired Glen's cool as he watched him work. His hands were swift and sure as he worked to properly connect all the blood vessels to the new kidney, and to make sure the connection to the ureter was solid. The only remaining evidence of the crisis was the absolute lack of the usual banter among the three men as Glen worked.

After a while, Glen set down his instruments and let out a long breath. "Ready to close."

Jeremy positioned the tray of suturing supplies within Glen's easy reach. More silence ensued as he sutured Mr. Abbott shut, layer by layer.

"Done." Glen stood straight and stretched his back.

"I'll start bringing him out of it," said Tim.

Jeremy stepped over to the operating table to apply a dressing to the wound. He vowed to adjust whatever protocols were necessary to avoid another close call like this.

CHAPTER 38

Jeremy's hand shook as he hung up the phone. He could feel the blood draining from his face as the news sank in. It was Mr. Abbott's personal physician, Dr. Callahan, and the report was grim. Indications of kidney dysfunction had resurfaced along with symptoms of necrosis. Emergency surgery revealed that the new kidney had begun to die. Mr. Abbott was not only back on dialysis but was also on massive doses of powerful antibiotics to ward off possible septicemia. He was in intensive care, and given his underlying frailty, the prognosis was uncertain at the moment.

It had only been a week or so since the implantation. Given how that had gone, Jeremy was surprised Mr. Abbott made it through the emergency surgery. Two major procedures so close together would be rough on anyone; that old bird must be tougher than he looked. Jeremy was grateful for that much.

Callahan hadn't sounded accusatory. He seemed to be merely reporting events as they happened. But Jeremy could connect the dots in his head. The next call would likely be from a lawyer.

A small, painful spasm slithered through his gut. He tossed it off as a reasonable response to the call he'd just received, and sent a quick internal message to Glen and Tim to come to his office right away. He wanted to have a word with them first, before calling in Brad Gilman, SomaGene's general counsel.

They arrived quickly and took their seats. "Well, this is mysterious. What's up?" asked Glen.

"Remember Mr. Abbott from last week? Well, I just got a call from his doc." He then explained what Dr. Callahan had relayed to him.

"That kidney tested out perfectly before the procedure." Glen then brought his hand to his chin, as if considering something very carefully. "But, when he had the arrest, I hadn't yet completed my resection. I had to secure the kidney quickly just to try to hold it in place during the defib. I wonder if something was damaged during that brief interval when he bounced around on the table."

Tim cast Glen a sharp glance. "Well, what was I supposed to do?"

Glen waved his hand in a dismissive gesture. "No, no. There was no choice. I know that. If anything, I held you up while I tried to secure it. I don't know what we could have done differently. If only he hadn't arrested right then—well, or at all."

Jeremy asked the question that scared him the most. "What about his pre-ops? Do we have any exposure there?"

Tim thought for a moment, then answered. "Well, his blood values were certainly borderline for surgery like that. But they were still just within our guidelines. The man is ninety, for crissake."

"But should we perhaps have more conservative guidelines? Could we have seen this coming if we'd looked more closely at the labs—or maybe at the lab values in combination with his advanced age?"

"No, I don't think so. I know *I* didn't see this coming. Sure, I took his age into account with the anesthesia, but he looked good enough going in that I wasn't overly concerned. If you're that worried about this happening again someday, then maybe we do tighten down what lab results we'll accept before going forward. Maybe we wouldn't have taken this one on, I can't say. On the other hand, I'd hate to exclude others who are borderline simply *because* they need our services. Seems like it could be counterproductive for most of our clients." Tim sat back and glanced at Glen.

"I agree with Tim. I think this was either unavoidable or something that, had we tighter screening criteria, might throw out the baby with the bathwater as far as our target clientele is concerned. We've had other cases where the labs were close to the line and this didn't happen."

"All right, I'll brief Brad so he's ready if Abbott lawyers up. Thanks."

CHAPTER 39

Amanda took a sip of her Chardonnay and glanced at Jeremy. She didn't like what she saw. Things had been going so well since his surgery, but today he looked preoccupied, as if something was terribly wrong. She sat back in the leather booth, set down her glass and cleared her throat.

"What?" Jeremy seemed to snap out of a daydream and fixed his gaze on her as if he'd just noticed her sitting there.

"We go out to a nice place, and you haven't said a word since we got here. You seem to be worried about something."

"Sorry." Jeremy shook his head and stared down into his wineglass. "I didn't mean to wreck the evening."

A waiter dressed in trim black pants and vest and a blindingly white starched shirt whisked by, refilled their glasses, and placed a basket of warm bread and butter on the table.

Amanda waited for him to leave, then asked, "What is it? It's obviously serious, for you to look like that."

Jeremy took a piece of bread, halfheartedly buttered it, then set it aside. His movements seemed automated, devoid of focus or intention. "We had a problem in a procedure last week. We didn't realize at the time how serious it would turn out, and I got a call today. Patient had to have the kidney removed due to necrosis."

"Necrosis? Why?"

"We're not entirely sure. He arrested during surgery, when the new kidney hadn't yet been fully resected. We think it suffered some damage while we defibrillated him—but we didn't realize it at the time. Got a call from his doc today that the kidney wasn't functioning and had become necrotic. He needed surgery to remove it and massive antibiotics." He took a small bite of his bread. "Looks like he'll probably pull through, but I'm sure we'll be hearing from his lawyer any time now."

"Oh, I'm sorry. What are you going to do?"

"Well, first I need to see if he pursues it. I suspect he will, though, and that's what worries me. Meanwhile, we're re-evaluating our pre-op testing protocols to see if we want to tighten them up. Problem is, if we do that, we might cut out a lot of patients whose only hope is one of our procedures. It's a tricky balance."

Amanda took a sip of wine as she considered Jeremy's dilemma. "I see what you mean. Frankly, I'm surprised something like this hasn't happened before. Your clientele is by definition in serious condition—their only advantage is their ability to afford your services to solve their problems."

"True enough." Jeremy grimaced.

"Are you OK?"

"Sure, fine."

"You're not having stomach pains again, are you?"

"A couple here and there. I'm sure it has to do with this problem. I just don't know how ugly it will get before it's resolved, and I really don't like being in that kind of situation."

Amanda frowned. "But you'd been totally symptom-free since recovering from the procedure. Are you sure something isn't starting up again?"

Jeremy shook his head. "I'm sure it's not related to that. If you'd received the call I did today, you'd have a stress-induced twinge or two yourself." He tried to smile.

Amanda wasn't convinced. "I don't know. Maybe. I'd keep an eye on it if I were you." She took another sip of wine and stared more closely at Jeremy. She didn't like the idea that he could be backsliding into Crohn's symptoms after doing so well. She hoped she was overreacting.

CHAPTER 40

"Yes, Brad, what is it?" Jeremy had been dreading this call, and gnawed on the end of his pen as he waited for his in-house counsel to update him on the Abbott situation.

"No real surprise. Abbott got himself a lawyer and is threatening to sue. He's asserting he paid his money, passed his pre-op tests, and should be happily done with dialysis now instead of still fending off possible septicemia after the kidney went necrotic."

"Well, sure, he did pass the tests, but despite that, he went into cardiac arrest at exactly the worst possible moment for the kidney—it was partly transplanted at that point and we had to deal with the arrest first." Jeremy realized as soon as the words were out of his mouth that it sounded like he blamed the patient for going into cardiac arrest. He grimaced in disgust at himself as he waited for Brad's response.

"You don't have to convince me. I get what you're saying. But Mr. Abbott feels the money he spent on the kidney and procedure should have pretty much guaranteed a perfect result."

"We don't guarantee any such thing in our standard release. Where does he get off?" Jeremy tossed the pen down and slapped his hand to his forehead.

"We *don't* make any such guarantee, true enough. But his lawyer will likely argue he was in a desperate situation, vulnerable in some way seeing as he's elderly, and the high fee and SomaGene's own stellar reputation set up some reasonable expectation on his part."

"You've got to be kidding." Jeremy's free hand clenched into a fist, seemingly of its own volition.

"I'm not saying I agree with that position. Not at all. I'm just walking through the argument they'll likely present to us, and what we have to be ready to counter. Have you had a chance to review his pre-ops? Do we have a weakness there? Was something—anything—missed that would have made this a foreseeable outcome?"

Jeremy rubbed his forehead as the hot, painful tendrils of a budding headache snaked through his skull. "We've looked them over. Multiple times now. They're on the edge, but still within our current standards. There was nothing that gave a clear indication this outcome could be foreseen. Just the same, we're looking at maybe tightening the pre-op test criteria to give a little more margin for safety. Trouble is, that would cut out some more borderline clients who have no other choice and could really benefit from what we offer. I don't like that tradeoff very much, but I don't want another Abbott, either."

"All right, sounds good. I'll be in touch. Meanwhile, I'll feel out opposing counsel and see what we might be able to negotiate to get this to go away—quietly."

"Thanks, Brad." Jeremy hung up the phone. His head pounded and he felt nearly queasy. He reached into his desk drawer for some aspirin.

"So, what do you have to report?" Jeremy glanced at Tim and Glen—and hoped they had something useful to share. They sat across from him in his office a couple of hours after his conversation with Brad Gilman.

"I think we have an idea that will address the risk and still not cut out potential clients." Glen gave a self-satisfied smile, sat back in his chair, and steepled his fingers.

"Let's have it, then." Jeremy rubbed his temples where the last remnants of his headache lingered, and waited for Glen to get on with it.

"We leave the pre-op protocols as they are, so we don't eliminate potential clients. But, we change the implantation procedure itself. Right now, we presume a very short window between removing the old organ and implanting the new one.

And for our clients who remain stable during surgery—all but Abbott, so far—this is appropriate. But if we simply alter our protocol so that the new organ remains bathed in the nutrient bath until it is *fully* resected into the recipient, we avoid the tissue death that must have been kicked off during the interruption in Abbott's procedure."

Glen leaned back in his chair with a smug look on his face. Jeremy wanted to smack him, and not for the first time. "But how? I didn't take that kidney out of the bath until you were ready for it. How do you propose to have it stay in the solution while you're actively resecting?"

"Shortly before surgery, we need to place a biofriendly wrapper around the new organ that would accommodate a layer of the nutrient fluid, sort of like a very thin wet suit. The blood vessels and other connecting points—like the ureter, in the case of a kidney—need to remain free for the resecting. We then remove the wrapper once the organ is totally resected. Any nutrient fluid that gets into the body cavity would, of course, be harmless."

Jeremy pictured the concept in his mind. "So it would be more of a self-contained little unit, then?"

"That's right. Granted, it will take a bit more dexterity to manipulate the slightly larger package within the implantation site, as well as to carefully break and remove the wrapper after resection. Given those factors, I suggest we use it for the higher-risk cases, not every single one."

The idea sounded brilliant to Jeremy. Had Abbott's kidney still been in a nutrient bath, it would not have mattered that it wasn't fully resected when the arrest interrupted the procedure. Besides that, the additional padding afforded by Glen's design would provide transplant organs a layer of protection from any jarring or bumping that might occur, like when Abbott received his defib shocks.

"That's excellent, Glen. Let's implement that right away for anyone near the borderline on their pre-ops, or who has any other pertinent risk factors that we might want to minimize. Thank you."

As soon as Glen and Tim left the room, Jeremy called Brad and explained the new protocol to him so he'd know they had solved the problem for future cases.

Jeremy sat back in his chair and rubbed his face with his hands. Glen's breakthrough idea was welcome news, but the Abbott matter could still inflict massive damage on SomaGene. He hoped Brad was a great negotiator.

CHAPTER 41

Jeremy was beginning to realize he shouldn't have been so dismissive of his symptoms. They'd started out some weeks back. At first, they were mild enough he was able to convince himself they were simply due to stress and that he could safely ignore them. Then they'd increased in frequency and severity, a little at a time, until denial became just short of impossible. Lately, they'd become severe and routine enough that he began to fear that his Crohn's was making a comeback. Even so, he really didn't want to face that fact.

Right now, he wished he'd at least taken an over-the-counter antidiarrheal before scrubbing for surgery. Another cramp passed through him as he tried to focus on the task at hand.

"Clamp." Glen held out his hand while keeping his gaze trained on the open chest before him. Today's client was receiving a new heart with clear, unblemished blood vessels to replace his tired, atherosclerotic heart. "*Clamp,*" he repeated when Jeremy did not immediately snap it into his hand.

Jeremy hastily provided the clamp with a trembling hand. He was relieved that Glen did not apparently notice the tremble and kept on with the procedure.

"Vitals still good," said Tim from his seat by the patient's head.

"All right, I'm nearly done resecting it onto the existing blood vessels." Several minutes passed in silence. "Done. Now I'm going to start removing the wrapper." Glen maneuvered a tiny surgical scissors to make the initial opening. "You know, this may work well to head off another Abbott-type incident, but I think we'd be better off coming up with a biodegradable wrap. I don't much like the removal process. Too much room for error."

Jeremy barely heard him as another wave of pain swept through his abdomen. He'd already had several painful and exhausting sessions in the bathroom before the procedure began, and he hoped he would be able to hold off until Glen closed up the patient. But he was already dehydrated from the morning and he was starting to feel lightheaded.

"Damn it—I nicked it a little bit. Sponge."

Darkness crept in at the edges of Jeremy's vision.

He stepped back and leaned against the wall behind him, trying to steady himself.

"Sponge!"

Jeremy felt his knees begin to buckle, and he slid to the floor. He tried to breathe deeply to stave off the dizziness. The pain intensified.

"Jeremy!" Tim jumped up and went over to him.

"What the hell is going on?" Glen broke his gaze from the surgical site and glanced over at Tim and Jeremy.

Jeremy mumbled to Tim, "Crohn's attack, thought I could make it through. Dehydrated…a little dizzy."

"Christ, Tim! Leave him on the floor so he can't hurt himself and help me wrap this up. Get me a couple of sponges."

Jeremy motioned Tim off. "Go." He leaned forward, clutching his belly and trying to breathe through the pain. He glanced up and saw Tim assisting Glen in the final stages of the procedure. He groaned slightly and hoped nothing changed in the patient's vitals while Tim abandoned his perch to assist Glen.

"All right, I can suture the outer layer myself. Better deal with the anesthesia."

"Right." Tim hurried back to his bank of monitors and dials. "Vitals still steady. I'll prepare to bring him out of it as soon as you've closed."

Jeremy bowed his head and breathed a sigh of relief.

Shortly after the patient had been taken to Recovery, Tim escorted Jeremy to a treatment room and started an IV running to counteract the dehydration. He added some drugs to the saline to help calm the intestinal spasming and pain. Alone now in the room, Jeremy lay on the exam table and gazed up at the ceiling as the saline dripped hydration and relief into his vein.

He felt somewhat better physically with the help of the IV, but now the gravity of what had happened began to sink in. He'd nearly compromised a surgical procedure because of his condition. He felt chilled to his core when he imagined what could have happened if the procedure had been at a more delicate point when he lost it. He dreaded the idea of going back on the full regimen of meds he'd been on before his surgery, but he couldn't let something like this happen again.

The door opened and Glen strode in. He wore an emphatic scowl on his flushed face. "What the hell were you thinking? Do you realize what could have happened?"

Jeremy shut his eyes. "I know. Believe me, I know."

"So what happened there? I thought you'd been doing great since the surgery."

Jeremy hesitated. He'd refused to admit to himself what was really going on. Answering Glen honestly would force him to admit not just to Glen, but to himself, that his Crohn's was back, and his little honeymoon of well-being was over. He'd even worked hard to hide it from Amanda. But now, a patient's life had been put in danger because of his denial, and he had no choice but to face it. He told Glen what had been going on.

Glen seemed to weigh the information carefully before answering. "Well, before your procedure, you'd reached the point where the meds were barely working, and the side effects were mounting. You did quite well when we replaced just the particularly compromised section of intestine. We need to run some tests to verify, but I suspect there were other sections that were compromised—just not so badly at the time—and they're deteriorating. I don't think you have a choice now. You need to replace the remainder of your intestinal tract."

Jeremy wasn't surprised by Glen's reaction. He'd wanted to perform the complete transplant all along. Nonetheless, hearing the words actually spoken felt like a physical blow. His mouth dry, he turned away while he frantically tried to think. He'd managed to sweet-talk himself into ignoring the ethical implications of the first, more limited, procedure because the Subject wasn't doing too terribly badly as a result. But if they took the rest of the Subject's intestinal tract…

"Of course it's your decision in the end. But I don't see where there is any choice left for you in the matter. You can't go on like this." He folded his arms. "And you certainly can't be relied upon in surgery any more until this is resolved. What happened today simply can't be allowed to happen again." He briefly checked and adjusted the IV flow. "You have a bit more of this left to go. Try to relax. I'll send Tim in to check on you in a little while."

After Glen left the room, Jeremy again stared at the ceiling without really observing it as he weighed his diminishing options. He knew on one level that Glen was right about what he needed to do to cure himself again. If only there were a way to cultivate intestines for transplant outside a human host. He sighed. It didn't matter. Even if there were, he didn't have the time to wait. His Crohn's was making up for lost time in tearing him back down.

He'd felt so great, so *normal*, once he'd recovered from his procedure. He had Amanda back, and they were so happy together. He had everything he wanted, until now. Jeremy felt shattered to have been cured and to have regained his life, only to have it snatched away again.

In the meantime, Tim's adjustments to the Subject's food had worked. He was actually doing quite well now—so much so that Jeremy had been able to take his guilt, package it up, and tuck it away where he didn't have to face it.

That wouldn't be the case anymore. No amount of special food or treatment would compensate the Subject's loss this time if he went ahead with the complete transplant.

CHAPTER 42

Amanda clicked her opener and pulled inside the garage. She noticed that Jeremy had beaten her home, which was highly unusual. She stepped out of her car and went inside.

"Jeremy—what are you doing home already?" she shouted as she set down her bag on the kitchen table.

No answer.

She shrugged. Maybe he was upstairs at the far end of the house. It was certainly big enough he might not hear her from there. She started up the stairs. "Jeremy!"

"Up here."

She frowned at the odd tone in his voice. It sounded tired and muffled. "What's the matter?" she asked as she quickened her pace and headed for their bedroom.

She opened the door and saw him sitting on the edge of the bed, his head in his hands. The shades were all drawn, throwing the room into a murky gloom. She turned on the light and sat beside him. "What is it?"

He turned to her with exhausted eyes. "I haven't told you…"

Alarmed at the expression on his face, she asked, "Told me what? What's wrong?"

He looked down into his lap, shoulders slumped. "It's back. I've tried to keep it from you—and from myself. But it's back, and it's bad."

"What, your Crohn's? I thought you just had a little stomach flu, is all. You've been doing great since your surgery."

"I *was* doing great. It started up a little at a time. I thought it was just nerves or whatever—you know, with that lawsuit and all. But it's been getting worse." He looked up at her again with bloodshot eyes. "Today I nearly passed out in surgery. I just sat there on the floor, helpless, while they closed without me." He shook his head and stared down into his lap again. "That could have been a disaster," he said softly. "Someone could have *died.*"

"Why didn't you tell me?" She put an arm around his shoulder.

"Because I didn't want to tell *myself,*" he snapped. He broke away from her, stood and began to pace. "Everything was going so well."

"Well, I suppose you'll have to start back on the meds. Maybe you can try a different regimen. They come up with new ones all the time, don't they?" She could feel his anguish, and she realized her comment sounded lame the moment it came out of her mouth.

Jeremy stopped pacing and glared at her for a moment. "I had the surgery in the first place because it had gotten to the point where there were more side effects than benefit from the meds. No, even the most current regimen available wasn't cutting it anymore." He clenched his fists and pressed them against the sides of his head. "Oh, God, I wish it were that easy. Glen's pushing me to get the complete transplant."

"Oh." Amanda felt like someone had just knocked the wind out of her. She suddenly understood why Jeremy was so upset, why he'd been in denial and kept his condition from her. Somehow they'd both managed to set aside the ethical issues with the first procedure and enjoy the benefits for these past months. Now the stakes had been raised. She knew full well the implications of the complete transplant.

Jeremy started to pace again. "Yeah, I see you get it."

Amanda flinched at his bitter tone. She knew she'd lost any hope of objectivity now that she was back with Jeremy. Before, she could at least try to consider the ethical considerations and take the high road—and then go home to her life. Too late now. She loved Jeremy too much to put the Subject's interests ahead of his. She couldn't bear the thought of watching him deteriorate when there was a solution. "Then that's what we do."

He stopped pacing and turned to her sharply. "You think it's that simple?"

"It is, for me. It's the only thing that will make you well."

"But what about—?"

"We work with Glen and Tim to figure out how to make it as… humane…as possible." She swallowed hard as she tried to think of how to make humane the taking of a person's entire digestive tract for the sake of another. Involuntarily, no less. She tried to convince herself the Subject probably didn't understand what was going on anyway. After all, he'd never been educated or socialized. He didn't know anything of the outside world. She did her best to relegate the Subject to the status of an *it*, not a *he*. It was the only way.

CHAPTER 43

Jeremy looked up and down the hall, and was relieved to confirm he was alone. He'd come again on another pilgrimage of guilt.

He opened the door and stepped inside the Subject's *home*. He made himself really think about that for a moment, forced himself to open up and allow the guilt to freely wash over him. The Subject had never known another environment in his relatively brief existence. He tried to imagine what that must be like, and could not. Here was a human being whose entire life and environment had been that of a captive lab animal.

He gazed at the Subject, who sat on the edge of his erstwhile bed and gazed blankly back at him. What else did he have to do? He couldn't read, so books were of no use to him. He had no concept of sports or movies, so a television wouldn't be anything more than a strange and useless curiosity to him.

The more he thought about it, the more puzzled he became. What sort of mental or interior life did the Subject have? Did he have anything like that at all? Given his circumstances, it might be more of a mercy if he *did* lack those things.

Despite Jeremy's professed resolution to do so back when he first learned of the secret project, he'd never had the Subject tested for his cognitive capabilities. Somehow he never did get around to it, partly due to the logistics of finding someone qualified, given the needed secrecy, and partly because he simply didn't want to face whatever the results might show. They didn't even have an informal clue as to his mental capacity, because no one had ever tried to provide any sort of education or socialization beyond the minimum interaction to feed and care for him.

Surely now no one ever would.

It would be so much easier that way. Jeremy knew what he was doing. He was working hard to dehumanize the very human-looking Subject who sat before him. It wasn't all that hard to do, really. For the most part.

He decided it would be better to just leave, to not approach the enclosure and try to examine the Subject more closely. The more distance, the better.

Jeremy had just turned to go when the door opened and Glen stepped inside.

"Oh. I didn't expect to find you in here." Glen glanced at the Subject, then at Jeremy. He eyed him warily, then asked, "What *are* you doing in here, anyway?"

"Nothing. Just checking in on things."

"Well, you can leave that to me. I'm going to do a pre-op check shortly to make sure everything is in good shape for transplant."

Despite his own efforts to objectify the Subject as nothing more than a donor, Jeremy winced inwardly at Glen's choice of words.

"You know, there is another issue for you to consider."

Jeremy waited, wondering if Glen had suddenly had an attack of ethics to wrestle with.

"The nature of your disease. You know it goes on attacking the intestinal tissue. The transplant isn't going to stop that; it's only going to give you a new start, for the time being. There will undoubtedly come a time when it begins to compromise your new organs."

"Yeah, that sounds logical." Jeremy wondered where Glen was going with this line of discussion.

"So eventually you're going to need another transplant, most likely. We have another batch of Ivan's tissue preserved for this purpose. We should take a portion of it and start to generate another Subject for that eventuality. I'm assuming we won't be able to regenerate the large and small intestine within this Subject's body after the procedure—although we should certainly try so we can learn if it is possible or not."

Jeremy glanced at the Subject. He still just sat on the edge of his bed, watching them both with a neutral look on his face. As if he didn't understand a thing that was going on.

At least Jeremy hoped he didn't understand.

He cleared his throat, then said, "Yeah, I suppose you should go ahead and do that."

Then he left the room without looking back at the Subject.

CHAPTER 44

"Yeah, Brad. Stop by my office." Jeremy set down the phone and ran his hands through his hair. Just what he needed. Brad Gilman wanted to talk to him. He just had a feeling nothing his corporate counsel could say would be good news.

A few minutes later, Brad knocked briefly, then entered. "Hey, Jeremy. How goes it?"

"All right, I guess. Depends on what you have to say." Jeremy glanced up at Brad and attempted a smile. At least he wasn't the stereotypical suited-up, gibberish-mumbling lawyer type. He was grateful for that much. Brad was a practical guy who understood SomaGene's business and typically got to the point in an intelligible way.

Clad in jeans and a black T-shirt, Brad dropped his lanky frame into one of Jeremy's guest chairs. He held a slim folder. "Got some movement on the Abbott matter."

Jeremy's shoulders tightened. His impending surgery had pushed the lawsuit out of his mind. It disturbed him he could have completely forgotten about something so important. His throat suddenly felt constricted. "Yeah, what do you have?"

"Well, Abbott lawyered up shortly after he got out of the hospital. No surprise there. Actually, I prefer dealing with an attorney on the other side. The *pro se*'s can make you crazy with their ridiculous demands." He chuckled briefly. "Anyway, he's come up with his wish list. Wants a new kidney generated, wants it transplanted under your new protocol. And he wants $50,000 cash for the privilege."

Jeremy dropped his head into his hands and groaned.

"Are you serious? Jeremy, this is great. It's not that much

money, and it avoids trial and all the related expenses and exposure. Best of all, I'm pretty sure I can get him to sign a confidentiality agreement if we agree to his full demands and maybe sweeten the cash component a little. That's more important than anything. You don't want a whiff of this getting out, and it looks like we can manage that. You've changed the protocol so it can't happen again. What's not to like?"

"Yeah, that makes sense. I didn't see it that way at first. It just seemed so overwhelming."

"No worries. I think this will settle easily. You pay him the money, do the procedure—all done." Brad looked at Jeremy more closely. "Hey, are you all right? You don't look so good."

Jeremy waved his hand. "I'm fine. Just a little tired, is all." He didn't dare mention he'd be having his own surgery shortly. Brad had no idea about the Subject and all that entailed, and he intended to keep it that way.

"OK then. When should I tell him to expect to have the surgery?"

Jeremy paused, not wanting to let on to Brad about his upcoming unavailability. Of course, there was no need for him to be personally present at the surgery. He could have several of the more recent hires handle it while he was convalescing. "I'll let you know. I need to check our queue and capacity first."

"Great. Let me know in the next day or two, so I can get back with Abbott's attorney." Brad sprang out of his chair and headed for the door. "Thanks. I'll let you know when there's an agreement to sign."

"Yeah, thanks." Jeremy put his head on his desk, relieved as hell, but just as exhausted.

CHAPTER 45

"Shut the door, Tim. I don't want any interruptions. I want to discuss Jeremy's upcoming procedure."

"Sure." Tim shut the door, then took a seat in front of Glen's desk.

"Jeremy gave his permission to initiate a second clone. I think we should get that process started as soon as possible. We have nothing to base a guess on how long it will be before his Crohn's attacks the new intestinal tissue."

Tim squirmed in his chair. "I suppose that's wise. It took a couple years for this Subject to be ready. I don't know how we could speed up the process without inviting problems. In fact, I still worry that getting this one to adult size as fast as we did might have some consequence that hasn't yet manifested itself."

Satisfied they had agreement on one point, Glen steeled himself to raise the next issue. He expected a difficult conversation, given the nature of some of Tim's remarks about the Subject. "All right, that's settled. We can initiate tomorrow or the next day. There is another matter we need to discuss before the day of the procedure."

Tim's brow furrowed. "What's that?"

"We need to agree on what is to be done with the Subject after the surgery—given that it will be a complete transplant this time."

"I…I don't know." He stared out the window.

"Surely you've considered the implications before now?"

"Well, yes, but I hadn't taken that next step in my mind. I was somewhat surprised Jeremy even agreed to the second procedure."

"Oh come on, Tim. What else could he do? You saw how he's deteriorated. Doesn't matter if he's uncomfortable about it, he has no choice. But that's really beside the point now. He's agreed to the procedure and we need to prepare for it. And we need to decide what to do about the Subject afterwards."

Tim cast him a sharp glance. "Well, sounds like *you* have some ideas about it. What have you been thinking?" He sat back in his chair with folded arms.

Glen had been hoping to tease out ideas from Tim, so that maybe he'd be able to get more buy-in from him. But the surgery was only days away and this had to be settled ahead of time. "Well, the way I see it, there are two main ways to go. Each has a downside. Consider that the Subject was generated for the sole purpose of providing Jeremy a solution for his Crohn's. So, unless Jeremy develops some unrelated problem, the Subject will be of no further use to him after this procedure. We could simply pull the plug. But then we have a disposal problem. We at least put off the disposal problem if we set up some indefinite form of life support to take the place of the digestive function."

Tim stood up, his face flushed. "How can you talk about doing that to a *human*—?"

Glen rose to his feet and leaned forward over his desk for emphasis. "A *lab asset*. Do not forget his origin and purpose. We grew him in the lab from a scrap of Ivan's tissue. We did so for this very eventuality. The sooner you stop thinking of him as a fellow citizen, the better."

"Jesus, Glen. Open your eyes!"

"Tim, he looks like a human because he was cloned from a human. *You* look at him. He sits there day after day. He probably has no interior life at all. He doesn't speak; he doesn't particularly interact any more than one of the lab animals in the room next door to him. He's *tissue*…tissue purposefully engineered to be put to a specific use." He leaned forward a bit farther. "And you know what? You assisted all along. It's a little late to try to wash your hands now."

Deflated, Tim flopped back down in his chair and rubbed his face with his hands. "I wish to God I hadn't."

Sensing victory, Glen sat back down. "So, can we get down to a meaningful discussion of what to do post-op?"

Tim let out a long breath before answering. "I just can't support pulling the plug. I suppose the thing to do is to come up with an alternate way to get him nutrition and fluids—and to try to do so as humanely as possible." Tim rubbed his ear with a noticeably trembling hand. "I suppose we can go with total parenteral nutrition through an IV. But it will mean he's hooked to a needle and tube the rest of his life, with a constant risk of infection, of course. It'll probably put more pressure on his kidneys than otherwise, but at least he'll be alive." He stared at the floor.

Glen chose to ignore Tim's defeated demeanor. "I'm glad we could get this figured out." He then turned to his computer monitor to break off the discussion.

Tim got up and left without another word.

CHAPTER 46

Katie glanced at the sheep-themed clock on the wall in Johnnie's room. Tim was certainly running late today. She knew he liked to give the little guy his bath each night while she got dinner ready, but it was just getting too late to wait for him this time.

"C'mon Johnnie, it's you and me tonight." She picked up the baby and headed for the bathroom.

She held him on her hip as she started the water and waited for it to get to the right temperature. She scowled as she thought about Tim. He'd been getting more and more distant lately, and came home in a foul mood more and more often. She knew he was losing sleep, too. He didn't think she could tell, but she could. He'd lie there next to her, shifting around, but definitely not breathing the calm breath of a sleeping person. She'd thought about reaching over and asking him what was wrong, but he usually liked to try to work things out himself, so she'd let it go.

It must be something at work. He used to speak more freely over dinner, regaling her with how well the business was doing, how many surgeries they did and what kind. He seemed so proud of his work at SomaGene, how much good they did their patients, and how no other clinic could touch what they offered.

But lately, he only spoke of his work in a very clipped sort of way. Single word answers, grunts—and he had to be prodded for even that much. Not only was that tone of pride gone, but he seemed to be keeping something from her. She wondered if something had gone wrong with a patient and he wasn't free to talk about it. They had such a great success rate, but maybe something had blemished it and wasn't public information.

Katie resolved to force the issue at the earliest possible opportunity. Whatever it was, it had gone on long enough—several months now, it seemed. And it was getting worse, not better.

She made sure the water was the right temperature, removed Johnnie's diaper, and gently placed him in his little plastic bath seat. He became excited, jiggling his legs and splashing the water with his tiny hands. He babbled as she began to wash him.

CHAPTER 47

A bolt of lightning cut through the early morning gloom and nearly blinded Amanda as she turned into the SomaGene driveway. Heavy rain drummed against the windshield as the wipers struggled to keep up.

Neither she nor Jeremy had uttered a word on their way to the facility for his second surgery. There was no need. They both knew full well what the other was thinking. No matter how much they had tried to talk it through, neither one of them was remotely at ease with the ethics of the situation.

But both of them knew Jeremy had no other choice.

Amanda parked the car in Jeremy's spot, same as last time. She harbored a slight superstition that it would bode well for him in getting through the surgery. Another thing they both knew and didn't openly discuss was the fact that such extensive surgery had never before been attempted.

At least, not to their knowledge. Amanda wondered if other labs hadn't successfully cloned humans for organ harvesting purposes and just kept it quiet to avoid the inevitable storm of controversy. Obviously, it was possible.

"Well, here we are." She turned to look at Jeremy. He just sat there, staring down and apparently wiping sweat from his palms onto his pants. He didn't respond. "Jeremy, you ready?"

He looked at her, his face pale, his eyes dark and tired-looking. He'd been back on the extreme meds to calm his digestive tract so he could be in the best possible condition to tolerate the surgery. He answered as if she had distracted him from deep thought. "Yeah, I guess so."

Amanda glanced at the driving rain and sighed. "Better

make a run for it. It's coming down pretty hard."

They swiftly exited the car and bolted toward SomaGene's front door. Once inside, they brushed themselves off and silently headed for Jeremy's office. The brief walk down the hallway felt like a grim replay to Amanda.

They stepped inside his office and hung up their rain jackets. Jeremy sat in his chair, and Amanda took one of the seats in front of his desk. They both stared at their laps and avoided conversation as they waited for the appointed time.

He lay down on his padded shelf. He was tired, so tired. He couldn't remember not being tired, but there must have been a time. He just didn't know.

His food still tasted terrible, but he tried to eat more of it because that White Coat seemed to want him to. That White Coat spent more time with him than he used to. Not like the other White Coat. That one didn't seem to like him much. He didn't understand why. It used to be harder to tell them apart, but they acted differently now so he usually could tell the difference.

The White Coat bringing his food was about the only thing that happened each day. He would hear the screaming and ranting from the room next to him, then a short while later, the White Coat would come in with food and would stand and stare at him until he finished it. Then he would go.

Not much else ever happened. Not White Coat came a couple of times. He always got a strange feeling inside when he came. He didn't know how to describe it, but it just felt funny through his insides. Not White Coat would just look at him for a while, and then go away again. He never brought food or anything. He couldn't understand why he came at all.

The door opened and both White Coats came in. He didn't know what to think about that. They rarely came at the same time any more.

Except that other time.

Panicked, he sat up and pressed himself back against the wall, as if he could push through to somewhere safe. The White Coats were getting closer to where they could open the door to his little enclosure and get inside. He didn't want them inside.

He suddenly remembered what happened last time they came together. Now he remembered when he used to feel better. He used to feel better before they came together that last time and took him out. He'd never been out before, and they both took him out into that strange room. The room with the painfully bright lights and that table.

He remembered more. He remembered being strapped to that table, unable to move, then feeling a sharp sting in his arm. Then nothing, until he woke up with a terrible pain in his belly. He remembered it all now, though he did not understand it. He woke up with white pads taped to his belly and it hurt so bad under those pads that he couldn't walk at first.

And it was ever since then that his food tasted so bad, and he was always so tired.

And they were back! They were going to do it to him again.

He opened his mouth and he began to scream, startling himself with the sound. He could barely breathe from the panic that had set in and tightened his chest and throat.

"Shut him up!" The White Coat that didn't like him quickly opened his enclosure and charged at him. The other one hung back for a moment, then joined him.

They had his arms pinned down. He twisted and tried to get away, but they were so much stronger. Then he felt a sharp sticking pain in his arm. He kept trying to break from their grip, but he felt weaker and weaker.

Then darkness.

CHAPTER 48

They waited until the Subject stopped struggling and fell under a light anesthesia from the intramuscular injection. Glen stepped to the door and checked down the hallway. "It's clear. Good thing this section is cut off from the main operation. I'll get the gurney." He left the room.

Tim sat on the shelf-bed next to the Subject. He looked down at him and felt almost physically ill at what had just transpired. He must be capable of memory, or why would he have reacted that way? Tim wondered how specific his memories were.

At least he was out for now, and he wouldn't awaken until the procedure was complete. He wouldn't form any new traumatic memories of being marched into the surgical suite and strapped down. Tim supposed that was some small consolation.

Minutes later, Glen arrived with the gurney. He wheeled it into the enclosure and they lifted the Subject onto it. Tim winced as Glen cinched the straps more aggressively than was necessary. He supposed he was driving home the point that the Subject was nothing more than a living container for the organs Jeremy needed.

They wheeled the Subject into the surgical suite and positioned the gurney alongside the one that would hold Jeremy. Both of them worked in silence to optimally position the carts, trays and various surgical instruments that would be needed.

Tim then began to prepare the Subject for surgery. He set up an IV, then hooked up the cardiac and respiratory monitors to his chest. He gazed at the screens for a few moments. Satisfied with the readings, he deftly intubated him and adjusted the gas flow. A cold feeling crept into the pit of his stomach as he watched Glen completing his own preps on the Subject.

Glen draped the surgical site as if he were draping a lab animal in preparation for a classroom demo. He performed his tasks roughly, as he exposed the Subject's abdomen and swabbed it with antiseptic. He stood back for a moment as if taking a mental inventory, then said, "All right. Ready. If everything's ready on your end, I'll buzz Jeremy."

"Yeah, he's stable."

Jeremy slowly set the phone down. "That was Glen. They're ready for me." He felt weak in the knees.

Amanda looked at him, her eyes wide. She looked like she was trying to keep from crying. "Oh," she said in a tiny voice.

Jeremy took a deep breath, stood, and walked over to her. "I'll see ya soon." He attempted a smile, then bent down and kissed her briefly.

She stood up and hugged him hard. He could feel her trembling. This was already tough enough and—though it was no surprise—it made it worse to know she was scared, too. He gently pried her off him and held her by her shoulders. He kissed her again, trying to ignore the tears that had started down her cheeks.

"Gotta go. I'll see you." The words barely made it out of his tightening throat. He turned and left the room while he still could.

He gently shut the door and started down the hall to the surgical suite. Once inside the vestibule, he saw the gown that had been left out for him. He picked it up and stared at it for a few moments as he thought about what he was about to undergo. Theoretically, he could still back out. But what would that solve? He couldn't go on as he had been. His disease was taking a brutal toll, and it wouldn't stop until it tore him apart as it had his mother.

He unfolded the flimsy hospital gown, sighed, and changed into it. Head bowed and shoulders slumped, he stepped to the swinging door, pushed it open, then entered the surgical suite.

A guilty chill ran up his back when he saw the draped and prepped Subject lying on the gurney next to his. Glen had told him that they were going to try to keep him alive after the procedure with some IV-based nutrition regimen. If he survived the procedure at all.

He gazed at the Subject for a moment longer before proceeding to his own gurney. He could see very little of him, actually, which was just as well. He was surrounded by wires, tubes, and monitors. The green surgical drapes placed around his abdomen framed his belly like a gift to be opened.

Jeremy supposed that was true in its own way. Whatever he thought of Ivan, and even if this was an ego-driven project at base, he had given him a gift. The gift of a new chance at life with a new colon and small intestine. Made just for him.

At least he tried to think of it that way, and not the other way—that he was stealing the lifesaving organs from an unwitting victim.

"We're ready for you." Glen motioned toward the empty gurney that awaited him. Jeremy had a brief, odd thought that he looked a little like a maître d' waving him to his table.

He stepped over to the gurney, his feet feeling numb and uncooperative. He got on it, lay down, and turned his head slightly away from the Subject to try to keep him out of his line of sight.

Tim stood over him. "OK, I guess you know the drill." He tried to smile. "I'm going to start the IV, give you a whiff of the gas to get you under. Then I'll do the rest and we'll get started. You ready?"

"Yeah, I guess so."

Jeremy tried to relax as he felt the stick of the needle. He could feel the slight coolness of the IV solution as it began to flow into his vein. *Odd, the little details that come to attention at times like this.*

Tim placed the mask on his face. "Now just breathe normally. It won't be long."

Jeremy took a breath and felt the workings of the gas pretty quickly. He felt like he was wrapped in cotton, soft and quiet. A couple more breaths and he was out.

CHAPTER 49

Tim glanced once more at each patient's monitors. He hesitated to make his announcement, because he knew that would mark the beginning of the dual procedures, the point of no return. He worried that, despite all their preparations and planning for various potential scenarios, something would happen that would be difficult to impossible for only two surgeons to handle. They'd managed just fine the first time, but this procedure would be so much more extensive, and such a transplant had never before been undertaken. What might they have missed in their planning?

"Well? Are you ready?" Glen sounded somewhat irritated.

"They're both ready and stable."

"All right, let's go." Glen stepped over to the Subject's gurney. "I'll open him up first, leave everything in place, then open Jeremy. Then I'll work on the transfer."

"We really could use another two surgeons for this—at least. It's a lot to do in a limited timeframe."

"Well, that's not an option, so we're just going to have to do our best. I don't want to have to call on you to assist, given you're trying to watch two patients yourself, but I may have to."

"They're both in pretty good shape, compared to some of our really elderly and infirm patients. But you never know, once they've been under a while. Things can happen."

Glen paused before making his first incision and pointed his scalpel at Tim for emphasis. "Let's be clear right now. If things get dicey with either of them, we focus on Jeremy. If it comes to excising the intestines and rushing to get them into Jeremy, I'll forgo tying off the Subject's blood vessels if need be. Is that clear?"

Tim didn't want to shortchange the Subject's care, but given the situation and the obvious tradeoffs, he couldn't argue with Glen's priorities. "Yep. It is."

"Good. Note the time, and… Go." Glen dexterously opened the Subject's abdomen, and placed metal clamps to hold it open. Tim noticed he sped up the process by quickly using the electro cautery, rather than clamping the blood vessels more meticulously.

Tim wondered how well the incision would heal, given that approach—or if there would even be a need for that incision to heal by the time this procedure was over. He shook the thought from his mind and tried to focus on the immediate situation.

Glen selected a fresh scalpel and turned to open Jeremy. Tim noticed that he spent more time clamping the blood vessels as he worked.

"How are they doing?"

"All good."

"Do you think you could work on removing the intestines from the Subject while I prepare to remove Jeremy's? It would speed this up considerably if we could do that simultaneously."

Tim glanced again at the monitors. "They've both been rock solid so far. Yeah, let's do that. I don't like the idea of them both under any longer than need be."

He rose from his stool strategically positioned at the patients' heads and went over to the Subject. The enormity of what he was about to do hit him, and he wondered if Glen had more in mind than merely speeding up the overall procedure time. He wondered if this was Glen's way of pulling him in even further so his hands would be just as unclean should something go wrong or if anything about the program eventually leaked. He decided that was pretty damned likely and there wasn't a thing he could do about it right now except to do his best to make sure both patients survived.

He readied his instruments and began lifting and separating the Subject's intestines from the abdominal cavity. He tried to work as quickly and carefully as he could as he went along, locating the various blood vessels that would need ligation, as well as the connective tissue holding the intestines in place. He fully realized he had the easier job, since the vessels only needed to be tied off and the ends of the intestines stitched shut. Glen would have to splice the blood vessels from the Subject's intestines onto Jeremy's oh, so carefully.

They both worked in silence, side by side, to prepare their respective intestines for removal. After about an hour, Tim completed his task and placed the intestines into a waiting body-temperature nutrient bath in a stainless steel container next to the gurneys. "I'm done."

"I'm maybe halfway through. This is tricky business because I have to leave all these vessels ready to resect onto the new organs. How about if they're both stable, just going ahead with closure on the Subject?"

"Good idea." Tim stepped over and carefully checked the monitors. "Still good. I'll get to work." He went back to the Subject and first verified that all the ligated blood vessels within the abdomen were holding properly. Blood vessels that would no longer be needed to nourish an intestine that would no longer reside in his abdomen. *What a bizarre concept.*

Other strange thoughts ran through Tim's head as he prepared to close. The intestines took up a considerable amount of space in the abdominal cavity. Aside from the obvious impacts of their removal, would there be any unforeseen problems from the simple lack of their presence in supporting the rest of the abdominal organs within the cavity? Tim began to work in a sort of reverie as he pondered the potential implications. He didn't hear the beeping.

"Tim—one of the monitors is going off! I can't stop what I'm doing."

Tim set down his instruments and rushed over to check the monitors. "It's the Subject. He's getting a little tachy."

"How's Jeremy?"

"He's good."

Tim rolled the crash cart over to the Subject's gurney.

"What are you doing?"

"Getting ready in case he arrests."

"Get that back over here. I don't want any delays in case Jeremy needs it or any other quick response."

"He's in danger of arresting any time now. I can't just stand by."

Glen slammed down his clamp and turned to Tim. "Dammit, Tim! I thought I made it clear before we got started—Jeremy comes first. Period. I can't deal with this and focus on what I'm doing. You'd better not lose sight of Jeremy's condition. I'm elbow-deep here." He turned back to his work.

The alarm went off, indicating full arrest. Tim grabbed the paddles and shocked the Subject without hesitation. He glanced at the Subject's monitor. *One more.* He hit him again. He glanced back and saw the Subject was back to a normal rhythm. He set the paddles aside and drew the back of his sleeve across his forehead to wipe away beads of sweat.

He picked up where he had left off—this time, using the electro cautery more frequently to secure the blood vessels as quickly as possible. He didn't want the Subject open for a minute longer than necessary. He knew the risks of trying to monitor two patients in complex simultaneous procedures.

He next focused on tying off the cut ends of the intestines. Since it was something he'd never done before, he had to make it up on the fly. He stitched them shut with dissolving sutures, then applied adhesive tissue patches for extra strength during the healing process. *It's not as if the Subject will ever eat or drink again, so there should really be no stress on these sutures. But, just in case.*

Tim then closed the abdomen, layer by layer, as fast as he could. Glen had made no effort to create the smallest possible incision. It was one long swipe from the bottom of the sternum to the top of the pubic bone. With all the electro cautery, this was going to be a large and ugly scar when all was said and done. Tim shook his head. The scar was the least of the after-effects the Subject would have to contend with.

He adjusted the IV, lightened the anesthetic just a bit, but kept the Subject under for now. He couldn't leave the room to deal with him while Jeremy's surgery was still under way.

"Done on this end."

"Good. I've just clamped the last vessel here, and I'm ready to implant the new intestine. Help me with that, would you?"

"Sure." Tim wheeled over the cart that held the steel container of harvested intestines. He glanced over at the monitors, and was grateful to see that all looked stable.

"All right, I'm ready." Glen carefully lifted out Jeremy's excised intestines while Tim extracted the Subject's intestines from the nutrient bath. They switched positions. Glen dumped Jeremy's intestines into the nutrient bath, then began to arrange the Subject's within Jeremy's abdominal cavity.

Tim moved closer to his usual station near the patients' heads so he could more readily observe all the monitors. He felt some relief now that only one patient was open. Yet he was still anxious for the procedure to be over, as both had been under for several hours now and he was getting more and more uncomfortable as time ticked on. The Subject had already arrested. He might not be able to survive another incident. And the longer they were under, the more risk there was of Jeremy having some sort of incident.

After another hour that seemed like four, Glen proclaimed he had resected all the necessary blood vessels and it appeared the new intestine was properly infusing with circulated blood. "I'm going to connect the ends of the intestine now."

Tim glanced at Glen and noticed he was beginning to look tired. They'd been at this procedure better than half the day now, just the two of them. It was insane to attempt such a thing with just two surgeons. Insane. But there was no way around that when only three surgeons were privy to the secret project, and one of them was under the knife.

Glen tossed a used clamp into a steel pan, sighed deeply, then did a small backbend to release the tense muscles along his spine. "Done. All that's left is to close." He bent down again to the task and worked swiftly, silently.

Tim continued to watch the monitors closely while Glen worked. He spotted an irregular beat or two on Jeremy's readings. He was concerned, but not panicked. Even so, he would breathe a lot easier when they were done and bringing both patients out of the anesthesia.

"That's it." Glen dropped the suture needle and clamp into the steel pan. "Note the time and start bringing them out of it." He rubbed his eyes with the back of his sleeve. "Jesus, I'm exhausted."

Tim took his cue and started to alter the gas composition. He could feel the tension lifting from his shoulders as the patients' anesthesia lightened and waned. Whatever happened next, at least they made it through the grueling double procedure.

CHAPTER 50

"I'm so thirsty." Jeremy rubbed his cracked lips together. "God, it hurts," he croaked out.

"Here, the doctors said to suck on an ice chip. They didn't want you swallowing yet." Amanda offered a small ice cube and stared at him with a concerned furrowing of her brow.

He took the cube, worked it around in his mouth. He'd never been so grateful for a little chunk of ice. When it had fully melted, he tried to smile and thanked her.

He shut his eyes. He felt like he was swirling downward in a mix of drug haze and pain both inside his abdomen and in the skin. The incision had to be longer than last time to get the job done—and it felt like it. He felt fragile, like he might break open if he tried to move. "Hurts."

"I'll call them and let them know."

Moments later, he heard footsteps. He opened his eyes to see Tim approach the side of the bed opposite Amanda. "How're you doing?"

"Hurts bad."

"I can give you a little more pain med." Tim reached for something on the tray next to the bed, and slid a needle into the port on the IV tube. "There. That should take the edge off in just a minute."

"What happened…to him?" he whispered.

Tim leaned closer. "You mean the Subject?"

"Yeah."

Tim hesitated, looked at Amanda.

"Tell me…"

"He's in recovery as well. Sedated. We've started special

nutrient IVs for him to make up for his… loss."

Jeremy looked from Tim to Amanda, and just noticed her face blanch before the room began to swirl, the pain began to lift, and he succumbed to the drugs.

CHAPTER 51

"You go ahead and go home, at least for a while. I'll stay on site in case there are any problems. Assuming nothing comes up, you can relieve me in the morning." Glen rubbed his eyes, took another sip of coffee, then leaned back in his chair and stretched.

"Are you sure? You look beat." Tim sat slumped in one of Glen's office guest chairs.

"Can't have both of us wearing ourselves out. We need to trade off. Jeremy's looking pretty good, all things considered. I think it's safe enough. Go home and rest." Glen waved his hand as if shooing Tim off.

Tim rose from his chair. "Well, thanks. I'll be back early tomorrow morning, unless I hear otherwise from you in the meantime." He turned to go.

Tim stepped outside the SomaGene entrance and blinked in the bright sunlight. He hadn't so much as looked out a window all day. The last he recalled, it had been raining buckets in the morning. Now the clouds had broken up and the late-day sun beat down on the moist ground and raised a curtain of humidity.

He shuffled out to the parking lot and got into his car. He slipped the key into the ignition, then paused. What was he going to say to Katie? He was completely exhausted and hadn't yet come to terms with the day's events, and she had been hammering on him lately about his work. She seemed to suspect he was keeping something from her—and she likely wouldn't rest until he gave her something to stop her questions.

He glanced at his face in the rear-view mirror. He looked every bit as haggard as Glen had. Maybe he could just beg off and go to bed when he got home and dodge her questions at least for tonight.

He started the car, backed out of his space, and left the parking lot. Once out on the main road, he realized he'd managed to pick the worst time of day to leave. The road was a main drag through this portion of Minnetonka, and the four-way stop sign at the next intersection guaranteed a long backup at the slightest provocation. Tonight was no exception. He leaned back in his seat and gritted his teeth. The city really needed to dump the stop signs and install traffic lights there.

Finally he got up to the intersection and broke free of the backup. His house was only a few miles from SomaGene, but at times like this, he might as well have had a long commute through Golden Valley. He grunted and pressed the accelerator to make up some time.

After what seemed like days, he pulled into his garage and went into the house. Something smelled good in the kitchen, but he wasn't quite sure what. He went in and found Katie stirring a pot of something and Johnnie rolling around in his playpen in the nook area.

"Hey, Katie."

She turned to glance at him, and the look on her face instantly changed to one of concern. "What happened to you today? You look awful."

"Long surgery. A bit touch and go for a while." He left it at that and hoped that summary would satisfy her.

Katie put down the ladle. "I've never seen you look this bad. What is it, really?" She put her hands on her hips.

"I'm really too tired." The cooking smell was making him especially hungry, but he thought the best plan would be to simply go to bed. He was certainly tired enough, and that would avoid further discussion that he wasn't up for. Once Katie put her hands on her hips, he knew from experience he'd be in for a long interrogation if he didn't cut it off pronto.

"No. Something's been going on for a while now, and I need to know what it is. You can't just come home looking all beat up like this and avoid the subject." She motioned for him to sit at the kitchen table.

"Really, Katie. I just want to go to bed." He started to leave the kitchen and head for the stairs.

She took a quick look at Johnnie in his playpen and shut off the stove. Then she followed him. "Not this time. We're going to talk."

He continued up the stairs to their bedroom, hoping to shake her from his tail. "Katie, I mean it. I'm way too tired to talk right now." He reached the bedroom, sat heavily on the bed and slipped off his shoes.

Katie stood in the doorway, wearing her most stubborn look. "Not till we talk."

He groaned and hung his head. He'd seen her like this before. She would not back off until she was satisfied. He had to tell her something, or she would stand there until hell froze. He weighed his response before starting. "I can't give you specifics, but I'm involved in a new project at SomaGene. Ivan started it before he died, and Glen and I have been working on it since, according to his wishes. It's very leading edge, never been done before. The work is…difficult, and Glen and I are not seeing eye to eye on some aspects of it."

Her eyes widened with curiosity. "What sort of project?"

He raised his head with an effort and looked up at her. "That's what I can't talk about. It's crucial it remain under wraps. But I can tell you, it is what's been stressing me. The work itself, as well as the conflict with Glen over certain aspects. That's really all I can say, but I hope you understand."

"Well, all right. You know I'd keep quiet if you did tell me." She looked at him imploringly.

"Maybe someday I can tell you more. But not now." He leaned back. "Can I please just go to bed now? I'm sorry about dinner. I just really need to sleep."

"All right. I'll get Johnnie's bath, too." Katie started to back out of the room.

"Thank you." Tim didn't bother to change clothes. He just closed his eyes and fell asleep within minutes.

CHAPTER 52

Jeremy stood staring out of his office window. He wouldn't have believed it possible, but time had flown by while he recuperated from his second surgery. The leaves in the trees now had that mature sort of green about them, looking tired and ready for the transition to fall in a few weeks. Such a stark contrast with how he felt now.

His recovery had gone remarkably well for such an extensive procedure. He was back on a normal diet after being initially restricted to only the most easily digested foods while his new intestines established themselves in his body.

Amanda had been with him every step of the way—and they had somehow managed to avoid the topic that lurked beneath his miraculous return to health. For that he was grateful. It had taken all his strength and concentration to convalesce as rapidly as he had. He couldn't have handled such discussions— and besides, what point was there? The procedure was done, and the Subject was being nutritionally supported. It's not like there was any turning back. So there was no sense in draining his energy constantly revisiting the opportunity to feel guilty.

And now, he was off the meds, pain-free, and feeling even better than after the first procedure. Life was certainly good now. But he had to wonder how long this respite would last. He still had Crohn's, and the disease would want to lay waste to his digestive tract. And it would—it just had new tissues to work on that would stave off the worst of it for a while. For how long? He had no idea, and neither did Tim or Glen.

What if it only worked for a couple of years—or less? How many more times over his lifetime would he need a transplant?

He didn't want to think about this, but eventually he'd have to face it. Would he need an indefinite supply of new Subjects to keep him healthy? Maybe there was some medication that he could take that would at least slow the process down.

A knock on his office door interrupted his thoughts.

"Come in."

Glen stepped in. "You have a few minutes?"

"Yeah." Jeremy returned to his desk and motioned Glen to sit. "What's up?"

"We need to talk about next steps. You gave me the go-ahead to start a new Subject from Ivan's tissues, and I did so."

"OK." Jeremy had to admit that this news gave him a feeling of relief. It also made him feel like a parasite.

Glen leaned forward in his chair with a rather enthusiastic expression on his face. "We anticipate it will be several years before it's ready to harvest from. We need to look at what drug regimen will have the least side effects for you, yet still retard Crohn's effects on the new intestines. That might be easier than before since you now have new, undamaged intestines. Personally, I suspect there may be something of a vicious cycle involved with Crohn's—once it gets some headway in damaging the tissue, there is more inflammation and it can attack more viciously. This is just a hunch, of course, since no one's ever observed a situation where it gets to start over in the same patient on an entirely new intestinal tract."

"I'd prefer to be off the drugs entirely, but what you say makes sense."

"We also need to look into whether we can get to harvestability any sooner than the first time. Could we, for example, increase some of the growth hormones and nutrients in the second Subject's diet to get there sooner? Worth a shot."

"Is there any risk inherent in speeding it up, though? Could it lead to anomalies?"

Glen paused. "That is something to consider, of course. We should probably only incrementally increase the nutrients and growth hormones over what we used with the first Subject. You know, I wish we could find a way to regenerate the digestive tract right within the original Subject. I just haven't figured out yet how to avoid some of the same pitfalls we encountered in trying to develop digestive tracts *in vitro*. The walls would adhere and seal the lumen shut, and we weren't able to generate the complex supporting structure that naturally develops *in utero*." He stood. "Well, that's all I have for now. I'll let you get back to what you were doing." He strode from the room and shut the door behind him.

Jeremy realized his new life came with a price. The Subject wasn't the only guinea pig at SomaGene.

CHAPTER 53

He lay on his thin mattress and gazed at the ever-present tube that led from just below his collarbone to the bottle suspended high above him. He rarely felt like moving around in his enclosure any more. Instead, he spent most of his day just staring at the bottle, watching as a bubble occasionally formed and the level of the liquid within slowly lowered throughout the day.

It was always sore where the tube connected to his body. Always. He didn't want to look at it, didn't want to touch it for fear of making it hurt worse. It made him want to draw into himself to escape it, but there was no escape.

The White Coats never brought him anything to eat any more. He heard the animals in the room next to him shout and screech every day still, and his stomach made noises and hurt. But no one brought him food. He didn't understand it. Even though the food had tasted bad since the last time the White Coats had taken him into that special room, he missed eating.

His body didn't even feel right ever since that day the White Coats came in and pinned him down. He couldn't remember what happened after they came in. His next memory was waking up and having pain in his stomach again. So much pain. He'd very tentatively reached his hand down and touched his stomach. Again, it had some large pad taped to it for some days.

Then one day the White Coats took the pad off and left it off. When they left him alone again, he reached down and touched the area. He felt a long, painful ridge that went halfway up him. And he felt something else. When he lay on his back, his stomach sunk right into him. And it hurt. Not just on the skin where the line was, but all through him inside hurt if he shifted position.

And that's why he hardly moved these days.

He tried to think, to find a connection. The only thing he could think of was when both White Coats came in, something always happened. And when that something happened, he would forget what it was, but would remember having pain afterwards. The first time was bad, but this time was so much worse.

What if they came in together again? Would it happen again? How much worse could he hurt? He couldn't quite fathom it.

He watched as another bubble made its way to the surface of the fluid, and the level in the bottle went down just a little bit more.

He turned quickly when he heard the door open. It was one person, Not White Coat. The one who always acted strangely when he came in, but at least he had never hurt him. He watched him approach his enclosure. He didn't feel sufficiently threatened to bother moving.

Jeremy's stomach clenched when he took his first look at the Subject since the procedure. He lay draped on his pathetic little shelf of a bed. He looked listless, pale, and...hollow. Even beneath his hospital gown, the concavity of his abdomen was apparent. Jeremy wondered what sort of sensation the Subject experienced, if he realized that his abdomen was devoid of any intestines.

A permanent IV drip had been installed into his subclavian artery. The bottle held an off-white fluid that provided total parenteral nutrition. The Subject could never be allowed to have solid food ever again. It would simply hit a dead end just below the stomach and turn into an indigestible bolus that would have to be removed one way or the other.

Jeremy stood rooted in place, staring. What kind of life did the Subject have? He couldn't imagine never being able to eat again; of course, he was able to eat whatever he wanted now. Food represented both sustenance and pleasure for him. The Subject had been fed lab rations all his life, had never experienced anything more than utilitarian meals meant to deliver nutrition, not enjoyment. But still, to never be able to eat, and to be hooked up to that IV for the rest of his life. It had to be its own sort of unique prison for him.

The door behind him opened. "Oh, I didn't realize you were in here." Tim entered, carrying another bottle of the fluid.

"Oh, um, yeah. I—"

"It's your first time in here since the procedure, isn't it?" Tim's eyes took on a weary, yet sympathetic, look.

"Yeah. I felt I should see how he's...doing."

Tim gazed at the Subject as he answered. "Well, he's doing as well as can be expected, I suppose. He appears to be absorbing the nutrients from the fluid reasonably well. We've managed to keep the needle site from getting infected, and we've been lucky he doesn't seem interested in pulling at it. In fact, he doesn't even touch it. It must hurt." He sighed. "Maybe that's just as well. I can't imagine what we'd do if he did actively interfere with it. Like it or not, it's his lifeline now."

Jeremy's mouth turned dry as cotton as he forced out the question that plagued him. "What do you think he's feeling? What must it be like for him, beyond not being able to eat solid food? What does it feel like to be missing his entire digestive tract?"

Tim glanced at the level in the current IV bottle, then quietly entered the enclosure and swapped it out for the new bottle before answering. He closed the enclosure door behind him and stared down at the nearly empty bottle in his hands as he answered. "I honestly don't know, Jeremy."

He turned the bottle over and over in his hands, appearing focused on the remnants of whitish fluid that sloshed within. "You know, he arrested during the procedure. I had just removed his intestines and set them aside for Glen. I was ligating blood vessels, and he started to go tachy, then he seized. I got the paddles and zapped him back. All the while, Glen was yelling at me to not bother, to keep focused on you and the rest of the procedure." He stopped, glanced at the Subject once more, then said, "Now I wish I'd done as Glen said. Excuse me." And he exited the room without another word.

CHAPTER 54

"Jeremy—what's the matter?" Amanda dropped her purse on the counter and hurried to the kitchen table where he sat.

Jeremy looked at her through eyes that stubbornly refused to focus. He didn't generally drink the hard stuff, but it seemed like a good day for it. He raised his half-full glass of whiskey in greeting. "I paid a little visit to my…benefactor today."

"What?" Amanda frowned in confusion.

"The Subject. First time I've seen him since he so generously gave up his entire intestinal tract so that I can have a good life." Jeremy took another sip.

Amanda stared down at her hands. "Oh. I thought you'd made some sort of peace with yourself on that."

"Yep, out of sight, out of mind was working pretty well for me. Then I made the mistake of actually looking." Jeremy put down his glass and pressed his face into his hands. "Oh, my God, Amanda."

"I thought they said they would come up with some alternate feeding method—"

Jeremy slammed his palms onto the table and glared at her. "They sure did." He waved his hand as if the Subject were in the room just off to his right. "Yeah, it's great. He's hooked up to IV nutrition for every minute of the rest of his goddamned life. There it is, nice bottle of white crap flowing into his veins all day every day." He pointed to a spot just under his collarbone. "Needle goes in here. And that's where it's going to stay. Forever." He paused, stared off into the distance and continued in a lower tone. "No solid food again. Ever. Unimaginable."

Amanda reached out and put her hand on his arm. "Probably

wasn't the best idea to go see him."

He glared at her again. "Well, too late now. The image is burned in my brain forever." He sat back in his chair, crossed his legs. "Tim doesn't feel too good about now either. Apparently, the Subject arrested during the surgery and would have died a peaceful death but for Tim's heroic acts with the defibrillator. He sure seems to have second thoughts about it now himself. We can only guess at the pain and discomfort the Subject's enduring." He shook his head. "My God."

"I'm sure they're making him as comfortable as possible. Jeremy, you had no choice. You know how bad you were getting. Something had to be done."

"No, they're *not* making him as comfortable as possible. There's an advantage to the needle site remaining sore—to keep him from trying to tamper with it. Isn't that great?"

Amanda opened her mouth, then shut it and stared down at the table. Tears began to stream down her face. She wiped them away, put her face in her hands, and began to sob.

Jeremy felt filled with poison, and wanted to try to drain himself of it in any way possible. "And I already gave Glen permission to go ahead and generate another Subject—because some day Crohn's will degrade *this* set of intestines and I'll be ready for a retread. I can inflict this pain on another Subject so that I can live." He took another gulp of whiskey. "Wonder how many times this little cycle will play out, how many Subjects I will leave in this condition and how long they'll live."

Amanda looked up, her face red and puffy. "You can't think of it that way, you just can't."

"What other way would you suggest?"

CHAPTER 55

Tim had closed his office door and set his phone to go straight to voicemail. Now he sat at his desk, his eyes fixed on his med school diploma on the far wall. He'd been staring at it for the last twenty minutes as he sat absolutely motionless.

He thought back to why he'd wanted to become a doctor in the first place. Unlike some of his classmates, who seemed driven by the prestige and money at the end of the rainbow, he'd gone to med school simply because he really liked the idea of learning the necessary skills to heal.

He remembered the day he completed his very first operation. He was so pumped that he was unable to sleep that entire night. He sat in his apartment alone, amazed at what he had done and grateful he had the knowledge and manual dexterity to do it well.

He'd gone into research because he wanted to be on the front line of developing new ways to improve people's health and lives. And for a number of years, that is precisely what he had done at SomaGene. He had been there in the early days with Glen and Ivan, developing the various protocols needed to cultivate and harvest the organs successfully, and refining the surgical procedures and physical environment to nearly guarantee a successful outcome. Of that he was proud, and always would be.

But now, thanks to Ivan's desperate desire to find a way to save Jeremy—as well as Glen's and his own hubris—he'd succeeded in reclaiming Jeremy's health at the terrible price paid by the Subject.

Ashamed, he turned away from his diploma, then stood and walked to the window. Several inches of fresh snow carpeted the ground and stuck to the branches of the pine trees on the wooded SomaGene campus. He usually liked the look of fresh snow. Today it just looked as cold and bleak as he felt in his heart.

He reflected on his encounter with Jeremy in the Subject's room several weeks ago. Even Jeremy, beneficiary of the procedure, could see it was wrong. Tim wondered how he lived with that knowledge—that his nearly normal health was completely due to an involuntary sacrifice on the part of the Subject. And the Subject—how much pain must he be in every single day of his life? What does he know or understand about what happened? Does he have a concept of time? Even if he did, he probably did not understand that his condition will never, ever improve.

Tim held his hands before his eyes and stared at them. Healing hands. And he'd participated in the procedure. He had removed vital organs from a living human being, sentencing him to a life of pain and continual dependence on his nutrition flowing through his veins and being processed by his kidneys.

He felt a stone settling in the pit of his stomach as he realized he truly meant what he said to Jeremy—that he shouldn't have intervened when the Subject arrested. He who only wanted to heal patients had admitted to another—and now to himself—that he would have preferred to let the Subject die.

If the Subject could truly comprehend his situation, what would he want for himself? Tim returned to his desk and pressed his face into his hands. He chided himself for thinking he could play God. But then…he already *had,* hadn't he? He'd played God, and he'd cooperated in putting a human being into a severely degraded physical condition.

Tim rested his hand on the knob of the door to the Subject's room. It had become harder and harder for him to go inside to perform the needed maintenance and deliver a fresh bottle of IV nutrition. Every time, the Subject's face seemed more hollow and more devoid of life and energy. Tim had started to see it in his dreams at night—that is, when he was even able to sleep.

He took a deep breath and entered. The Subject lay on that

thin mattress, just as always. Today he seemed to be just staring aimlessly at the ceiling. He didn't seem to even notice Tim's entrance. Maybe he just didn't care anymore.

Tim approached the enclosure for a closer look. The Subject languidly turned toward him and regarded him with glassy eyes.

The White Coat had returned, the only one that came any more. He couldn't remember seeing the other White Coat since that time they pushed him down and he went to sleep, only to wake up in pain. He didn't like the other one very much. In fact, he didn't like either one of them after what they did to him to make him hurt, but this one seemed a little different from the other one. He still came by, and he hadn't hurt him any more since then. That was something anyway.

The White Coat was looking at him strangely. He didn't know what to think of that. Just looking at him strangely and standing there.

He looked up at the bottle that hung above him. It was nearly full. Usually the White Coat didn't come until the bottle was nearly empty. Something strange was going on.

The White Coat started to open the door to the enclosure. The Subject shrank back toward the wall. He feared he had come to take him to the strange room again. The room that always brought more pain.

Tim felt a pang of guilt as the Subject drew back against the wall when he entered the enclosure. There was a time when the Subject did not fear him. Of course, that was when he brought the Subject food that was halfway palatable, and had never hurt him in any way. Now he had taken him through two painful surgical procedures and put him in the piteous state he was in now. The Subject had every right to be afraid.

"It's all right. I won't hurt you anymore." Tim felt odd speaking to the Subject. No one had ever really tried to converse with him or bothered to teach him rudimentary English. He wondered if the Subject had picked anything up just from overhearing him talking with Glen on prior visits. He hoped he could at least sense that he wanted to help him.

He stepped all the way inside the enclosure and shut the door behind him. He crouched down, doing everything possible to avoid being threatening or intimidating. "It's all right." He carefully reached for one of the Subject's hands and gently stroked it to try to soothe him.

The Subject at first recoiled and pressed himself even more tightly against the wall. Then he looked at Tim very intently and relaxed a little. He allowed Tim to take his hand, and he continued to stare back at him as Tim tried to soothe him.

"I'm so sorry. I should never have done what I did. I am so sorry." Tears slid down Tim's face as he continued to hold the Subject's hand.

He reached out and gently touched the tear. Many nights, as he lay alone in pain in the dark, such things had come from his eyes and run down his face. He wiped them away as he wiped them away from the White Coat's face now.

Maybe the White Coat *can* understand.

He gazed along the length of the tube leading from him to the bottle above him. He thought of all the pain, of how it hurt to move anymore. One tear, then another, then a stream of them, began to flow down his face. He turned to the White Coat, hoping he could make him understand.

Tim observed the Subject's movements and tears, and then it hit him like a blow to the gut. The Subject was trying to communicate with him. Tim had imagined the Subject must be miserable, but now he knew it. The Subject's facial expression, the way he looked at the IV setup, then at Tim, with tears in his eyes. That was his way of communicating just how miserable he was.

Tim reached out and gently wiped the Subject's tears away with one hand. It was time for the pain to stop.

He released the Subject's hand and stood. He reached into the pocket of his lab coat with a trembling hand and took out the syringe he had prepared. He maintained eye contact with the Subject and muttered soothing words as best he could as he grasped the tubing in his left hand. He popped the cap off the needle and inserted it into a port in the tubing, then hesitated.

The Subject continued to gaze up at him with wide, trusting eyes brimming with unshed tears. He looked relaxed now, not fearful.

His heart pounding, Tim took a deep breath, then slowly pressed the plunger until the syringe emptied its contents. He broke his gaze from the Subject for a moment as he glanced at the tubing. He could see the clear fluid he just injected form a segment in contrast to the white fluid from the IV bottle. The clear fluid began to make its way down the tubing toward the Subject. When it was mere inches from where the needle entered the Subject's subclavian artery, Tim set the syringe aside, sat next to the Subject on the bed, and took his hand in his.

He looked into the Subject's eyes and waited.

The White Coat had done something with the tube, but he didn't understand what. Now he sat beside him, very close. No one had ever sat that close to him without causing him pain.

But there was no new pain. And the old pain was fading a little. That felt good. It faded more. That felt better. Soon the pain was gone entirely for the first time in so long. He looked up at the White Coat. His vision started to get fuzzy, and he started to feel like he was floating. It felt good to feel painless and weightless. He started to get tired and sleepy. He yawned, then relaxed. He closed his eyes and smiled.

Tim waited several minutes, then checked the Subject's pulse. It was over.

He gently set the Subject's hand down at his side, then stood and stopped the flow of the IV. He turned and very gently pulled down the Subject's hospital gown to reveal the site where the needle fed into the artery. Gently, so gently, he removed the tape holding it in place, and, as carefully as with the most sensitive patient, he slid the needle out and set the IV assembly aside. He pulled the hospital gown back up over the wound.

Then he sat on the bed next to the Subject, put his face in his hands, and cried as he had the very first time he lost a patient.

CHAPTER 56

"You can see from the graph that the wait time for procedures started to trend up in the last six months or so. We already have the capacity to increase the number of organs being cultivated simultaneously, but I think we need to add two or three more surgeons to keep up with the associated implantations." Glen held in his lap several printed graphs he wanted to discuss. He flipped to the next one as he waited.

Jeremy traced a finger on his monitor as he reviewed the graph Glen had just discussed. "I see what you mean—" His face suddenly twisted into a grimace as he paled alarmingly. He screamed in pain, clutched his abdomen and nearly fell from his chair.

Glen jumped up and went over to him. "What's the matter?"

"Pain…like a knife…worst ever…" Jeremy gasped. Drops of sweat formed on his pallid forehead.

Glen reached for Jeremy's wrist. His pulse was thready and racing. "Let's get you to the treatment room." He crouched to get Jeremy's arm over his shoulder and half-dragged him out of his office as he continued to moan.

Once inside the room, he helped Jeremy up onto the exam table and loosened his upper shirt buttons. Then he opened the cabinet and grabbed a syringe and a vial of a fast-acting sedative and painkiller. He hurriedly drew a dose into the syringe and injected it into Jeremy's arm. "There, that should ease the pain pretty quickly. Are you OK to just stay put a minute while I go get Tim?"

Jeremy drew himself up into a fetal position. "Yeah, I think so," he said through clenched teeth.

Glen hit the call button and paged Tim, then took off down

the hall to see if he could find him any faster. As bad as Jeremy had been hit with attacks of his Crohn's, he had never seen him have such a sudden and excruciating onset. They needed to stabilize him and run tests—and fast.

As he sprinted down the hall, he saw the door to the Subject's room open slowly. Tim emerged, looking every bit as pale as Jeremy.

"What are you doing in there? Didn't you hear the page?"

Tim regarded him with red-rimmed eyes. "What? No, I didn't hear it."

"What the fuck is wrong with you?" Glen pushed Tim aside and took a quick look inside the Subject's enclosure. "What the hell is going on in here?" He strode inside and saw the Subject had been disconnected from the IV and was lying beneath a blanket. He turned to Tim. "What happened?"

Tim started to open his mouth, but nothing came out.

Glen grabbed his arm and began to steer him toward the treatment room. "No time right now, Jeremy's in crisis."

They arrived moments later to find Jeremy still lying in the fetal position. He appeared to be in slightly less pain than when Glen had left him.

"All right, Jeremy, so what happened?" Glen reached for the blood pressure cuff and stethoscope.

"I don't know. I was fine one minute, then this incredibly sharp, burning pain went through my abdomen. Just all through it. The drug is helping some, but it's still pretty bad." He wiped sweat from his forehead with a shaking arm.

"Hook up the monitors." He gave Tim a little shove to get him moving. "I'll start an IV drip." He deftly took Jeremy's blood pressure and shook his head. "Low. I don't like it." He removed the cuff and tried to start the IV. It took him multiple attempts to get a vein that would cooperate.

Several minutes later, Jeremy lay amid a nest of wires and tubes. Glen studied the monitor screens. "Rhythm good, but a bit fast, probably from the pain. I'll give you a little more of the med." He quickly administered a second dose through the IV port. Then he slipped an electronic thermometer beneath Jeremy's tongue. "One hundred two. Tim, draw blood for a CBC. May have some fast-moving infection." He turned to Jeremy. "OK, I'm going to have to palpate your abdomen. Please try to relax as best you can." He helped Jeremy uncurl from the fetal position. He began to palpate, then stopped. "He's absolutely rigid—but it feels like it's *inside*, not in the muscle wall. I've never felt anything like it."

"What's happening to me?" Jeremy asked in a small, tight voice.

"I'm not sure. I want to get a look at the labs first. Try to relax." Glen turned to Tim. "Make sure he's stable, then come to my office when you have the labs. We need to talk."

CHAPTER 57

Glen looked up from his computer monitor as Tim entered his office. "What do the labs say?"

"They point to inflammation—and something else."

"What?"

"Tissue death. On a pretty large scale." Tim rubbed his eyes. "I'm worried about the transplant. I think something may have gone wrong."

Glen sat back in his chair and shook his head. "I don't get it. If there had been a problem with the surgery or the resection of the blood supply, it should have presented long before now. Hell, he was fully healed from the procedure and had been doing perfectly well."

Tim sat silent, head bowed, shoulders slumped. He did not make eye contact with Glen. His hands twisted and fidgeted in his lap as if of their own volition.

Glen let out a frustrated sigh. "I hate to do it, but I don't think we have a choice. Let's get him stable and prepped for an exploratory. I'd like to begin with a laparoscopic exam to keep it minimally invasive. If something needs intervention, then we open him up."

"Sure. I'll monitor him for a bit longer. He was stabilizing reasonably well, but was still in a lot of pain despite the meds." Tim started to get up to leave.

"Wait a minute. We have something else to talk about, don't we?"

Tim became even paler as he sat back down.

"What happened to the Subject?"

"He's dead."

"I got that. What happened?"

Tim stared at his hands in his lap.

"What *happened*?"

Tim raised his head, looked Glen in the eye. "That was no way to live. He was in constant pain and misery."

"Well, for someone who was so damned adamant about bringing him out of arrest during the procedure, that's quite a turnaround."

Tim bowed his head again. "I finally grasped just how miserable an existence I sentenced him to by saving his life that day, and I couldn't live with that anymore."

"Frankly, he had no further use for us anyway—unless we were going to try to develop a new intestinal tract within his abdominal cavity. Guess that's out now, but it would have been interesting to try." Glen scratched his head as he pondered the implications. "The main problem this raises is that of disposal. Since he never existed in the normal sense, there would be a lot of uncomfortable questions if we disposed of the body as we would a deceased patient."

"I hadn't thought that far ahead. I just couldn't watch him suffer like that another day."

"Well, now we have to deal with the problem, don't we? I suppose we could store it in the freezer for the time being, maybe disposing of it in parts in medical waste over time." Glen slapped a hand onto his desk. "I'd hoped to avoid having to face this issue for some time. Let's just put it in the freezer for now, so we can focus on Jeremy. We'll think more about disposal later."

"What's the matter with me?" Jeremy glanced anxiously at Glen and Tim.

"We're not entirely sure. Signs point to some sort of infection and inflammation. There appears to be tissue damage as well, but it's not clear why or how that would happen at this point." Glen glanced at the monitors. "Tim, what do you think?"

"Probably as good as we're going to get."

"What are you talking about?" Jeremy tried to sit up, grimaced, and lay back down.

"We need to see what's going on in there. I'm planning to use the laparoscope. It's tiny, and we can get a little camera in there. From there, it all depends what we see. It's possible we may have to do something more extensive. I just don't know. Whatever we do, we need to move quickly."

Jeremy looked away. "Oh, God. Can someone let Amanda know?"

"No time right now. We'll let her know afterwards. Tim, prep him."

Glen maneuvered the slim metal tubes and tiny camera inside Jeremy's abdominal cavity. "Still stable, Tim?"

"Heart rate is a bit higher than I'd like, but so far, so good."

"That's not a surprise, given the labs. All right, just about in position here." Glen nearly felt sick when the camera and light revealed the problem. "Oh, dear Christ."

"What is it?"

Stunned, Glen quickly ran the camera over the rest of the abdominal contents to verify what he'd seen, then switched on the external video monitor so Tim could see for himself. "The entire intestinal tract. Look at it—it's darkening. Looks like total tissue death. Gangrene can't be far behind. We're going to have to go in and remove it all." He slid out the laparoscopic tubes and set them aside. He drew his gown-clad forearm across his forehead. "My God. Adjust the anesthetic while I get ready."

"You're going to remove it all?"

"No choice. If it stays in it'll kill him. I suppose it was useful to have the Subject around as long as we did. Jeremy's going to have to go on the same total parenteral nutrition IV regimen until the second Subject is ready to harvest." Glen paused as he arranged his instruments. "We're going to need to use that time to figure out what went wrong here, and how to avoid it next time. It was so strange. I was in Jeremy's office. He was fine, then this came on so suddenly. Like someone flipped a switch."

CHAPTER 58

Jeremy awoke in a pain-laced haze. His mouth felt like he'd been eating sand; his entire abdomen felt as if it were on fire. He struggled to open his eyes; his eyelids felt weighed down. He tried to focus, to figure out where he was and why.

Amanda gazed down at him with a frown of obvious concern. "Hey, hello there." She did not smile.

He tried to form words, but his mouth couldn't properly coordinate. "What—?" Uttering the single word tore at his dry throat.

She made shushing sounds. "Don't try to talk right now. You came out of surgery just a little while ago."

He tried again to speak, but this time his throat just clicked painfully. He wanted to weep, but knew the pain would be even more unbearable.

"All right, I'll tell you, but you're still pretty drugged up right now. They said you started having severe pain, they ran tests and decided they'd better do an exploratory." She fought off tears.

He tried to form a questioning look to prod her for more information.

She swallowed hard, hesitated, then said in a small, frightened voice, "And they found that the intestinal tissue had all died, and they were worried about infection."

Jeremy feared what she would say next; feared that he knew what was coming.

"Jeremy, they had to remove it. They said they had no choice, that it was already too far advanced." The tears won out and began to stream down her cheeks.

The news knifed through the drug haze as the implications made themselves known. He'd seen the Subject firsthand, and so knew what it would mean to be completely dependent on an IV bottle for all his nutrition. He wanted to scream, but only a small croak escaped his lips.

Amanda paled, then turned and pressed a button. Moments later, Glen, looking drained and worn, entered the room.

"What's going on?"

Amanda told him what she had revealed to Jeremy.

"I see. Jeremy, I know you're upset. We had no choice, none at all. We'll do everything possible for your comfort, but you will need to be on parenteral nutrition for the time being. No solid food. But it's temporary. I had already initiated cultivation on a new Subject after we spoke a few weeks back. I'll work with Tim on seeing if we can speed the process up in light of this development. You just need to hang on and be patient for a while. You tolerated the surgery well, and we were lucky we realized what was going on as quickly as we did."

Jeremy moved his cracked lips. "Pain," he whispered.

"Sure. I'll increase the meds a bit." Glen injected the contents of a syringe into the IV port. "There, you should feel a little better in a few moments. Might even drift off again for a while. Just relax and let it happen."

Gradually, Jeremy felt enveloped in a soft warm cloud. The pain felt more distant. He closed his eyes and let himself float off and forget for a while what he would have to face.

CHAPTER 59

Glen adjusted the oxygen infusion level of the nutrient solution for the beginnings of Subject Two. Cell division and overall development were proceeding as anticipated, but with Jeremy in his current state, it just wasn't fast enough. Nothing could be fast enough. He wondered how much more growth hormone he dared add to the solution.

A beep sounded, and the door to the sequestered lab opened. Tim stepped in and closed the door behind him.

"Glad you're here. I want to talk to you about the growth hormone concentration in the solution we're using."

Tim shifted his feet uneasily. "I didn't come to discuss that."

Glen didn't like his tone at all. "So what did you come to discuss?"

"My resignation."

"You've got to be kidding. How can you resign? Jeremy's living off IVs while we're trying to get this ready in time for him." He motioned toward the glass container that held the new, developing Subject.

Tim looked Glen in the eye. "We've gone too far. Way too far. I didn't think the project was right when Ivan first proposed it. But I didn't think it would ever come to fruition, so I didn't object at the time. Then I let myself become involved, and I let you sink me in deeper as we went. I'll never forgive myself for that, and I'll be damned if I'll let myself get involved in another round of this madness."

"But what about Jeremy? He's going to need surgery again when the organs are ready for him."

"I feel terrible for him. I really do. But I don't know how

he lives with himself. He saw the Subject afterward. He saw the price he paid so *he* could live a normal life. Yes, I assisted the first time, and there hasn't been a day that goes by that I haven't regretted it—even though it gave Jeremy a normal life until now. It was wrong. The entire project should never have been undertaken." Tim stared at the second Subject with a pained expression.

Glen swept his arms wide, palms up, in a gesture of appeal. "How am I supposed to do this myself when the organs are ready? You know it's already tight and terribly risky with just the two of us in a procedure this complex."

Tim tore his gaze away from the new Subject and glared at Glen. "You're not hearing me. That's no longer my problem. I became a doctor to help people. Sometimes saving someone's life feels a bit like playing God. But deliberately harming another human being to help another? That's too far, and I won't be a part of it any more. That's it." He turned toward the door to leave.

Glen trembled as the numerous implications of Tim's decision hit him. "Who are you going to tell?"

Tim paused with his hand on the doorknob and looked back over his shoulder. "Don't worry. I have no intention of going public with this. I have too much to lose to risk that. I *am* going to tell Jeremy, though. He deserves to hear it from me firsthand." He turned and left the room.

Glen sat down heavily on a lab stool. His legs felt weak and his hands shook. At least Tim wasn't going to publicize the project. But how was he going to handle the prep and eventual surgery by himself? He could think of no other staff member he dared to let in on the secret.

He'd find a way to work it out. He just had to.

Tim poked his head into Jeremy's office. "Can I have a word with you?"

"Sure. What is it?"

Jeremy sat at his desk, his face pale and drawn. He'd taken to wearing button-down shirts on a daily basis, so the tubing from the needle site in his subclavian artery could be threaded out the nearest gap between buttons. His constant companion, the IV rack, stood at his side behind the desk.

Tim's heart sank at the sight, not only because of his role in the project, but for what he was about to say and what it likely meant to Jeremy's eventual fate.

"I'm not quite sure how to start." Tim shifted in his seat. "Guess I should just get it out. I've come to resign."

Though it would have seemed impossible, Jeremy became even paler. "What? Why?"

"I probably gave you a hint that day some months ago when we ran into each other in the Subject's room. I've never felt comfortable about this project. But after the second procedure, it was just too much." He paused and gazed off into the distance. "Every day when I saw him, what he'd become, it hammered it home to me. He didn't understand what had happened to him, and he surely had not consented to that—and wouldn't have, had he been given the opportunity and ability to speak for himself."

"Well, I'm living the same way now, and *I'm* managing." Jeremy's face reddened. "How bad can it be for him—especially if he doesn't understand the implications of his condition?"

Tim took a deep breath to steady himself for what he had to say and how Jeremy might react. "Not an issue any more."

"What are you saying?"

Tim glanced at Jeremy again, this time seeing him in a new light. Seeing him as someone who, aside from this unanticipated setback, had done nothing but reap the benefits of the project without really having to deal with the downsides, as Tim had.

Suddenly he wanted to rub some of the dirt in his face, even though at the same time he saw how he was suffering so much despite all their efforts—or perhaps because of those efforts. "He's dead. He's no longer suffering. I eased his pain with an overdose of sedative. Best I could tell, I think he would have wanted it that way. He just couldn't express himself verbally."

"You did *what*?"

"Don't act so above it, Jeremy. You're here today because of what he gave up—involuntarily, I might add. I don't see why you should be concerned. He'd already given you all he could. He didn't have another set of intestines, so he was useless to you and Glen at this point."

"But you…deliberately…?"

"I put the drug in his IV tube. True enough. And I'll have to live with that. But surely you realize his death warrant was signed as soon as we all decided to remove his intestines and give them to you. He had no life left, not really. At least you have the second Subject in the works to bail you out." He waved his hand in the general direction of the IV rack. "He would never have had that chance."

"Tim, don't think this has been easy for *me*. All you see is the medical side, and the various procedures that you've conducted. You don't know how I feel about this, what guilt I've had about it. Do you think I'm not human? I saw the Subject for myself that day. And now I get to experience firsthand what he was going through—poetic justice there, I suppose. Do you think I really have a choice in this?" He looked imploringly at Tim.

Tim considered Jeremy's words for a moment before answering. "It's hard to say. You could have refused the procedure. I don't honestly know what I would have done in your place. Maybe it's too easy for me to say you could have just said no. At any rate, there is the matter of disposal of the body. He's in the freezer now."

"My God." Jeremy stared down at his desk. "Who else knows?" he asked softly.

"I told Glen. That's it. I'm not going to make this public. I just can't be a part of it any more. I wanted to tell you myself, so you could understand my reasons." He stood, then turned to leave. "Goodbye, Jeremy."

After Tim left and shut the door behind him, Jeremy rested his head on his desk and tried to grasp the implications of his resignation. He felt utterly hollow inside, drained and hopeless.

He constantly felt weak and subpar since the most recent surgery and his resulting dependence on the IV for nutrition. He relied on Glen and Tim to keep SomaGene running while he showed up each day—or tried to—and barely got anything done. Now with Tim gone, Glen would have to pick up the slack on that front—and he would have to perform the eventual surgery unassisted. Jeremy didn't like that idea at all, but he was running out of choices.

If he didn't want Glen performing the surgery solo, then he was going to have to drag some other staff physician into it. He couldn't think of anyone he dared trust with knowledge of something like this.

And Amanda. She was already doing the best she could to help him. He knew he was a handful to deal with, his mood alternating between helpless self-pity and angry frustration at his condition. Stuck in the small circle of those who knew of this project, she had no one she could confide in or share her burden with.

It was all such a disaster, and now it felt like a noose tightening on his neck, rather than the way back to a happy and healthy life.

Maybe Tim was right. Maybe he should have refused to participate in such a scheme from the get-go and taken his chances with his Crohn's. He wouldn't have had Amanda back—but he wouldn't be putting her through all this, either.

He glanced up at the IV bottle. Was the price worth those extra months of disease-free living that he'd enjoyed? It had been laid in front of him, and, despite high talk to the contrary, he'd set aside his moral concerns and gone for it. He could have turned it down if he had really wanted to, but he wanted his life to be healthy and normal. He wanted a chance back with Amanda. He'd managed to rationalize and compartmentalize what it had cost the Subject, who had no say at all in the matter.

He put his head back down on his desk. He was too exhausted to think about it anymore.

CHAPTER 60

Tim pulled into his driveway and switched off the ignition. He wasn't quite ready to deal with Katie, and he didn't want the sound of the garage door opener to alert her to his arrival just yet. He sat for a moment, preparing himself for what he had to do, what he had to face. It was early afternoon; he rarely came home this time of day. Katie would be surprised to see him. She'd be even more surprised when she heard what he had to say to her.

He glanced at the massive maple tree that dominated his front yard. Scarlet already tinged the edges of some of the leaves. Minnesota autumns were intensely beautiful, and cruelly brief. They left no doubt that an end had arrived. He faced an end of sorts himself, and wondered what would come of it.

He took a deep breath and let it out slowly to try to calm himself. It didn't help much; his stomach still felt jittery and tense. Then he got out of the car and quietly entered his house, feeling a bit like an intruder sneaking in like that.

At this time of day, Katie was probably in the playroom with Johnnie. He headed for that room and stood outside the doorway, silently watching them playing together on the floor for a few moments before announcing his presence. He wanted to capture and savor that peaceful memory before he revealed the information that would forever change their lives.

He cleared his throat. "Hi, Katie."

She glanced up quickly, startled, and pressed one hand to her chest while she held Johnnie with the other. "I didn't hear you! How long have you been standing there?"

"Not very long."

A frown creased her forehead. "What's the matter? What are you doing here this time of day anyway?"

"I have something I need to tell you. Can you put Johnnie down for his nap now?"

"I'm not sure he'd go down quite yet. I'll just put him in the playpen. He'll be OK there." Scowling, Katie picked up the squirming baby and laid him down gently in his playpen. She gave him his little teddy bear and tucked a blanket around him as she made soothing noises to try to get him in the mood to perhaps nap, or at least not get agitated.

She stood and tucked a stray lock of hair back behind her ear. "What is it?"

"Let's go sit down." Tim led her to the living room, where they seated themselves on the couch. One glance at her worried face told him this would be even harder than he had imagined.

"What's the matter, Tim? You're scaring me." Katie's tense shoulders rose to nearly touch her jaw. She folded her arms so that she held an elbow in each hand.

Tim couldn't muster the momentum to start while he was looking at her. He leaned over, elbows on knees, chin in hands, and stared at the coffee table as he began. "Remember I told you about the special, secret project I was working on with Glen, and how we were at odds on it?"

"Yeah." The word came out in a tiny whisper.

"Well, it all has to do with that. I'm going to tell you some things that you absolutely must keep to yourself. You'll see why soon enough. I need you to promise that first. Do you?" He looked her in the eye.

"I don't even know what you're going to say, how can I—?"

"I need you to promise."

"All right." Katie's lips pressed tightly together.

"Thank you." He took a deep breath, then began, knowing there would be no turning back. "This project involved human cloning."

"What? Clones?" Katie's eye widened.

"Please. Let me get through this. It's more difficult for me than you can possibly know yet."

"All right."

Tim chose his words carefully to avoid violating doctor-patient confidentiality as best he could, given that Jeremy had been his patient. "Ivan wanted to develop a transplant protocol for the treatment of Crohn's disease. We developed a full-grown human from a tissue sample. There was a targeted recipient. We initially transplanted a small portion of intestine. That worked well for a while, and the implications for the clone were not too terrible. He needed additional nutrition, but that was about it. After a while, the Crohn's did enough further damage to the recipient that he needed another transplant. This time, we took the entire remaining large and small intestine from the clone." He bowed his head. "I'd always thought the project was going too far, but that took it over the line for me."

"What happened?"

"The clone made it through the surgery—barely. I had to bring him out of cardiac arrest. But without an intestinal tract, he could never eat again. He had to be kept alive with IV nutrition. Forever."

"Is that possible?"

Tim sighed. "Yes, it is, technically. There are IV formulas for that purpose, anyway. But typical patients who receive that sort of nutritional support do so temporarily or are elderly or in end-stage disease and have no other choice. In this case, the clone was the equivalent of a young adult."

"Was? Did he die?"

Tim looked at Katie and took both her hands in his. "He is dead. I hope you understand why I did what I did."

"What are you saying?" Katie's hands began to tremble.

"He was suffering so much. He never learned to speak, but he communicated to me in nonverbal ways. I'm sure of what he was trying to tell me. I gave him an overdose of sedative. He went peacefully." Tim stared into the distance.

Katie began to tremble all over. "Oh my God."

"I never dreamed I would become involved in something like this. I never should have agreed to participate from the start, but I did, and I got sucked in deeper and deeper. But that was too much. I couldn't go in there and look in his eyes again and see that suffering day in and day out. Lab animals get better treatment."

Tim spat out the last words, then sat silent, waiting for Katie's reaction.

"You actually *killed* him?" Katie began to gnaw on a fingernail, something she hadn't done since she was a teenager.

The truth of her words struck Tim like a physical blow. Even if he could finesse the overdose as a mercy killing, he knew in his heart that his participation in the full transplant was the first step in killing the Subject. "Yes." He let the word slide out in a whisper.

"Wha…what do we do now?" Katie appeared on the edge of hysteria.

Tim girded himself to deliver the rest of his message, come what may. "I resigned today. I promised I would not go public with any of this, so they have nothing to fear from me. Of course, if I were to blow the whistle on them, I would blow it equally on myself." Tim again looked her in the eye. "And that is why I needed your promise to keep this to yourself. We're going to have to move somewhere else. I'll need to find a new job so we can start over. But I'll have to live with what I've done the rest of my life. I'm not looking forward to that. I feel that I betrayed my reason for being a doctor in the first place, and I will need to spend the rest of my life trying to make that up in any way I can."

Katie suddenly stood and rubbed her upper arms as if she were freezing cold. "I…can't believe all this. I need to digest it, but I'm not sure I can." She briefly paced the room as if she didn't know what else to say or to do with herself. "I'm going to go check on Johnnie." She ran from the room.

Tim rubbed his eyes and bowed his head. He hoped Katie just needed time to absorb all that he had revealed. He didn't want to destroy their family on top of everything else he'd done.

But if he lost them, it was his own damned fault. He'd allowed himself to get involved in something dangerous and destructive, and he'd pay the price forever. He began to sob.

CHAPTER 61

"**W**ell, here we are again." Jeremy slumped in his chair as Amanda hung up her coat in his office.

"Yeah." She tried to smile, but he noticed how thin an attempt it was.

More than a year had passed while they'd waited for Subject Two to be ready. More than a year with Jeremy hooked to the IV of life. The situation tested the mettle of their relationship, as well as his physical and emotional endurance. Glen had not escaped the stress; he had run himself ragged trying to ready the latest clone as quickly as he dared and preparing himself—logistically and psychologically—to perform the eventual transplant unassisted.

Jeremy had wasted away to nearly a living skeleton. Life had become a series of days he waited out like someone serving a very long and indefinite prison term. He couldn't eat; he couldn't easily go out. His tether to the IV kept him from moving freely—as if he had the energy to do so anyway. Amanda had to wait on him hand and foot. She had been doing very well in her new job, but finally had to quit to take care of him this past year.

And of course, she'd had to make up a cover story about why she had to care for him so intensely. She couldn't reveal to anyone how hard it was caring for someone who had no intestinal tract—and especially why he was bereft of such a thing in the first place.

And Glen. He wasn't even looking very good these days. Since Tim left, he'd been solely responsible for not only all of the care and cultivation of Subject Two, but also all of Jeremy's care. He'd had to manage the day-to-day operations of the business as well, since they didn't dare let any of the SomaGene staff see Jeremy in his present condition. He had to stop performing commercial SomaGene surgeries because of the numerous burdens.

No one had heard directly from Tim since the day he resigned, but there had been rumors that he'd snagged a research position out in L.A. Jeremy couldn't blame him for wanting to get as far away as he could from SomaGene and all that had happened. He thought back to the last day he'd seen Tim. He'd found his moral compass—granted, a bit late, but at least he found it. In a way, Jeremy admired him. But he just couldn't bring himself to turn down another chance at living, not after what he'd been through.

He glanced at Amanda. She stood gazing out the window, her arms folded. She looked lost in thought, and so very tired. He wondered if maybe it would be best if he didn't survive the surgery, then tried to wipe that thought from his mind before it took root.

"It'll be OK, Amanda." Maybe if he said it aloud, he'd believe it as well.

She turned to him, the dark circles under her eyes exaggerated by the angle of the light. "Will it? They never did figure out what went wrong last time. How do you know we won't be going through this same little tableau in a year or so?" She shook her head. "I'm sorry. That was cruel. I didn't mean to—" She started to sob. "It's just been so hard."

He rose on unsteady legs and went to her, IV rack in tow. He put one arm over her shoulder. "I know. I know you didn't mean it that way. Believe me, I've had the same thought."

They stood together, silent for several minutes. Then Jeremy's phone buzzed.

He picked it up. "Yeah, OK." He looked at Amanda. "It's time."

She went to him, kissed him. "I love you. See you afterwards, OK?" She tried to smile, but the tears gave her away.

Jeremy did his best to smile, but knew he'd also failed. "Yeah. See you soon," he whispered, then turned and made his way to the door while he could still maintain his composure, for both her sake and his own.

Knowing that Glen would be busy with preparations, Jeremy understood he'd have to walk himself to the surgical suite unassisted. That was fine with him. He could be alone with his thoughts for a short while without wasting energy trying to put on a good front for anyone. But it seemed to take him forever to make his way there, between just feeling so tired and weak, and having to scoot the IV cart along with him.

He glanced up at it. He was utterly sick of having it continuously connected to him for all this time. The site where the needle penetrated his subclavian artery was constantly sore and he didn't even like to look at it. Didn't like to touch it. He knew it repelled Amanda, too.

He felt so very fragile. And now he knew firsthand that, though he couldn't converse or otherwise express concepts verbally, the Subject had surely experienced all the same miseries, perhaps more.

And now there was a second Subject to endure the same experience. Jeremy felt so guilty—yet so helpless.

Finally he arrived at the vestibule outside the actual surgical suite. He was supposed to change into a gown, but that posed a challenge to accomplish unassisted. He would have to maneuver it over the tubing coming from beneath his collarbone. He tried to decide what to do. Certainly he couldn't walk into the sterile surgical suite in his street clothes. Finally he removed his clothes, let them fall to the ground, and just draped the gown over himself as best he could and went into the suite.

An all too familiar sight greeted him—aside from Tim's absence. There was Glen, checking monitors and arranging his instruments.

The Subject. Somehow Glen had managed to get him in there and sedated. He lay on the gurney next to the empty one that awaited Jeremy. He was hooked to tubes and wires and was already draped and ready to go.

Jeremy averted his eyes from the sight. "Hey, Glen."

Glen looked up from his work. "Hey, Jeremy. You ready?"

"Suppose so." Jeremy dragged his IV cart over to the waiting gurney and lay down. He made himself as comfortable as he could, which wasn't very. "All right. Let's do it."

"OK, Jeremy. The Subject is ready. Let's just get you under."

Jeremy welcomed the mask over his face as it delivered the

gas that mercifully and quickly brought peaceful sleep.

Glen silently cursed Tim for his attack of conscience. Now he had to perform the complex dual procedure solo—and hope nothing went wrong that would sidetrack him from simply getting it done as swiftly and precisely as possible.

He'd put a delayed-release sedative in the Subject's dinner the night before, so he had been easy to subdue in the enclosure and slide onto the gurney. So far, so good with his vitals. After all, he had not been weakened by prior surgery, so that would be on Glen's side.

Jeremy, however, was another story. He'd spent over a year living off nothing but IV-delivered nutrients and limiting his activity because of the omnipresent IV rack that constrained him. His general physical condition had seriously degraded just due to those factors. Glen also suspected Jeremy was depressed—perhaps not clinically so—but nonetheless depressed. Who could blame him, really? He'd been doing so well, then that newfound health had been taken from him so suddenly and so dramatically.

Glen thought for a moment as he intubated Jeremy and adjusted the anesthetic gas flow. He'd never been able to figure out why the implanted intestines had just suddenly died like that, long after Jeremy had recovered from the procedure—and that worried him. If he didn't know what happened, how could he avoid repeating it? Was it something he could have prevented with some change in regimen, or how the organs were transplanted? He shook his head. Better stop mulling over that and focus on the present. Jeremy and the Subject were ready, and he had to work quickly yet pay careful attention, because no one had his back today.

He'd leave Jeremy intact until the organs were ready for transplant, even though that meant a delay in the implantation. He felt he'd rather minimize the risk of Jeremy being open longer than necessary—the organs would wait in a body-temperature nutrient bath in the meantime. It would have to do.

Heedless of aesthetics, he swiftly made a lengthy incision in the Subject's abdomen and hastily cauterized all the blood vessels, rather than taking the time to apply clamps. He reached inside and began to lift the intestines up and out, cauterizing a path behind them as rapidly as he could.

The thought occurred to him to simply take the organs and skip the cautery in the interest of time, but he decided to preserve the Subject if he could. He still wanted the opportunity to attempt an *in vivo* production of a new intestinal tract in the Subject's living body.

He worked quickly, glancing at the monitors periodically to check on vitals. At last, all the blood vessels were dealt with. Then he cut the end of the small intestine just below the stomach and tied that off. He cut and tied off the final portion of the large intestine, then lifted the ungainly mass and lowered it into the waiting nutrient bath. He drew his sleeve across his forehead and took a breath before turning to Jeremy.

Glen stood over his patient, his scalpel poised. Jeremy's abdomen sported evidence of the prior procedures in the form of three long, dark pink, ropy scars. He calculated a tradeoff between speed and ease of healing, and decided in favor of speed. He made a longer incision than before so he could work quickly and close as soon as possible to minimize the risk of complications. Jeremy would just have to live with yet another major incision and some additional post-op healing.

He used the electro cautery liberally, then applied metal clamps to hold the flaps of abdomen open and out of his way while he worked. His jaw clenched as he viewed the surgical field and grasped just how tedious this was going to be. Thankfully, he'd had the forethought to use special clips on the ends of the blood vessels when he removed the failed transplant. That would make those vessels easier to spot and grasp and hopefully easier to resect onto the new organs. However, he would still have to carefully snip each vessel just behind the clip before resecting because the opening would be sealed shut permanently at the actual site of the clips.

Tedious, yes, but at least those vessels would be resectable. He worried about the ones that had been too small to clip in the prior surgery. Those had been cauterized. He wondered how many of those he would be able to resect today, and if it would be enough to perfuse the new organs with adequate circulation to avoid tissue death. He shrugged and got started. He would just have to work with what he had.

He glanced up at the monitors. Jeremy's pulse had become a bit rapid and weak. He looked back into the abdominal cavity and spotted one blood vessel that was leaking. He quickly clamped it then checked the monitor again. The pulse steadied, but he knew every minute Jeremy was open was risky.

Wishing he somehow had more than two hands, Glen lifted the intestines from their nutrient bath and gently laid them in Jeremy's abdomen. He decided to connect each end of the intestines first, then work from left to right, top to bottom to get all the blood vessels properly attached. He knew he was going to be exhausted after this procedure, and that there would be no rest for him because he was the sole person who could do the post-op monitoring. He groaned to himself and kept working. No point in focusing on that. Not now.

Hours later, he straightened up and stretched his back while taking another look at the monitors. Jeremy's vitals could look stronger, but they weren't out of line with his general condition and the fact that he had been under for some time now. Glen bent back down and made sure all the blood vessels were properly sealed and connected, no leaks. Satisfied, he began to close, stitching and cauterizing as fast as he could.

Then he turned to the Subject. He had delayed closing him in favor of getting through Jeremy's procedure as quickly as possible. He hastily closed the Subject's abdomen with as few stiches as he could get away with.

Glen realized he was in a quandary. Who to bring out of the anesthetic first? He couldn't handle both of them at once. He decided to bring Jeremy out first. He could put him in Recovery and let Amanda stay with him while he brought the Subject out and set him up in his enclosure with his permanent IV. It would have to do.

CHAPTER 62

Amanda had parked herself in one of Jeremy's office chairs, and had barely moved since he'd left. She knew a lot of time had passed, but had no idea how much. She didn't really want to know, and so deliberately hadn't looked at her watch. She'd just sat and stared into space the entire time.

She knew he was absolutely miserable in mind and body, and that he harbored a lot of guilt for what had happened to the first Subject. If this procedure didn't restore his health, she wasn't sure he would want to come out of the anesthetic. She wasn't sure she would want him to—and she felt guilty for even being able to form such a thought.

A knock at the door startled her back to the here and now. Her heart pounded in her chest. "Yes?" she said weakly, fearing the worst but hoping for the best.

Glen came in, still wearing his scrubs. His face mask dangled onto his chest; his surgical cap still covered his head. His eyes had the hollow look of utter exhaustion. He looked so bad, she wondered how difficult the procedure had been.

"Jeremy's in the recovery room now. He's just beginning to come out of the anesthetic. I'd like you to wait with him there, so I can get the Subject squared away. I've no one to assist, you know."

"Sure." Jeremy had told her what happened with Tim and why he had resigned. The idea of Glen having to perform the procedure singlehandedly had weighed on them all in the interim. "How is he?"

Glen spoke quickly, as if he needed to get everything said before he collapsed from exhaustion. "So far, so good. I'd have preferred to have completed the procedure faster and had him under for a shorter time. To speed things up, I had to make a larger incision to make access easier. I'm afraid he will have a bit more healing to do because of it, but it was a tradeoff I needed to make."

"I understand."

Glen led her down the hall to the recovery room and motioned her in. "If anything seems amiss, don't hesitate to press the call button. I have a portable receiver—it'll buzz me wherever I happen to be." He turned and left.

She went to Jeremy's bedside, took a seat on the rolling stool that had been left there, and examined him closely in the cold hospital room light. His color wasn't as good as it had been after the prior procedures, but he had gone into this one in a much more weakened state.

His eyes began to flutter open. He looked dazed as he tried to focus on his surroundings.

"I'm here." She reached out and took his hand. "Don't try to talk. The surgery is over. You're in Recovery now."

He blinked and gave a slight nod.

Glen removed the breathing tube from the Subject's throat, then wheeled his gurney from the surgical suite back to his enclosure. He struggled to singlehandedly transfer him onto the bed-shelf without having him fall to the floor. He had to push and shove and rearrange the Subject's inert body a number of times to get him properly positioned.

He pulled down the front of the hospital gown to reveal the area just below the collarbone. Then he connected a long section of IV tubing to a full bottle of parenteral nutrition that hung from a rack above the Subject, and let it flow for a moment to get the air bubbles out of the tube before connecting it to the needle. Quickly, before the Subject could come out of the anesthetic, he swabbed the area with antiseptic, then inserted the large gauge needle. He adjusted the flow, then applied tape to secure the needle where it entered the Subject. Then he raised the hospital gown back up to cover the site.

Glen sat down on the bed next to the Subject to rest his tired back and legs while he waited for him to regain at least minimal consciousness. He didn't like energy drinks and artificial stimulants, but this called for a can or two of the stuff. He'd go get some from the break room as soon as he made sure the Subject was stable enough to leave alone.

After a short while, he could see the Subject's eyes start to shift beneath the lids. Then they opened and stared back at him with a questioning look. He groaned softly and closed his eyes again.

Glen checked his pulse and found it satisfactory. He'd be good enough unattended for a while. Wearily, he rose, locked the enclosure behind him, and headed for the break room.

He opened his eyes. Slowly, his surroundings swam into focus. He couldn't seem to concentrate. Something was wrong. He tried to move, but his breath caught when a searing pain shot through his midsection. He felt so tired, so broken, but didn't have the mental language to comprehend it more fully.

As the pain became increasingly intense, his vision began to clear. He was back in the place he lived, the only place he'd ever known.

But there was something new.

There was something hanging above him. A bottle of whitish fluid, hanging from a gleaming metal rack several feet up. He wondered what it was. Then he noticed that a tube ran from it toward him. He followed it with his eyes, and could just move his head enough to see that it attached to him high on his chest.

He reached one hand up and gingerly felt the area. There was something there that didn't belong, and it hurt him. He removed his hand and tried to understand what had happened to him.

He couldn't remember anything since some time after he ate his food last night. Nothing at all until now. He moved his head and looked around his enclosure. Nothing had changed, except for that bottle hanging high above him—and the pain.

His chest hurt where that thing attached, and his abdomen burned with a consuming pain. He reached his hand to where it hurt and touched carefully. There was some sort of padding there.

He closed his eyes and tried to go back to the sleeping place he'd come from, before the pain came.

Glen had taken the energy drinks back to his office to consume. He didn't want to run into any of the other staff doctors in the break room and have to explain what he had been doing that had exhausted him so.

Despite downing both drinks in rapid succession, he had been so tired that he'd dozed for little while with his head on his desk. He awoke abruptly and panicked when he realized he had been out for about half an hour. He tried to convince himself he would surely have awakened had Amanda pressed the call button. The buzz of his receiver unit could wake him out of the soundest sleep.

Nonetheless, he decided he'd better go check on Jeremy. He rubbed his eyes, smoothed his hair a little so he wouldn't look like he'd just been asleep, and went to the recovery room.

He opened the door and peered inside. Amanda sat next to the bed, holding Jeremy's hand. Thankfully, it appeared *she* had managed to stay awake to keep an eye on things. "How's he doing?" He whispered to her as he approached to avoid disturbing Jeremy.

"He seems all right. He's been dozing on and off."

"Good. I put a sedative in his IV to help ease things for him as he came out of the anesthesia. I didn't want the post-op pain to hit him all at once." Glen took a look at the monitors. "I think he's progressing well, all things considered."

"So what's next?"

"I'd like to keep him here a little longer than last time, since he went into the procedure in a more weakened state. It must have been pretty uncomfortable for you sitting there like that all this time. I could wheel another bed in and you could stay here with him if you like." He absently ran a hand through his hair. "Actually, if you would do that, I'd be rather grateful. We could both keep an eye on him, since there is no one else to do it."

"Neither of you could convince Tim to at least assist through this operation before leaving?"

"No. He was determined to cut ties—immediately. He didn't even pack up his office. Just marched in and told Jeremy he was resigning, and never looked back."

Amanda gazed at Jeremy's sleeping face as she spoke. "I can understand it, actually. We've had many discussions about this, and grateful as we are for the chance this gives Jeremy, I'd be lying if I didn't admit there is a dark side to it."

"Well, this is probably not the time to discuss it, but I've never seen it that way. The Subject is a mere product of a process that involved some tissue that Ivan donated—donated to help save his son from a terrible fate."

Amanda shook her head and sighed. "You're right. I'm not up to discussing the ethical aspects right now. I'm ashamed to admit it, but I've tried hard to avoid dwelling on that. Given we've gone ahead and taken advantage of it, it seems disingenuous to look the gift horse in the mouth."

"Sorry. I know this must be difficult for you, especially after what you both have been through in the last year. I'm tired and not being very diplomatic." He tried to smile.

"Thanks. I understand. We're all pretty tired about now, I suppose."

"Yeah. Well, I'll check back in later. Remember to buzz me if you notice anything that concerns you."

"Will do." She smiled, then turned back to gaze at Jeremy.

Glen shut the door behind him. Jeremy did look like he'd weathered the procedure in decent shape. That much was a relief. He decided to go lie down on the couch in his office and take a real nap for a while. He desperately needed the rest, and figured he should take advantage of a quiet point to grab some before Jeremy needed further post-op attention.

CHAPTER 63

He awoke to even worse pain than before. Only the small lights were on now in his enclosure. The darkness didn't usually frighten him, but this time he felt so cold and alone and he hurt so very badly.

How could he get the pain to stop? He wanted to curl up in a ball in the darkness, to shield his belly from the terrible, searing pain. He squirmed, tried to get onto his side. Another pain—worse than all the rest—shot through his stomach when he moved. He flinched, accidentally kicking his feet against the wall and toppling himself over the edge of the narrow bed and onto the cold cement floor.

He heard a loud crash when he fell. He wasn't sure what it was. He reflexively clapped his hands to his upper chest as he experienced a new, tearing pain there. It was warm and wet where his hands were.

There was even more pain in his stomach. He reached down to his belly. The pads there were wet, sticky, and warm. He lay there, uncomprehending, as his vision grew dimmer and dimmer in the dark. The pain became mercifully hazier along with his vision. He was too tired to get back up on the bed, so he just curled up on the floor as the darkness came.

Glen flung his forearm over his face as a ray of early morning sunlight attempted to penetrate his eyelids. He rolled over to settle back into sleep, then realized where he was and why. His eyes snapped open and he took in his surroundings. He was all crunched up on his office couch, and sunrise was creeping through his window already. He'd slept there the better part of the night and still felt completely drained.

He groaned as he forced himself to a sitting position. His back still ached from the long surgery and his limbs were stiff from sleeping on his couch in such an awkward position. He tried to stretch out the kinks as he planned his day.

Maybe he should check in on the Subject first and replenish his IV bottle, then take the time to give Jeremy a more thorough exam. That sounded like a good plan. Jeremy had looked pretty good when he last saw him, and he would have heard the buzzer had Amanda tried to reach him. He wasn't quite up to dealing with her yet anyway. After she voiced her ethical concerns, he realized he walked a fine line with her that could lead to a confrontation he didn't need right now. He wanted to get Jeremy stable enough to leave his immediate care, so he could get some real rest.

He headed for the restroom down the hall to splash some water on his face and make himself presentable. He looked in the mirror and decided the night's rest on the couch hadn't done him nearly as much good as he had hoped. Dark circles lay beneath his bloodshot eyes and made him look ten years older overnight. He sighed and resolved to try to sneak in another nap later. He smoothed his hair and left the bathroom to go check on the Subject.

Planning only a brief visit, Glen entered the Subject's room, only to discover he'd fallen to the floor with his back to the door. The IV rack had toppled and the bottle had shattered on the hard cement floor. He groaned at the prospect of having to heave the Subject back up onto the bed and clean up the mess.

Annoyed more than anything, Glen stomped over to the enclosure and let himself in. Only then did he notice the blood. Two large pools of it lay on the other side of the Subject.

He scooped the Subject up to get him back up onto the bed, doing his best to lift with his legs to avoid wrenching his already aching back. Glen didn't like his color, especially the blue tinge on his lips. He reached down and checked for a pulse. Barely there. He took a closer look at the damage.

The needle apparently ripped out when the Subject fell and tugged the IV down, leaving a tear in the subclavian artery that had flowed pretty freely before partially clotting. Though it had mostly stopped bleeding, he didn't dare touch it and risk getting it flowing again before he had the materials on hand to try to suture it shut.

But the needle tear was the least of it. Blood soaked the hospital gown where it lay over the abdomen. Glen lifted the gown and peered beneath the bloody bandages. His shoulders slumped as he realized what had happened. The fall onto the cement floor had been hard enough to rip open some of the fresh external stitches. He wiped aside some of the blood with the edge of one of the bandages and confirmed his even greater fear—not only was the incision bleeding, but the fall must also have reopened at least one other blood vessel internally. Blood seeped both from the edges of the wound and from within the abdominal cavity.

Glen sat on the bed next to the unconscious Subject and wearily weighed his options. He could drag him back into surgery and try to stem the flow of blood and repair the damage. But why? He'd hoped to try to develop a new set of intestines *in vivo* using the Subject, but that was a long shot and he was far too tired to try to perform another singlehanded surgery now. Given the amount of blood loss, any such attempt would probably be a waste of time and energy anyway.

He checked the pulse again at the carotid artery. Very weak and thready. He was nearly gone. *Screw it.* He'd deal with the mess later. Glen decided to let it go, and just focus on Jeremy's care.

Jeremy suddenly awoke screaming in pain. His color was terrible, and he clutched at his abdomen.

Amanda looked at him, wide-eyed. "What's wrong?"

Jeremy screamed and moaned, "Not again!"

Amanda grabbed the call button and frantically pressed it.

Glen shut the door to the Subject's enclosure and tried to think of when he was going to get the time—let alone the energy—to get back in there and clean up the mess. He would have to park the body in the freezer with the first Subject and deal with them both later. He shook his head. He was just way too tired to deal with these complications now.

He was already on his way to check on Jeremy when his buzzer went off. "Shit!" Forgetting his exhaustion in a surge of adrenaline, he sprinted down the hall to the recovery room.

He burst through the door and ran to Jeremy's bedside. One look at his patient triggered a panicked déjà vu. He could draw blood for tests, but feared he already knew what it would tell him.

"What's going on?" Amanda stood near the bed, pale and taut, her hands pressed to the sides of her face. She appeared right on the edge of hysteria.

Glen decided not to share his suspicion with her until he verified it. He hoped he was wrong, though in his gut, he knew he wasn't.

"I need to take some blood. I'll let you know as soon as I get the results." He hastily drew the blood, administered some additional painkillers through Jeremy's IV port, and left the room before he could get into a discussion with her.

He ran to the Subject's room and hurried to the enclosure. He pressed a trembling finger to the Subject's carotid, knowing and fearing what he would find. Death.

And now he had his answer. He now knew why Jeremy's first transplanted intestines had failed. The donor Subject had to be kept alive at all costs. But that didn't do him any good now.

He slumped from exhaustion, exhaustion that was magnified because he knew what he would have to do, how long it would take, and that he would have to do it all unassisted.

CHAPTER 64

It's the same damned thing. I know it. Jeremy's blood chemistry profiles matched the ones run when the first transplanted intestines began to die inside of him. Glen rubbed his eyes and groaned. To be perfectly, professionally certain, he should confirm with a laparoscopic exploratory, but neither he nor Jeremy could spare the energy.

He knew what the problem was, and now he knew the cause. If only he hadn't been so cavalier about letting the Subject bleed out. Even if he'd just done some minimal patching, rather than extensive surgery, it might have been enough. It's not like he cared about brain damage. He just needed to keep the Subject alive, however minimally. *Too late now.*

"God damn it!" He slammed his fist onto the desk. To have brought the project this far, only to come to this. Again. And this time without any assistance whatsoever to do what needed to be done.

And now he had to go deliver the news—if Jeremy hadn't already figured it out on his own. He might have, if he wasn't too drugged to realize it.

He cursed Tim again. Not just for leaving at such a critical point, but for actually *causing* the critical point. If he hadn't let his emotions drive him—rather than his brain—he wouldn't have killed the original Subject and none of this would have happened. Jeremy would have continued to enjoy good health until his Crohn's eventually made its move—and who gave a damn about the Subject? Tim never did get it through his head that the Subject was a piece of tissue created to serve a purpose. Nothing more.

Glen gritted his teeth. No matter how stupid and misguided, what was done was done. Now he had to go face Jeremy and Amanda and have a very hard conversation.

Amanda didn't like the way Jeremy was breathing. It was labored, and there was a noticeable hitch in it now and again. She was grateful for his sake that Glen had sedated him—the pain he experienced appeared to be far worse than any pain she'd ever witnessed and she couldn't bear the sight of him enduring it. But on the other hand, she didn't like that he was out of it and unable to communicate his wishes to her. The situation seemed serious enough that it was important for her to know what he wanted. Or what he would not want.

Almost superstitiously, they'd diligently avoided the topic before this latest procedure, as if somehow that would shield them from having to face such a situation. But now she wished they'd discussed what he might want if something went badly and he couldn't speak for himself. At what point and under what conditions would he want to be allowed to...? She couldn't even think the word to herself, despite her previous reflections on the quality of his life and whether he was really happy living it.

She took his hand in hers. It was damp with perspiration. He must be feverish, by the feel of it. She pressed it to the side of her face. Where the hell was Glen? When was he going to come back and explain what was going on? Did she even want to hear what he would have to say? Despite her high talk about ethics, she knew she'd do anything to have Jeremy well again. Anything.

A knock sounded at the door. She quickly wiped away her tears. "Come in."

Glen stepped in, a notepad in his hand. "Hi, Amanda. How's he been?" He approached the bedside opposite of her.

"His breathing worries me. It sounds terrible." She looked up at Glen, her eyes burning with tears. "What is it?" she asked in a small voice.

Glen glanced at the monitors and made a show of taking Jeremy's pulse and giving him a visual onceover before answering. He pulled a rolling stool to Jeremy's bedside and sat down on it heavily. "It is serious, Amanda. I won't kid you."

Amanda's stomach felt hollow. She didn't know what was coming, but she already knew it would be dismal.

"Remember the last time, when he'd healed and the transplanted organs failed and began to die? Well, that's exactly what's happening again. So not only have the organs ceased to function, but he's being hit with toxicity from tissue death and infection."

Amanda remembered all too well. Jeremy had been rushed into emergency surgery, only to emerge tied to the IV full-time until he could get another transplant. And it was all happening again. "Why?"

Glen hesitated before answering. "You're going to find this a little difficult to believe, but best I can tell, there appears to be a clear correlation. Last time, this happened right after Tim terminated the Subject. This time, it happened right after the Subject expired due to a hemorrhage. It happened in the same way, with the same timing."

She tried to grasp what he had said. The Subject had to stay alive for Jeremy to stay alive. She knew of no precedent for such a connection in normal organ transplants. All she knew was that Jeremy had lapsed into a very precarious situation because of it. "Couldn't you stop the bleeding? Couldn't you have taken more care?"

Glen waved his hands as if to ward off her rising anger. "I didn't realize the correlation until this time, or I would have tried to do more, believe me. It still seems preposterous to me, but it's too tightly coupled to ignore."

"So what the hell do we do now, watch Jeremy die?" Anger began to overtake her fear. She'd been through so much with Jeremy—he'd lived to taste good health, only to have it snatched away. Again. She wanted him back, and healthy. It wasn't fair to go through all he'd been through, only to end up like this. She glanced at him. His breathing was no better. Worse, if anything.

Glen looked like he'd been physically beaten by some invisible entity. He spoke in a soft, defeated tone. "The intestines are dying inside of him right now. If nothing is done, gangrene will set in, shock will ensue. He's in the early stages right now." He stared down at the floor, as if trying to find his next words there. "There isn't a lot of time. He needs to have the dying organs removed. Just like last time. Or they will certainly kill him. Then he needs to go back on the IV as before, until a new Subject can be developed."

"What are you waiting for? You can't just let him die!"

"Amanda, it's complex surgery. I'm completely exhausted, and Tim is gone. I'm not sure I can handle it."

"You have to try. If you don't, you already said what would happen, right?" Amanda wished she could will energy directly into Glen to get him to do what Jeremy needed done.

"It's tricky surgery. I just can't do it alone." Glen looked at her. "Can you assist? I don't know who else I can ask."

"Me? I'm a research scientist, not a surgeon. I don't know about instruments or anything. I might do more harm than good."

Glen dropped his head into his hands. "I can't let anyone else here in on it, and I sure as hell can't do it alone, not after the long procedure yesterday. I can about guarantee I'll miss something—and the end result will be the same as doing nothing."

Amanda stood and began pacing the room. "I can't accept that. There has to be a way. We can't just give up on him and leave him like this." She stopped pacing as an idea struck her. It wasn't without its problems, but it was probably Jeremy's only hope. "I have an idea."

"What?"

"I know—or knew—a surgeon who could handle this."

"No one outside these walls can know about this project."

"At the cost of Jeremy's life? I'm not willing to make that trade."

"Don't you understand what it would mean if this got out? The scandal would bring down SomaGene. This wasn't meant to be a public project, not as it was originally designed. Maybe someday, we could redesign the approach to raise fewer ethical hackles. But not now."

"I don't give a shit about SomaGene. I only care about Jeremy. Besides, there might be a way to convince this person to keep quiet. It would be a small price to pay to save Jeremy—and protect your precious SomaGene." She stepped back over to Jeremy's bedside and folded her arms. "Jeremy owns the company. I'm going to contact this person and offer him whatever I need to—on Jeremy's behalf."

She suspected she was on thin legal ground, but didn't care. She saw only one way to save Jeremy, and she'd do whatever she had to do. She figured if he were able to speak for himself, and knew of the person she spoke of, that he would do the same.

CHAPTER 65

Amanda adjusted Jeremy's bed sheet and gazed at his sleeping face for a moment. He still looked deathly pale and fragile, despite the heavy antibiotics. If anything, he was starting to look worse and time would soon be running out.

Glen had left her alone with him a while ago after her bold announcement that she knew who she could call on to help. He didn't seem to believe she would be able to pull it off, but at least he quit fighting her about keeping absolutely unbroken secrecy around the project. He'd just have to trust that she could handle the negotiation in a way that wouldn't expose SomaGene. Hell, she'd been involved to some degree herself and any scandal would likely harm her reputation and employability as well. They all had plenty to lose if she screwed up—and Jeremy had everything to lose if she didn't find help.

She leaned over and kissed his clammy, feverish forehead, then left the room to make her call.

Amanda sat at Jeremy's desk and took out her cell phone. She set it down in front of her and gathered her thoughts before making the call. While Jeremy's welfare was paramount, she wanted to be careful not to needlessly create any permanent repercussions. She anticipated this conversation would be very tricky to navigate.

She glanced at her watch. It was already late in the afternoon. She picked up her cell and hit the speed-dial while she still had her nerve up.

After several rings, voicemail kicked in. She gritted her teeth and punched Jeremy's desk as she prepared herself to leave a message. It had to be just the right message.

"Hi, Rick. It's Amanda. It's really, really critical that I speak with you as soon as possible. Please call me." She left her cell number and hung up.

She couldn't sit still. She stood up and walked to the window and stared out for a few moments, then paced around the office. Adrenaline surged through her system and her heart raced. She knew this was a life and death call, and she was forced to wait, helpless. Would he even call her back, given how they had parted nearly two years ago now? Would he even remember her?

Even if he called back, would he call in time, let alone agree to what she planned to propose?

She sat back down and rifled through Jeremy's desk drawers, hoping to find at least a stale granola bar. She realized she hadn't eaten much in the last forty-eight hours—she'd only munched here and there on some hospital-type food Glen had brought to Jeremy's room. Her hands trembled from stress and low blood sugar.

About a half hour after she'd left her message, her cell rang and nearly startled her right out of her chair. She grabbed it and looked at the display before answering. Her heart hammered so hard she could hear it in her ears.

"Hello, Rick?"

"Yeah. Didn't expect to hear from you after all this time. What's up?"

Amanda took a breath and tried to calm herself, then began. "Rick, I'm involved in a very strange situation up here in the Twin Cities. You're the only one who can help."

A pause, then Rick answered, his voice taking a guarded tone. "What sort of situation?"

"We need a highly skilled surgeon to at least assist, possibly lead, in an urgent procedure. The patient needs to have his entire intestinal tract removed." She cringed as she waited for his response.

"What? Why is this an emergency and why do you need to recruit someone? Surely you have numerous capable surgeons in the Twin Cities."

"The intestinal tract is dying—the tissue is quickly becoming necrotic and toxic. We need help because we're down to only one surgeon who is familiar with the patient and the procedure, and he can't perform the procedure unassisted."

"That still doesn't answer why there isn't someone local who can assist—hell, there should be whole teams available to assist up there. Why would you attempt it with only two surgeons, anyway? I'm no more familiar with the patient than anyone else, and I've never performed such a procedure. Why the hell is the entire intestinal tract necrotic? I've never heard of that."

Amanda realized she was going to have to risk revealing more information to have any chance of getting him to bite. "Rick, the patient is in this situation because of an experimental procedure. We can't recruit just anyone to assist for reasons of confidentiality, and we need someone with exceptional talent in leading-edge procedures."

"Who is 'we' and what sort of experimental procedure led to this?"

"The experimental procedure was a full intestinal tract transplant. Something has gone wrong and the transplanted organs are dying. For the time being, they must be removed to save the patient's life. As far as the 'we,' I'm not actually part of the team that performed this. I'm a...very good friend of the patient's. I can't think of who else we could bring in to help, and we're running out of time to save him. Please, Rick."

"Who is this team? Are they part of an institution? I can't just perform surgery wherever I feel like. My employment contract limits me, you know."

"I'd rather not go into the details of the program. I'm probably not the best person to discuss that too deeply anyway. I can tell you a publicly funded institution is not involved. This is a skunk works project at a private company. Only a small staff was working on it, and one of them left—that is why we're short a suitable surgeon."

"So you're asking me to drop everything and head up there to perform an urgent, extremely risky surgery on a patient I'm not familiar with—who's part of some experiment that I'm not involved in and know nothing about?"

Amanda sighed. "You're right. That about sums it up. For myself, I'm asking as a favor. I know I have no right to. The patient is the President and CEO of the company in question. He's not in any condition to negotiate anything right now, but I doubt I'm going too far out on a limb to say if you saved his life he'd be very grateful and would compensate you appropriately. Pay, maybe a position on the team if you wanted. I can't promise specifics for him, you understand."

"Does this have anything to do with those visits to your alleged girlfriend who was having surgery?"

"Yes. It does. This has been going on for a while at various stages. Rick, I really need to know. Will you do it?"

"Save his life so he can try to live without an intestinal tract? Is that really doing him a favor?"

"This is not the first time this has happened. They do have a protocol for nutritional support after the removal. It's not pleasant by any stretch, but it buys him time until they can try again."

"That could be a long time. The chances of an organ donor with a good tract and a solid tissue match are not terrific."

Amanda decided to keep the cloning aspect of the project in her pocket for now. "True enough. Rick, will you?"

Another long pause. "You caught me at a bad time. I have some things I can't get out of. I need all of tomorrow to get matters in a state where I can leave for a few days. I can be there the day after tomorrow. Best I can do."

"Thank you so much, Rick. I hope that will be fast enough. I'll have Glen Hawkins, the other surgeon, contact you with specifics as to location and all that, OK?"

"All right. See you in a couple of days."

"Rick, thank you. I mean it."

"You're welcome, but this had better be worth my while."

Amanda hung up and let out a long breath. She'd promise just about anything right now to save Jeremy's life, but she didn't think she could speak for him on exactly how he would want to repay Rick for his efforts. They'd just have to work that out later. If Rick didn't arrive in time to save him, it wouldn't matter anyway.

CHAPTER 66

Amanda shut the door behind her and approached Jeremy's bed. She was relieved Rick was coming, but still very worried it would not be in time. She gazed at Jeremy. He looked about the same as when she left him to make her call. She supposed that was about the best she could hope for under the circumstances.

She realized she didn't know where Glen was or how to find him in the facility, so she simply pressed the buzzer to get him to come to the room.

He arrived several minutes later, looking tired and alarmed at the same time. "What's going on? Did something change?"

"No, he's about the same as before. I just didn't know how else to find you. I found a surgeon to assist."

"You're kidding."

"No. It's Rick Granada. He's a regenerative medicine surgeon and research scientist down in Rochester. Soonest he can be here is the day after tomorrow, but at least he agreed to come."

"I've heard of him. He has an amazing reputation. He'd be perfect. How much does he know?"

Amanda explained what she had and had not revealed to Rick. "So he's going to have some questions, no doubt about that. And he's going to want to know what's in it for him. I didn't promise specifics—I don't think I'm in a position to. That's something Jeremy will have to speak for. I told him to expect your call concerning logistics."

"Sure. I'll take care of that. Meanwhile, we're just going to have to do our best with supportive care for Jeremy while we wait." He turned to her with a quizzical look. "How did you know to contact him, anyway?"

"We used to date."

CHAPTER 67

Glen led Rick into his office to meet and prepare for the procedure. He'd brought him in through a rear entrance, not only to dodge potential encounters with other SomaGene employees, but also to circumvent showcasing the high-tech lobby and spending precious time on any sort of distraction. He wanted to avoid anything that would delay getting the surgery underway as quickly as possible.

He sat behind his desk and motioned for Rick to take a seat. "I just checked on the patient, and he's about the same. I think you've arrived not a moment too soon. We need to operate before he gets even more toxic."

Rick held up a hand. "Before we get started on the details, I have some things I'd like to address."

Glen felt the tension build in his shoulders. Of course it wouldn't be so simple as having one of the most brilliant regenerative medicine surgeons take a little trip up to the Twin Cities to just do a little procedure for fun. There would be expectations, implications. Might as well find out what they were and deal with them as best—and as quickly—as he could. "Yes?"

"What exactly is going on here, and what led to this situation? I was not aware that SomaGene had developed a protocol for intestinal transplants. If you expect me to become involved, even by simply performing this procedure and nothing more, I need to know what I'm involved with."

Glen stared down at his desk. "I can tell you, but I must ask that the information not leave this room. This is a highly confidential project within SomaGene, and must remain so for reasons that will become apparent. Even the rest of SomaGene is unaware of this project."

Rick tilted his head, folded his arms, and sat back in his chair. "Why should I get involved in this? My skills are in high demand, and are under contract with my current employer. I'm likely about to violate the terms of my employment agreement—without any promised compensation—and you also expect confidentiality? Ridiculous."

Every minute that ticked by felt like a palpable added weight on Glen's shoulders. Every minute decreased the chances Jeremy would survive at all. He was afraid the great Rick Granada would come at a hefty price. If only Tim hadn't left when he did… No point rehashing that. "Rick, tell me what you want. I don't have the time or the inclination to play cat and mouse here."

Rick considered his answer for a moment. "I need to know what led up to this, what I'm participating in by agreeing to perform this surgery. I can't agree to it blind. There may be an ethical line I'm not personally willing to cross. I can't know that without you being honest with me. That said, it's clear that confidentiality is very important to you. But it comes at a cost. If your program interests me, I will want to join the team—appropriately compensated, of course. It sounds like you're short a good surgeon, so there should be an open position. If your program is not of that much interest, I will perform the surgery for a one-time fee. If I choose to not perform the surgery because of ethical issues, I will accept a one-time payment for my trouble in coming up here, and will be on my way. In any of these scenarios, you would have my silence."

Glen rubbed his face with his hands as he tried to think of a suitable response. He knew SomaGene was doing quite well, so money likely would not be a problem. But how much? That would be Jeremy's call, but he was in no condition to deal with a negotiation right now. "All right, I'll play."

Glen explained the origins of the program, as well as the key milestones and the various procedures Jeremy had undergone to date. He decided to soft-peddle Tim's reason for leaving—and what he had done to cause the first Subject's death. "You must understand, Jeremy would be the one to decide the specific amount of compensation. I can assure you he would agree to appropriate compensation—it's only right. I just wouldn't want to make a specific promise I didn't have the authority to make."

"Fascinating. Absolutely fascinating. You know, one of the things that frustrates me about my current position is that they're so conservative. There is no way on earth they would dare undertake a program like this because of the way they're funded. You say your partner left some months back and you're flying this project solo? You've got a lot of work ahead of you—beyond today's procedure. You're going to need a partner to work through that and determine how to make the next transplant the last Jeremy needs. I'd like to join the team, permanently." Rick stood up and offered his hand.

Startled, Glen stood and shook hands. He was sure he could get Jeremy to approve the hire—if he survived the surgery. If not, all bets were off at SomaGene anyway.

At least Rick didn't have the qualms that Tim had. Indeed, he'd make a great partner on this project. Glen smiled. "Welcome. Now let's get this done."

CHAPTER 68

Glen finished inserting the breathing tube and adjusted the anesthetic gases. He still didn't like Jeremy's EKG. They'd provided all the supportive fluids and meds they could throw at him, but the added delay in getting him to surgery had taken a toll. He looked borderline shocky, and he'd have to be monitored carefully during the procedure. Glen turned to Rick, who stood by the instrument tray, scalpel ready. "Let's go. And we're going to have to move fast, judging by these vitals."

"Got it." Rick bent to his work, starting with a rapid incision to expose the abdominal contents.

They had quickly conferred on how to approach the procedure before prepping Jeremy. Given that Glen was still so worn down from handling the prior surgery and ensuing post-op work alone, they agreed that Rick would be the primary surgeon and Glen would assist. Rick would be far fresher and likely to move through it much more rapidly and surefootedly.

"My God, I'm amazed he's alive. I've never seen such extensive internal organ necrosis—in a living person. I like the idea of clamping the major vessels for easier resection next time. This should go pretty quickly."

Keeping one eye on the monitors, Glen watched Rick work. He was like a machine. He'd pick up another clamp, seal off another vessel, clip it off, then repeat the process just as fast as seemed humanly possible. Glen had to admit to himself that even on his best day, he wasn't nearly that fast.

Rick continued making good progress and had been working in silence for maybe another hour when Glen noticed some irregular beats on the EKG. "How close are you, Rick?"

"Maybe three-quarters of the vessels are clamped off. Still need to get at that last quadrant—and detach the tract at each end. Why?"

"There've been some irregular beats. Nothing big, but I have a bad feeling something may be coming."

"I'll keep going fast as I can. Let me know if you have to defib."

"Yeah." Glen pulled the crash cart closer so he could be ready. He didn't like the feeling in his gut.

About ten minutes later, his gut was vindicated. "Get back! Clear!" Rick nimbly jumped out of the way, instruments still in his gloved hands. Glen gave Jeremy a jolt with the paddles and checked the monitor. Still showed a chaotic heart. "Again!" Another jolt. He again glanced at the monitor. "Flatline!"

Rick tossed his instruments onto the tray and picked up a syringe with a long, thick needle. He quickly drew a dose of epinephrine into it from a nearby vial and moved close to Jeremy. He tugged the surgical drape down, felt for the intercostal space with his left hand, then, without the slightest hesitation, plunged the needle in up to the hilt and pressed the plunger. He yanked the needle back out, tossed it onto the cart and began to vigorously thump and compress Jeremy's chest.

Glen stood back from the whirlwind that was Rick and stole another glance at the monitor. Miniscule heart rhythms appeared to replace the flatline. He alternately watched the monitor and Rick's aggressive pumping.

"Come on! Come on!" Rick shouted at Jeremy as he frantically continued his compressions.

Glen took another look at the monitor, fearing the worst. *A rhythm!* "He's back! Got a beat. Hurry, wrap him up and close."

Rick shot a quick look at the monitor, stepped back in position, and quickly got back to work.

About twenty minutes later, he lifted the excised intestinal tract out of Jeremy's abdominal cavity and hastily tossed it in the waiting receptacle. "All right, quick check for any leakers... good. Closing now."

Several minutes later, Rick stood up straight and stretched his back. "Done. Closed for speed, not aesthetics. You can bring him out of it now."

Glen breathed for what seemed to be the first time in an hour, and began to adjust the gases to bring Jeremy back out of the anesthetic.

CHAPTER 69

Acouple days later, Jeremy lay in his bed in the recovery room. He'd been in and out of consciousness since the surgery. Today he was beginning to feel somewhat more alert, though he was still quite tired and in a fair amount of abdominal pain. His ribs hurt, too, and he didn't know why—so much so, he didn't like to take a deep breath.

A knock sounded at the door, then Glen and Amanda came in, accompanied by someone he didn't know. Amanda hurried to his bedside and took his hand. She looked tired, but happy. "Jeremy, you're looking a lot better today." She smiled and gave him a brief kiss on the cheek.

Glen stood near the foot of the bed with the stranger. "Jeremy, I'd like you to meet Dr. Rick Granada. He assisted me in your surgery. Quite impressively, I might add."

Rick stepped forward and offered his hand to Jeremy. "Pleased to meet you. We were able to completely and cleanly remove your necrotic intestinal tract. Nothing escaped into the abdominal cavity, and so I think we're past any fear of acute septicemia. You were in a pretty degraded condition by the time we began the procedure, and it was a little dicey here and there. You may have some soreness in your ribcage because we had to hit you with the paddles and a shot of epinephrine. I did some pretty aggressive compressions to get things going again. I'm sure that was all due to your compromised condition going in— nothing permanent to be concerned about."

Glen spoke up. "I think we have a pattern identified, that if the Subject dies, so does the transplanted intestinal tract. I don't understand the mechanism at all. We're going to have to study that more closely. Meanwhile, I've started a new Subject from Ivan's tissues and will look at ways to speed that up. Until that's ready, I'm afraid, we're back to the IV nutrition." He nodded toward the bottle hanging above and slightly behind Jeremy.

Jeremy panicked as he realized that Glen had just mentioned the cloning project in front of this new person. He tried to signal him with his eyes.

Glen apparently picked up on his body language. "Jeremy, I couldn't have performed this latest procedure by myself—not after doing the transplant and all the post-op care. And as it turned out, that cardiac event would have likely been fatal had I been operating alone. We recruited Rick because I absolutely needed another very capable pair of hands in surgery, and fortunately he agreed to come up."

"I called him, Jeremy. We needed to get someone here who could help." Amanda squeezed his hand.

Glen shifted his feet for a moment before continuing. "I made him a promise on your behalf, since you were in no condition and it needed to be done. I promised him a position at SomaGene—specifically on our project. He comes to us as an expert in the field of regenerative medicine, and I can tell you from firsthand observation—he's a helluva surgeon." He smiled at Rick, then Jeremy. "We needed to replace Tim, and Rick is actually a far superior surgeon."

"Have you explained this project is not public knowledge?" Jeremy winced a little; talking aggravated his rib pain.

Rick took over. "They absolutely did. I'm clear on that. As a permanent member of your staff, I would of course keep all this information in absolute confidence."

Jeremy got the point. Whether he liked it or not, he had a new staff member who expected to keep working on this project. At least he was clearly a brilliant surgeon. He nodded. "Sure. Welcome, Rick. And thank you." He licked his dry lips. "If you all don't mind, I'm a little tired right now."

"Of course. I'll be in to check on you later." Glen turned to leave.

"Glen and I will be taking shifts to monitor your progress until you're ready to recover at home." Rick gave a brief wave and followed Glen out the door.

Amanda turned to him. "I'm so glad you made it through. You don't know how scared I was. You looked really awful right before the surgery." A tear ran down her cheek as she lifted his hand and kissed it. "I'll go now, and let you sleep. I could use a little myself." She smiled at him, then left and shut the door.

Jeremy closed his eyes and tried to rest. So much swirled around in his head; it was hard to absorb it all. The surgery was over, and now he was back on the IVs—for how long this time? And this Rick Granada. Where had he come from? He supposed he should be grateful, from the sound of it. The guy did seem sharp. Maybe they could figure out a more humane way to provide intestinal transplants…maybe Granada could help do that, and they could break this parasitic cycle he'd found himself on…

Exhaustion overcame him and he fell back asleep.

CHAPTER 70

"Here, let me help you with that." Amanda deftly collapsed the telescoping IV rack and bent to maneuver it into the back seat of the Pathfinder.

Jeremy stood in the garage by the driver's door, holding the IV bottle in one hand and his keys in the other. The ever-present tubing snaked out of the top of his snow jacket and led to the neck of the bottle. He loved Amanda, and he appreciated all she did for him, but this daily dance with the IV setup—rain, snow, or shine—felt degrading to him. But he couldn't tell her that. She believed she was helping him, not humiliating him. He didn't know how to tell her the truth without hurting her.

"Thanks. I'll see you later." He gave her a quick kiss and awkwardly slid into his seat while holding the IV bottle aloft. He hung it from a makeshift hook on the passenger seat's headrest so the fluid would continue to flow by gravity while he drove to work.

He watched her step to the door that led into the kitchen, turn around, smile broadly, and wave at him before going inside. Every day she did that. She seemed so grateful for his very existence ever since the latest surgery. He was doing better, as these things went but she insisted on taking care of him at all times when he was home. She hadn't given any indication she intended to return to work any time soon, even though he was out of crisis mode.

Every day it became that much more claustrophobic.

And he had to wonder about Rick. She'd finally admitted that she had called Rick because she knew him—not solely because he happened to have the right qualifications. Turns out he was the man she left him for a couple of years back. What a small world it was. So something about that guy had been attractive enough to take her away from him once. Could it happen again? Especially in his present state? She'd left him before because of his health, and his health was nowhere near this tenuous back then. Rick had relocated to Minnetonka, so he wasn't that far away.

Was she seeing him now? What should he think when he didn't see Rick at SomaGene during a given day? Was he just busy in another part of the facility—or was he busy with Amanda?

Jeremy tried to push those thoughts from his mind. It wasn't fair for him to think such things. Amanda was totally devoted to him and had been since his original surgery and the beginning of this long ordeal. He started the car and headed for the office. He needed to try to be busy. This line of thinking was just not healthy.

Jeremy sat down behind his desk and sighed wearily. It took him maybe twenty minutes just to get out of the car and into his office every morning, and it wore him out mentally and physically.

He hated that IV rack and trying to wrangle it out of the car every single morning. Then every single evening when he was ready to go home, it was the same thing in reverse, only Amanda wasn't with him to help out. Tonight it would be especially frustrating because it was supposed to snow some more during the day. So he would have to drag the damned thing out to his car through the snow and try to get it loaded up, all while trying to keep his IV bottle at the right height and properly flowing.

He sent Glen a message to come see him ASAP.

Glen knocked and entered. "You wanted to see me?"

"Yeah, sit down."

Glen sat, then crossed his legs. "What's up?"

"I should ask you that. What's the status of the new Subject?"

"Coming along. I know you wish it could go faster, and so do I. We've been testing out some ideas for how to accelerate the development, but so far they've all come with warning signs. The indications we've seen are that tampering with the speed any more than we have would lead to anomalies that might be far more dangerous than remaining on your current IV regimen in the interim." He nodded toward the IV rack. "Sorry. I wish I had better news on that front. We just don't want to take any needless chances. It has to be right this time."

"What does Rick think?"

"Oh, he agrees. He's even more concerned about the various accelerants than I am. Funny, I figured he'd be more of a hot dog, but he can be quite conservative on protocols, it turns out."

I'll bet. He'd probably love for me to remain in this helpless limbo state for as long as possible. He knows an opportunity when he sees it, that's for sure. Jeremy tried to shoo the thoughts away and focus on reality, not fantasy. "What have you figured out on why the organs failed both times?"

Glen leaned back in his chair and tilted his head. "Ah, that's another story. Rick and I don't see eye to eye on that one, and there isn't much we can do to test our various theories, for obvious reasons."

"What are your theories?"

"Well, you have to remember, he wasn't present for either of the events. So he can't see the pattern as clearly as I do. On the other hand, maybe that is a strength of his theory, that he isn't blinded by the proximity of events. He thinks I'm confusing correlation with causation."

"How so?"

"Well, in each case, the Subject died, and you immediately began to show symptoms. Immediately. There was no way on earth you could have known the Subject had died at that moment, so it couldn't have been psychosomatic on your part. Further, you obviously had real physical manifestations. No amount of self-induced symptomology could cause necrosis of internal organs. Period. My theory, therefore, is that some sort of connection is created between you and the Subject when the full transplant occurs. If something happens to the Subject, his intestinal tract dies with him. If it's implanted in you at the time, well, we've seen what happens. Necrosis and emergency surgery."

Jeremy considered the theory for a moment. The connection

certainly seemed to be there, but it was a bit too metaphysical for him to accept so readily. "And what is Rick's explanation?"

"He reminds me, rightly so, that this is not a statistically significant sample, and so this could be simple coincidence. He thinks there is some causation at work, but is not willing to believe that the mere demise of the Subject is that cause. And of course, we have no way to test and prove either of our theories."

"So what can you do to get to the bottom of this?"

"The only thing I feel safe doing. Next time we transplant, we do whatever it takes to keep the Subject at least minimally alive, even if it means artificial life support. We just can't take the chance that it's a coincidence. The stakes are too high."

Jeremy couldn't argue with that logic. "How far have you gotten in developing some other way to achieve this—some other way to cultivate an intestinal tract? Not just for me, but for the broader market—all those who suffer from Crohn's."

Glen shook his head. "Not very. We keep coming up against the same major roadblock. The intestinal tract's very structure works against us. It's tubular, and extremely long and flexible. We're having a devil of a time trying to figure out what sort of scaffolding we could use to generate the tissue in the proper configuration. With tracheas, they're rigid and of finite length, so we can create a scaffold for the tissues to adhere to and keep that shape. Not so with intestines."

"Maybe there's another way. Maybe something with the same functionality but perhaps in some form that doesn't remotely resemble natural human intestines."

"That's the sensible alternate plan. The trick with that is to completely engineer something that performs all the functions of the large and small intestines—but from scratch. We're not sure where to begin. So for now, we're thinking we need to keep on with the clone method. It works—as long as the clone remains living."

Jeremy suddenly felt too tired to continue discussing the topic. He hadn't received any of the news he had hoped to hear. All the same dead ends and ethical snake pits. "Well, thanks, Glen. That's all for now."

Glen stood. "Hey, Jeremy, I know it must be tough for you. Believe me, we are working on this as hard as we can. It's just an incredibly complex problem to solve. At least we have our original protocol to fall back on. We know that works, but you'll have to be patient for some more months, probably more like a year, I think. I need to check the growth chart again. I'll let you know." He turned to go.

Jeremy gazed out his window and absently fingered the tubing where it emerged from his button-down shirt. Suddenly remembering, he glanced up and noticed his IV was getting low. He reached into his drawer where he kept spares and took out a new one. He stood, unhooked the old one, and swapped it out for the fresh bottle, which he hung aloft. He placed the old one in his trash, then sat down again.

Funny, in some ironic ways, the IV saved him time. He didn't need to eat or drink—in fact, he couldn't do either. So he didn't need to buy groceries, didn't need to make or get lunch. Didn't need to cook. Put a lot of time back in his day. Time he could use to be miserable.

He mulled over his conversation with Glen. Looked like nothing new had happened, or was going to happen. It would be the same protocol and procedure as last time. Wait for a new Subject to be ready. Have another surgery. And shift the burden and pain of living like this onto the new Subject. For the rest of his natural and unnatural life. Because this time, there would be no escape, natural or assisted. Glen would see to that.

All so he could live a healthy life. Until Crohn's destroyed the new intestinal tract and the whole cycle would begin anew.

CHAPTER 71

Jeremy lifted his head and rubbed his eyes. He'd fallen asleep right on his desk. Not that uncommon for him anymore, since he had such little energy. Glen, and now Rick as well, had taken over day-to-day operations and shielded him from the rest of the SomaGene workforce while he was on the IV regimen. He just couldn't handle a normal workday any more, and he didn't want the rest of the staff to see his condition. He couldn't remember the last time he assisted in surgery. He spread out his hands before him. What a waste. He had been a good surgeon.

He sat for a moment as the cobwebs of sleep cleared away. He gazed out the window at the sad, weak, late winter light. He felt just like that light. Tired, pallid. Hopeless.

He reached into his center desk drawer and rummaged through the disorganized mess until he found what he was looking for. He held up the scissors and examined them closely. Then, before he could change his mind, he grasped the tubing several inches from where the needle lodged in his subclavian artery and he snipped. He grabbed a metal binder clip and clamped it onto the end of the tubing to seal it. He unhooked the bottle from the rack and tossed it into the trash.

He stood, free of the IV cart for the first time in many months, and stepped out of his office.

He headed down the hall to the sequestered cultivation room, stepped inside and locked the door behind him. He did not wish to be disturbed.

Jeremy approached the glass receptacle that held the developing clone of his father. It rested on a suspended Lucite slab like an obscene jewel case. He stopped and stared down at it, both mesmerized and disgusted. The clone was the size of a small child now, one that would look like a young adult in about another year.

The receptacle was shaped like a small glass coffin with tubes that entered to serve intravenous nutrition and drugs and exited to remove waste and other by-products. The clone lay on his back, eyes shut. They kept him in some sort of suspended animation so he could spend all his energy in rapid growth.

He lifted the lid and carefully set it aside on the floating Lucite slab. He stared down at the face of the clone. He looked much like he did as a small boy. That made what he had to do all the harder. But he had to do it. He couldn't sentence yet another human to the fate he had in store.

He wondered how sentient the clone was at this stage of development. He wasn't sure what exactly was being done to keep him in that state, and whether he could sense anything despite his apparent lack of consciousness. He decided not to take any chances on possibly causing him any pain or discomfort.

He turned and searched in the supply cabinet for something suitable. Most of the contents consisted of topical antibiotics, rubbing alcohol for disinfecting needles and other items, liquid nutritional supplements and other items for mixing into the perfusion fluid. He kept looking until he found a vial of sedative. Didn't really matter what kind, as long as there was a sufficient amount to do what was necessary. He grabbed a large syringe and filled it with the liquid.

He turned toward the clone and gazed at him once more. He could still change his mind, return to his office, replace his snipped tubing and wait for his turn to live normally again. After all, it was his parting gift from Ivan. You know what they say about gift horses and their mouths. He set down the syringe and turned away from the little glass coffin.

Jeremy thought again about what he had been about to do. He'd been about to kill his brother. Or was it his father?

Then he reminded himself of what was going to happen if he didn't act. That *child*—whatever its relationship to him—would grow prematurely into an adult. He would live in a lab, and he would be deprived of his intestinal tract and put on an IV for the rest of his miserable existence. Jeremy gazed down at the section of clamped tubing that hung from his upper chest.

He turned, picked up the syringe, and swiftly injected the entire contents into one of the inflow tubes. He gently placed his finger on the child's carotid artery, and waited while the pulse slowed, slowed…then stopped. He carefully lifted one of the eyelids. A dilated, blank pupil stared back at him. He quietly placed the glass lid back on the little coffin and paused a moment out of respect for the newly dead.

Then he turned to the small incubator on the other end of the Lucite slab. And there it was—the glass vial containing the remainder of Ivan's tissue sample, floating in that pinkish nutrient bath. He took out the vial and held it up for close inspection.

His father's tissue. The source of all the suffering and hubris. He turned toward the workspace on the other side of the room, set down the vial, and found a book of matches. He pulled a Bunsen burner into position under a metal rack, placed the vial on the rack, and lit the burner.

He watched as the liquid warmed, then began to boil. He let it keep boiling until all the liquid was gone and the tissue began to char. It looked like evil itself as it withered and blackened in the glass. Satisfied he had adequately destroyed it, he shut off the burner and left everything as it was.

Once back in his office, Jeremy shut the door and locked it. He went over to his desk and called home.

"Hello?"

"Hi, Amanda. How're you doing?"

"Fine." Her voice took on a suspicious tone. "You never call during the day. What's the matter?"

"Nothing. Just calling to say I love you. And to thank you for all you do for me. I don't say that enough."

"Oh, I love you, too. I just want to make things easier for you while you wait for the new transplant. Then everything will be better again. I know it will."

"Yeah, it sure will. Well, that's all I called to say. I need to get back to some paperwork here."

"OK. Hurry home. I miss you!"

"Will do."

Jeremy hung up. Then he grabbed two pieces of paper and a pen.

Glen and Rick,

I appreciate all you've done for me, but I no longer wish to be a part of an experiment that should never have happened. I couldn't keep living like this, and I couldn't live with being responsible for another human—the next Subject—having to live like this after the eventual transplant.

I've destroyed the Subject, as well as the rest of Ivan's source tissue. This experiment cannot continue.

If you both wish to take over SomaGene after I'm gone, you have my approval. With one caveat—that this line of experimentation cease forever. If you still wish to find a transplant-based cure for Crohn's, do so in a way that does not involve harvesting organs from captive clones.

He then took the second sheet of paper and began to write:

Dear Amanda,

I'm sorry for having to do this. I love you—I always have and I always will—but I couldn't go on living this way, and I couldn't bear knowing that yet another human being would have to live like this so I could live normally again. This experiment has gone too far, and I have taken steps to make sure it never happens again.

I want you to have the house and everything that was mine. Money isn't everything, but I want you to be comfortable and have a good life going forward.

Jeremy reread both letters, signed them, placed them in envelopes and addressed them. Tears welled in his eyes, but his resolve remained firm. He set the letters on the desk in front of him. They would be easy to notice.

He unlocked his bottom drawer and reached inside. There was the vial of lorazepam and syringe he'd placed there some weeks back, when this idea first came to him. At the time, he'd just tucked them away as a sort of security blanket, in case things ever got too difficult to bear. After a while, he'd nearly forgotten he'd stashed them there. He'd tried to look forward and think of when he would be healthy again. He'd tried to set aside his guilt, as he had before. And it worked, for a while.

Today was just the last straw. Glen didn't understand the terrible twin pains he faced. On the one hand, his current life was miserable, and it looked like it would remain so for some time yet because they couldn't accelerate the clone process. On the other hand, he'd now lived like this for two separate periods. He knew how wretched such an existence was, and he knew what he would be inflicting on the third Subject. Worse yet, the Subject could not even be allowed to die, or the whole cycle would begin again.

No, Glen just worried about the clinical aspects as if both he and the Subject were simple lab animals.

No more.

Jeremy drew up a syringeful of the drug. He reached down to the tubing, and then realized that, without gravity pushing the fluids down from the bottle, he would have to assist the drug in moving through the tubing and into his waiting artery.

To shorten the pathway, he moved the clamp closer to where the IV needle entered his artery. Then he slid the syringe's needle into the rubber tubing. He took a deep breath to steady his nerves and paused for a moment to make sure he'd thought through everything. He decided he'd best push the drug in fast to make sure there were no mistakes.

He placed his thumb on the plunger, and pushed it home in one swift motion.

Jeremy tossed aside the syringe and squeezed the tubing to be sure all the contents were delivered. He felt warm and carefree for a few moments as the drug began to course through him.

No more pain…

Floating…

Darkness.

EPILOGUE

He awoke to what seemed a soft, sweet dream. He felt weightless and free. Gradually he became aware of a faint bubbling sound. It soothed him. He opened his eyes and saw light and shadow performing a slow dance across his field of vision.

He stretched, feeling lazy and warm and comfortable. But something felt wrong. He wasn't breathing; he didn't *need* to breathe. He craned his neck to look around and discovered he only had a limited range of movement. He flailed his paddlelike limbs. What had happened?

He opened his mouth to scream, but he made no sound.

Glen stood with Rick in the sequestered cultivation room. He gazed down at the glass container that held the early-stage Subject in its bath of warm, filtered saline fluid. An artificial umbilical cord provided its nutrition and drew away its metabolic waste products.

"I'm pleased with its development so far. We've managed to increase the rate over prior Subjects with that adjustment to the hormone mix." Glen smiled and glanced at Rick.

"It is amazing seeing this firsthand, from the start. It'll be especially interesting to see how the gene splicing works out. Are you certain you don't carry any genes implicated in Crohn's?"

"Far as I know, I don't. Anyway, it's not like we had a lot of choice. It was either you or me to provide the genes to splice into the cells we took from Jeremy." Glen sighed. "Unfortunate what he did. Another Subject would have been ready for him soon enough."

"But he did give us the chance to try a gene-splicing approach this time."

"Yes." Glen smiled as he glanced down at the Subject, who appeared to be frozen in the throes of a silent scream. "Yes, he did."

ABOUT THE AUTHOR

Lisa von Biela worked in Information Technology for 25 years, then dropped out to attend the University of Minnesota Law School, graduating magna cum laude in 2009. She now practices law in Seattle, Washington.

Lisa began writing short, dark fiction just after the turn of the century. Her first publication appeared in *The Edge* in 2002. She went on to publish a number of short works in various small-press venues, including *Gothic.net, Twilight Times, Dark Animus, AfterburnSF,* and more. She is the author of the novels *The Genesis Code, The Janus Legacy, Blockbuster, Broken Chain, Incidental Findings,* and *Down the Brink,* as well as the novellas *Ash and Bone, Skinshift,* and *Moon Over Ruin.*

Curious about other Crossroad Press books?
Stop by our site:
http://store.crossroadpress.com
We offer quality writing
in digital, audio, and print formats.

Enter the code FIRSTBOOK
to get 20% off your first order from our store!
Stop by today!

www.ingramcontent.com/pod-product-compliance
Lightning Source LLC
Chambersburg PA
CBHW051505030726

47592CB00006B/2113